BATTLEFIELD MADONNA

also by James McConnell

THE BENEDICTINE COMMANDO

BATTLEFIELD MADONNA
James McConnell

HAMISH HAMILTON
London

First published in Great Britain 1985
by Hamish Hamilton Ltd
Garden House, 57/59 Long Acre, London WC2E 9JZ

Copyright © 1985 by James McConnell

British Library Cataloguing in Publication Data
McConnell, James
Battlefield Madonna

ISBN 0–241–11497–7
Phototypeset by Input Typesetting Ltd, London
Printed in Great Britain at The Pitman Press, Bath

for Daphne
her divine sculpture

In July 1944 the Americans and British were preparing to break out of the Normandy beach-head and strike towards Paris. The Russians had advanced into Poland and were threatening Warsaw. Hitler's enemies within Germany were plotting to assassinate him and save their country from a defeat that now seemed inevitable.

And still Edmund was stuck in the War Office. He had a nine-to-five job in a department of the Military Intelligence Directorate which prepared surveys of countries where the British Army might be called on to operate. He had been responsible for the volume on Italy and had written the piece on Florence himself. Most of his colleagues were married dons or schoolmasters. They did not share his frustration at being cooped up in the War Box.

Helen saw more real action than he did. She drove a Salvation Army tea van in the East End. That part of London was now getting the full brunt of Hitler's new terror weapon. When a flying bomb landed, her tea-van was often the first on the scene. She made it a point of honour to be there as fast as the rescue services.

Then one morning in the middle of July his posting came through. In an innocent-looking buff envelope from the Adjutant General's office.

T/Capt E V R Brudanell, it said, was posted from the War Office, Int Directorate to the Commission for the Protection of Art Treasures in War Zones (COPAT), 15 Army Gp. He was to report to the Air Transport Officer Hendon at 0600 hrs 18 July for air transportation to Caserta, Italy.

Rome had been captured on 4 June 1944. Seven weeks later, after a rapid advance through central Italy, the Allied armies were fighting in the Chianti hills just south of Florence. German resistance had stiffened and it looked as if the enemy were going to stand on the line of the River Arno. General Alexander, the Commander-in-Chief, had moved the head-quarters of 15 Army Group to the shores of Lake Bolsena, midway between Rome and Florence. The four officers of the Commission for the Protection of Art Treasures had been relegated to the extreme edge of the encampment where they had been allotted a couple of 160 lb tents.

This was not exactly front-line stuff. Indeed Lake Bolsena was a far more peaceful place than London, but Edmund knew why he had been summoned. The officer he was replacing had driven over a Teller mine buried deep under a road near Perugia. The Army, hunting through the files for an expert on Florentine art, had dug up Edmund's name. As soon as Florence was captured he expected to have a bigger slice of the action. Meanwhile the job was not uninteresting. The officers of COPAT had the advantage of being almost totally independent, though nominally they worked under the Allied Control Commission.

On the last Wednesday in July Edmund had been forward to Siena and Arrezzo to assess the damage there. Siena was a good twenty miles behind the front, not even in sound of the guns, but that was at least better than staring out of a War Office window on to Whitehall Court. When he returned that evening, security round the camp was much tighter than usual. Instead of being able to slip in by a track that led along the lakeside to the COPAT area, he had to go round by the main gate. Military Police, spiced with Field Security sergeants, were checking the identity of everyone entering the headquarters.

Edmund as usual made his report to Colonel Parkinson, an officer in the Allied Control Commission. He had a mous-tache that was as grey as the wispy hair on his balding head and wore a row of 1914–18 ribbons.

Siena, Edmund told him, was not badly damaged. The Germans had mined the city but their engineers' plan had been found and little damage was done. The worst casualty was a statue by Vecchietta in the Loggia della Mercanza which had lost its right eye. The Simone Martinis, Duccios and Lorenzettis had been successfully hidden away.

2

'Yes, I see.' Parkinson's eyes had glazed a little as Edmund reeled off these foreign names. 'You went to Arrezzo too?'

'Yes.' Edmund could feel the sweat cooling on his back. 'The town was sacked by the Germans but the Piero della Francescas in the church are OK – apart from a few stains, due to roof damage.'

Parkinson's fingers teased the little pile of papers on his blotter. Edmund realised that the names of the Italian Masters meant nothing to him.

'What's all the flap about, Colonel?' he asked. 'The security on the main gate is worse than the War Box.'

'We're expecting a Very Important Person.' Parkinson said pompously. 'I'm not allowed to tell you who it is but no doubt you'll find out tomorrow.'

The Officers Mess at dinnertime that evening was full of rumours. As usual Lovejoy, a young and very brash Intelligence Corps Major was holding forth. He had an exaggerated idea of his own importance and took great pleasure in putting down Military Government and Control Commission officers. Like all the old hands in this campaign he was bronzed a deep brown. He could see that Edmund was fresh out from England and treated him as a raw recruit.

'I was talking to Terence Airey today,' he declared to everyone within earshot, rolling the name of Alexander's Chief of Intelligence round his tongue. 'It's Winston. Bound to be. He's coming out to console Alex for having the Frogs taken away from him.'

Having recently been in the War Office, Edmund could understand this remark better than most. Alexander was about to lose seven divisions – four of them French. Lovejoy's eye roaming around the table lighted on Edmund's comparatively pallid face.

'He's bound to want to see you, Brudanell, and find out what Cowpat are doing to win the war.'

This remark was accompanied by a wink to his crony, the SOE staff officer, but it did not raise the hoped-for laugh. Edmund had won more respect than he realised during his week in C Mess.

He had the tent to himself that night. His colleagues had gone to San Gimignano and Incisa Val d'Arno. He slept badly, disturbed by a letter from Helen, the first he'd had

3

since he left. It had reached him in five days. She did not tell him much but reading between the lines he guessed that the new 'doodle-bugs' were giving London a real pounding. He could not help feeling thankful that they'd not had time to start a family before the war began.

His batman driver brought him a lukewarm cup of early-morning tea. Scroope was an unsatisfactory Cockney who reckoned he'd landed a cushy job driving these Cowpat geezers around. Edmund washed in cold water and shaved in a mirror hanging from the pole of the tent. It was another glorious morning and the day promised to be very hot. The lake shimmered in the sunlight. Waterbirds fussed among the reeds by the shore.

When he had polished his shoes – Scroope could not be trusted to do the job properly – he walked along the grassy track that followed the shore. Being at the edge of the camp had its advantages. Beyond the COPAT tents there was only a sparse wood. He'd found a convenient bush to pee behind and was just buttoning up his flies when he heard voices. Two men were coming along the track which curved into the wood before leading back towards the centre of the camp. They were talking earnestly in low tones. As they came into view he saw that both were hatless. They were wearing the regulation dress for British troops in Italy – shorts and shirts with sleeves rolled up. Only the scarlet tabs on their collars showed that they were of high rank. Both had several rows of medal ribbons on their chests. But whereas the chubbier man had suntanned knees and forearms, the other had the tell-tale white skin of a newcomer from England.

Edmund had no difficulty in recognising Alexander with his trim moustache, his slightly swaggering walk, his general air of confidence and authority. He hurriedly fastened the last button. How should a junior officer react when the Commander in Chief catches him doing up his flies? Rather than be seen skulking behind a bush, Edmund decided to step out into the open.

It was then that he had his second shock. Alex's companion was a small man of about the same age. The hair of his slightly tapering head was cut short back and sides. A signet ring glittered on the little finger of his left hand. He kept his eyes on the ground as he listened but when he looked up his

4

cheeks were wrinkled in a smile. Edmund realised then that this was no freak resemblance. The man ten paces away was King George VI.

Edmund stood there rooted to the spot. In fact, it was the best thing he could have done. As he was wearing no head-dress it would have been improper to salute. Alexander glanced up and saw him. A slight frown was evidence not that he was displeased but that he was searching his memory.

'I know you, don't I?' The alert eyes swept over Edmund's tall and lanky form in a split-second inspection, taking in the one unfastened shirt button, the Dunhill pipe stuck into the turn-down of the left sock, the fair hair that Edmund had not had time to get cut before leaving England. 'Now, where was it we met?'

'At Dunkirk, sir.'

'Ah, yes. It's Brudanell, isn't it? I remember now. Your unit had to hold the perimeter so that the rest of us could embark. We thought we'd lost you.'

'I got wounded, sir, and was put in the bag but I managed to escape and get back home through Spain.' Edmund smiled. 'Took a longish time.'

Alex nodded thoughtfully, his eyes staying on Edmund's face. 'Good man,' he said, and the words meant as much as having a medal pinned on your chest. 'You're not with the regiment any longer?'

'I was grade C when I got back to England. They found me a job in the War Office and then after Siena was captured I was suddenly sent out here.'

Alex was glancing round, trying to get his bearings. 'We seem to have lost our way. Do you know how we can get back to my caravan from here?'

'Just follow the lake shore along, sir, and you'll come to the NAAFI canteen. You turn left there and – '

'Oh, yes. I see where we are now.'

The C in C seemed to regard it as the most natural thing in the world that he should be taking a stroll in the Italian sunlight with the King of England. He was unaware of the unconscious humour of a supreme commander who'd lost his way in his own camp. He started to move off. He had made no attempt to involve his companion in the conversation. The King however had been studying Edmund's profile.

5

'I believe I too know you.' He spoke with that slight impedi-
ment which gave a peculiar emphasis to his words. It was
more a hesitation than a stammer. 'You did some work for
us at,' a short pause, 'Windsor.'

For the first time Edmund looked the King in the face. He
could see now that his forearms were already pink after only
half a day in the Italian sun.

'Yes, Your Majesty.' Edmund was a good six inches taller
than the King. He found it a little embarrassing to be looking
down at his Sovereign. 'I did an inventory of the Leonardo
drawings in the Royal collection.'

'Oh, yes. I remember now.' The King fingered the sleeve
of his shirt as if he was itching to roll it down. 'You're an
expert on Florentine art. Are you with the – Allied Control
Commission here?'

'Cow – Commission for the Protection of Art Treasures,
sir. We work under the ACC.' Edmund glanced at Alex but
the C in C was unperturbed by this unscheduled conversation.
'My job is to go into Florence as soon as we capture it.'

'Oh, yes.' A frown of concern wrinkled the King's brow.
'Such a beautiful city. One can't help hoping it – it won't be
damaged.'

'I believe there's a chance it may be declared an open city,'
Edmund ventured, knowing that he was forcing the pace.

'Is that so?' The King looked at Alexander for confirmation.

The C in C's expression had become a little less relaxed.
'Field Marshal Kesselring is putting in 1st Parachute Division to defend it,' he said crisply. 'That hardly inspires confidence in his willingness to treat it as an open city. As usual
Hitler has put his commander in the field in an impossible
position. On the one hand he's told him to resist on the Arno
as strongly as he can and on the other to try and preserve
Florence. He's never forgiven Kesselring for not blowing the
Rome bridges.'

'You have that from Ultra, I suppose?'

Alex shot the King a warning glance but the reference to
that Most Secret Source meant nothing to Edmund. Realising
that he'd committed an indiscretion, the King changed the
subject.

'As a matter of fact there's a picture of ours in Florence.

We lent it to the Italians before they declared war on us. For an exhibition of Renaissance painting.'

'Oh, yes, the Mostra del Rinascimento, sir? I've always thought that was the most beautiful painting in the Royal collections.'

'Yes.' A remarkably tender smile creased the King's cheeks. 'It's my favourite too. I always think La Simonetta looks her best in that picture. I hope one day we shall have her back.'

Edmund was uneasy about a conversation from which the C in C seemed to be excluded but, when he glanced towards him, he saw that Alex was looking at him with particular intentness.

'Then we shall have to see that you do, sir,' Alex said. 'Won't we, Brudanell?'

'Yes, sir.' Edmund had read the message in Alex's eyes. 'We will.'

As the two men moved away, immediately renewing their eager conversation, Edmund again stiffened to attention. Long after they had forgotten him he still stood there, slightly dazed by that improbable encounter.

Of course, it made sense that the King should come out to visit his forces in Italy. Alex commanded divisions not only from the British Isles but from South Africa, Canada, New Zealand and India. That slight figure ruled an Empire on which the sun never set.

Edmund could see the *tondo* now, hanging in its circular gilt frame on the wall of the ante-chapel in Buckingham Palace. The Madonna herself was flanked by four angels, each with the tender youthful countenance of a young fifteenth century Florentine. Her own exquisite face with its faintly sensuous mouth wore an expression of resigned sadness. The long graceful fingers supported on her lap a Child. In one hand he held a cluster of grapes and in the other three nails, symbols of future torment. In the infant's eyes could be read a question. 'Can ye drink of the cup of which I drink?'

Mario Benvenuti lived with his wife and two children in a third-storey flat on the southern side of the Arno. His study window commanded one of the most beautiful views in Florence. In the foreground he could see the Ponte Vecchio with its three arches supporting the double row of houses where the jewellers had their little shops. The green and brown shutters provided spots of bright colour against the chrome yellow of the stonework. The Arno had never divided Florence. The smaller southern section had always been linked to the north by a fraternity of bridges. Seen from above they gave an impression of mysterious intimacy. On either side ran the ancient palaces with their balconies overhanging the water and their quaint loggias like miniature temples on their roofs. They completed an amicable ensemble that had a fortuitous artistry about it which no deliberate planning could emulate. He loved that view and in the peaceful days before war came to Tuscany he could sit and watch the people strolling past the statue of Benvenuto Cellini or gaze into the changing reflections in the water flowing quietly below.

This morning he had no eyes for beauty. Already the sound of artillery could be heard to the south. The battle was approaching Florence. It was evident from the behaviour of the Germans that they were preparing to withdraw. He was more reluctant than ever to leave Ornella and the children.

'Keep them indoors,' he warned her. 'You heard, the radio says that the Americans may bomb the bridges.'

The air raid in March had been a grim reminder to the Florentines that their city was not immune.

'Papa says Marshal Kesselring wants Florence declared an open city.' Ornella reached up to fasten a button on Mario's shirt. 'He heard it from the German consul. That means there will be no fighting here.'

'We can't be sure of anything. Last night L'Impruneta was bombed and there were no Germans in the town.'

He put his arms round her waist and kissed her on the forehead. She had put on weight since their marriage and was no longer the pliant girl he had courted. After the birth of their second child she had responded less warmly to his advances. At times he almost felt that she was shrinking away from him. But she was a good mother and had given him two lovely children. It was understandable if she felt that one boy and one girl were enough.

'Do you have to go, tesoro?' Her anxiety had made her more breathless than usual. 'So many young men have been rounded up and taken away to labour camps.'

'I must.' Not even Ornella could be told about the crisis that had developed. Captain Carità, the incongruously named chief of the security police, had raided the secret radio station the previous evening. Those who had not been killed had been taken to the torture chambers of the 'Villa Triste' in the Via Bolognese.

'Try to see Papa and Mamma. I know they are worried about the children.'

He nodded, not promising anything. 'Did you take your pills this morning?'

Ornella put a hand to her mouth. 'Madonna! I forgot all about them.'

A few months ago the doctor had discovered that her breathlessness and headaches were due to high blood pressure. He had advised her to lose weight but in spite of food shortages she had shed only a few pounds.

Mario tried to conceal his exasperation. 'Well, be sure to take them as soon as I'm gone.'

He stooped to kiss his son and daughter. Stefano was a serious little boy of five. Anna, two years younger, was a vivacious and extrovert little minx. 'Be good and do what Mamma says'. He took a mental photograph of their upturned faces. 'No going down to play in the piazza.'

When you parted from loved ones these days you always wondered if you would see them again. In Tuscany the anti-Fascist struggle had been particularly bitter and the counter measures correspondingly brutal. Stories of pillaging and atrocities were rife. It was rumoured that the partisans were preparing to rise against the retreating Germans. If that happened the reprisals would be atrocious. Not even women and children were safe.

The narrow Via Romana was busy. Military vehicles were moving up towards the front, pulling aside for the ambulances

9

bringing wounded back to the hospitals. The civilians on the sidewalks were either old men or women. Any young men to be seen were in uniform – mostly German SS or Fascist Black Militia. The others had gone to ground with the partisans or been rounded up for transportation to labour camps. The people were cowed and apprehensive. And hungry. Rationing was very strict, food scarce. On the black market an egg cost a day's pay and a chicken a whole week's.

His way took him past the front of the massive Pitti Palace, once one of the great art galleries but now denuded of pictures. Crossing the big square he threaded his way past the Pitti to a corner of the Boboli Gardens. He walked through a small courtyard, at one end of which was a grotto adorned with carved figures. Beside the grotto was an inconspicuous brown door. He used his own key to let himself into a high but dark corridor.

Vasari had built this corridor for Cosimo de'Medici on the occasion of Francesco de'Medici's marriage to Joan of Austria in 1565. It was about three hundred yards in length and its purpose was to connect the two Medici establishments at the Pitti and Uffizi. Later it enabled Cosimo to proceed from the palace to his secretariat in the Uffizi without setting foot in the street – where by no means everyone was his friend. In modern times it was used to house the Uffizi's famous collection of self-portraits by the world's most famous artists. These had now been dispersed with the other paintings.

Il corridoio Vasari carried Mario across the Arno above the now shuttered shops on the Ponte Vecchio. He stopped once when he heard the drone of an aircraft. Through a round window he could see it high in the blue sky. The tiny object contrived to appear incredibly menacing. He shivered, alone there in the empty corridor. He wished he had not been so brusque with Ornella.

Once across the river the corridor took a right turn along the Lungarno, supported for a hundred yards by tall arches. It led him up a flight of stairs to a door which opened directly onto the art gallery itself. Once again he used his key and a moment later was passing the empty rooms. Here in happier days had hung pictures which were as much a part of his life as the blood that flowed in his veins – Cimabue's *Madonna*,

Giotto's *Madonna in Trono*, Michelangelo's *Sacra Famiglia*, Botticelli's *Primavera*.

Mario Benvenuti was a Florentine through and through. He came from one of the city's oldest families. There was even a street named Via de'Benvenuti to remind him of bygone wealth and influence. He was prouder than a Roman of this lineage and the city that had nurtured his roots. The great age of Athens had only lasted a hundred years, that of Florence lasted from the year 1250 to 1500. This small community of no more than a hundred thousand had been the fountainhead of political, intellectual and artistic ideas which had flourished to this day. His artistic sense had been awakened early. That was not surprising, since a walk down any street brought reminders of a centuries-old cultural tradition. Even such utilitarian objects as the lamps above archways, the rings to which horses had once been tethered, the grills across ground-floor windows, the very paving stones had been arranged with artistry and imagination. As a boy he had admired the soaring spires and *campanili* of the dozens of churches and the proud towers of the old families. He had loved to wander in the narrow streets with their hundreds of small craftsmen's shops, pausing now and again to gaze through the archway of some grandiose *palazzo* at the paradise of greenery and flowers in the enclosed courtyard. Most of all he was fascinated by the Lungarni, those promenades along the banks of the Arno, and by the bridges which so gracefully emphasised the unity of the city. A spot which had special meaning for him was at the northern end of the Ponte Santa Trinità. Here Dante had stood at nine o'clock on the morning of his eighteenth birthday and received from the passing Beatrice that one glance which had been the inspiration of his Divina Commedia. The number three and its multiples held a fascination for Mario as it had for Dante. He was now approaching the age of thirty three and he was certain that something of major importance in his life would happen near the time of his birthday.

At the age of nine he had been taken by his mother on his first visit to the Uffizi Gallery. That very day he had conceived the ambition to become Director of the Soprintendenza delle Belli Arti, the organisation which supervised the art treasures of the city. His ambition had motivated him through nine

11

years of schooling at the College of the SS Annunziata and five years in the Fine Arts department of the University of Florence. When the post of assistant curator at the Uffizi had become vacant in 1932 there had been fifty candidates. Mario's burning enthusiasm, his eager face and persuasive manner had got him the job.

Perhaps a factor in his success was that Fabio Pantano, one of the selection board, had seen a resemblance between this young man and the only known self-portrait of Michelangelo. He had the same forward-thrusting brow, the same intense gaze and the same strong though sensuous mouth.

By 1940, when Italy entered the war, Dottor Mario Benvenuti had risen to the position of Assistant Director and was in line to become the next director.

He hurried now along the broad main passage on the third floor of the Uffizi. The place was empty and silent, the lifts out of commission. He descended the long broad stairway and used an inner doorway to reach the offices of the Superintendancy in the Via della Nina.

He found Fabio Pantano in the Director's office on the third floor. Pantano was a vigorous sixty-year-old with a bald head and a body as hard and rotund as a pumpkin. By contrast his face was soft and fleshy. Since the autumn of 1942, when the Germans and Italians were routed at El Alamein and the Allies landed in Algeria, he had been forced to make agonising decisions. Not all of them had been justified by events.

He pushed himself up from his chair as Mario entered with his quick eager step. The downward sag of his jowls showed how desperately tired and worried he was. Mario knew at once that his superior had received some bad news.

'Fabio! What's happened?'

'I've just come from the Kommandatur.' Fabio pulled out a huge silk handkerchief to wipe the crown of his head. 'Colonel Lansdorf told me that the Kunstschutz have orders to remove all the paintings. . . .'

'But that is contrary to the assurance we had from Consul Wolf!' As always when he was angry Mario's head was thrust forward. When he talked his hands dipped and soared like a pair of mating swallows. 'And what about the Mostra del Rinascimento? Those paintings do not belong to us. We hold them in trust.'

'I know, Mario.' Fabio shook his head despairingly. 'The Consul himself deplores it. But these orders come from Himmler. Their excuse is that they are removing them for safe-keeping – so that the Americans can't steal them.'

'Pah!' Mario instinctively felt for a cigarette, then remembered that he had finished his last packet the night before. 'It is the Germans who are the looters. Who removed three hundred paintings from the Pitti last week? Not the Kunstschutz! That was done by an infantry battallion. And we still don't know who made off with the Finaly-Landau collection.'

'I know, Mario, I know. Terrible things are happening. And still no news from Bussola. I am afraid he may have been arrested or killed crossing the lines. Who knows what the fate of our deposits in Chianti will be?'

That had been one of the Director's mistaken decisions, though he had made it on the basis of information available at the time. When Mussolini declared war on Britain in 1940 no-one dreamed that the war would ever come to Italy. The main threat to Florence's art treasures appeared to be from British and American bombers. By the end of 1942 they were flying in their thousands to pound German cities. The first raid on Hamburg had virtually obliterated the free port and killed 50,000 civilians. The sensible course seemed to be to disperse the art treasures and store them in the villas, churches, even railway tunnels of the surrounding countryside. During the winter of 1942/43 some of the most famous statues and paintings in the world were transported to places as far away as Cortona. Botticelli's *Birth of Venus* was taken to Poppi along with Leonardo's *Adoration of the Magi*, Raphael's *Veiled Lady*, Filippo Lippi's *Madonna and child* and several hundred hardly less valuable paintings. Michelangelo's sculptures of *Day*, *Night*, *Dawn* and *Dusk* from the Medici chapel had gone to the huge Martini villa near San Donato in Collina. Donatello's *Saint George*, perhaps the most treasured piece of sculpture in Florence, had found refuge at the Villa Medici in Poggio along with the same artist's *David*. Literally thousands of priceless masterpieces were distributed among thirty-two different deposits. Those that could not be moved, such as the frescoes on the walls of churches, were boarded up. A brick wall was built round Michelangelo's *David* in the Accademia.

Yet this great effort proved to be in vain. The Allies invaded Sicily on 10 July 1943 and two months later were on the soil of Italy. The unthinkable had happened. The King kicked Mussolini out and negotiated an armistice. That did not prevent Italy from becoming a battleground. The country was now divided by the advancing line of the front. The Germans, enraged by the defection of their ally, took over the whole central and northern part. Instead of allies they were now an occupying power and it was soon evident that they intended to fight for every inch of the peninsula. Although no invader in history had ever conquered Italy from the south it had to be faced after the break-through at Cassino that the war would come to Tuscany.

Then occurred what seemed like a miracle. Rome was declared an open city. The fighting by-passed the capital and it escaped almost unscathed. Surely Florence could not expect less? The decision was taken to bring all the works of art back into the galleries.

This proved to be a more difficult undertaking than the dispersal. Tuscany was now under the heel of the German and Fascist SS. Petrol was in short supply and the Soprintendenza had only two lorries to transport thousands of objects. The Allies advanced rapidly. Travel by day was out of the question, for their air forces ruled the skies and attacked anything seen moving on the roads. The Germans, hard-pressed themselves, could not help. In fact, when approached, they requisitioned one of the lorries for their own purposes.

On 29 June the remaining lorry was leaving Arezzo with one of the Soprintendenza directors at the wheel. On board it had a load of the finest paintings of Piero della Francesca. A 1,000 lb. bomb landed a few yards from it but failed to explode. After this, it was decided to establish some kind of contact with the Allied air forces. A clandestine radio station was set up near Piazza Beccaria. The Allies were informed of the movements of the lorry so that they could avoid straffing the road it was using. Even as the fighting approached Florence, this system was still working.

Then the spies of the Sicherheitsdienst had got word of the secret transmitter and Carità's men had sprung a surprise raid. If the teams of operators had been killed the casualties would have been acceptable. Young Italians had been reluctant to sacrifice their lives for Mussolini's imperial dreams but they were prepared to die for their art treasures. A worse fate than death was to fall into the hands of Carità and his squad of torturers. Small wonder Fabio's face was haggard.

'Is there any news from Via Bolognese?' Mario asked.

Fabio shook his head and his cheeks quivered. 'I have not slept all night, thinking about it. The man Carità is a devil in human form. If the SD learn that we have been in contact with the Allies they will arrest us all as spies . . . .'

'We've only been trying to save the pictures from Allied bombers.'

'The SD, Mario! You know them.' Fabio could not keep still. He was prowling about the room picking up objects and putting them down in the same place again. 'Any excuse is good enough for them. Then who would be left to protect our pictures?'

Mario had heard the stories of what went on in the house that had been named the 'Villa Triste'. Men and women had been suspended by the wrists for hours. A girl he knew had been made to stand with her forehead against a wall for one whole week. Many had suffered the water torture until their guts had burst; Carità had improved on the technique by using scalding hot water. Beatings were commonplace. This form of direct violence suited his perverted taste better than the more refined electric tortures. He took particular delight in eating and drinking before the eyes of his battered and bleeding victims. Some of his accomplices added a bizarre horror to this hell's kitchen. There was a defrocked monk who played Neapolitan songs on the piano as an accompaniment to the victim's screams. Carità's mistress was sexually aroused by watching him torture men and urged him on to worse excesses.

Fabio stopped his prowling as footsteps pounded on the stairs leading up from the entrance in Via della Nina. The two men stared at each other.

'It's all right.' Mario relaxed. 'Those aren't German boots.'

The young man who burst into the room was pallid. Like all the partisans who had gone underground, he had not been exposed to sunlight for weeks. He was one of the team who manned a hide-out in the old post-office adjoining the Uffizi.

'Carlo has just come from Via Bolognese,' he panted, still

15

recovering his breath. Carlo was a former member of the intelligence organisation SIM who had joined the Italian SS so that he could pass on information to the partisans. 'He saw Viviano. Oh, God! They had him tied to a wooden triangle and were beating him with a steel-cored whip. Carlo says his flesh was hanging in tatters. Professore, what are you going to do? He cannot endure that, and when he tells them . . . .'

'Calmo, Attilio, calmo.' The skin of Fabio's cheeks had gone grey. He turned instinctively to his younger aide. 'Mario, you can help. You must talk to your father-in-law. He knows the German consul. Surely he can do something.'

Mario had made a good marriage. Ornella was from a wealthy and aristocratic Florentine family. The Lamberti had through the centuries been as influential as the Pazzi and the Strozzi. Lorenzo de'Lamberti, Ornella's father, had made sure of preserving his fortune in 1924 by declaring total support for Mussolini and the Fascist movement. Palazzo Lamberti had been the family home since the fifteenth century. It stood on the northern side of the Arno about two hundred yards back from the river. Like all the palaces of the Florentine nobility it presented a deliberately aggressive exterior to the outside world. The walls were faced with *rustico*, huge blocks of rough stone that protruded six inches from the pointing and seemed to say, keep out. There was only one entry, from the Via de'Lamberti.

The big archway with its heavy studded doors was topped by the family crest elaborately carved in stone. The wooden ceiling within the archway bore colourful paintings between its thick beams. Passing beneath it the visitor entered the verdant, enclosed world of gracious living. The *cortile* of Palazzo Lamberti was a complete contrast to the exterior. It was filled with colourful shrubs and flowers. An elegant fountain played over the well in the centre. To the casual observer Florence seems a place of narrow streets and crowded buildings. Its open spaces are behind walls, inaccessible to the common herd.

The days when a noble family and their retinue could occupy a whole palace were long gone. The present Count's father had converted the square building into five separate residences. Ornella's father had tried to persuade Mario to live in one of the flats but he had insisted on having an independent home. He found the Lamberti with their wealth and influence a bit too over-powering.

It took him no more than ten minutes on that sunny July morning to walk from the Soprintendenza to Via de'Lamberti. As always when he visited the *palazzo*, he felt glad that he did not live behind that prison-like façade. It was still very much a Lamberti enclave, for the occupants of all the residences had some connection with the family.

The door to the main family residence was opened to him by old Susanna, one of the two servants remaining of a domestic staff of ten. Susanna was sixty-three and had the rugged but respectful features of a peasant schooled to serve nobility. Even in wartime she was wearing a freshly starched apron.

Yes, she told Mario, Il Conte and la Contessa were at home. So was la signorina Rosalba. And la signorina Caterina had arrived early that morning.

'La signorina Caterina?' Mario's heart instantly quickened its beat.

'Sisignore.' Susanna's wise old eyes dropped so that she would not betray any surprise at Mario's eager repetition of the name. Caterina was a cousin of Ornella's and about the same age. Though she was married, the servants still used the name by which they had known her as a girl. Her husband was Jacopo de Angeli. He had been one of the first to join the partisan movement and had departed for the mountains in the summer of 1943 when the Black Militia had started rounding up men of military age.

Susanna escorted Mario up the grand stairway to the first floor, the *piano nobile*, and announced the visitor in the tones of one who brings good news.

'Mario, my dear, how nice to see you!'

The Countess had risen from an armchair and was coming towards him with a smile. Her features were unmistakeably aristocratic and she had the confident poise of a woman born and bred in luxury. She was still striking to look at, with dark intense eyes and the straight Florentine nose that does not dip into the brow. Her hands were extremely graceful with long expressive fingers. Her jet-black hair was drawn back to a *chignon* that hung at the nape of her neck. As always she was elegantly dressed.

She presented each cheek in turn to be kissed by her son-in-law. 'And how are my little treasures? They must be terrified by all this gunfire.'

'I think Anna is a little frightened, but Stefano is enjoying it. His soldiers' games are coming to life.'

Mario turned towards Ornella's father. The Count had been slow to rise from the desk placed behind the sofa, as if Mario's arrival had interrupted his study of an important document. He took off his glasses and held them between finger and thumb.

'Ah, Mario. Come va, figlio mio?'

'Non c'è male.'

His father-in-law was unusually tall for an Italian, with a heavy body, large head and a dark complexion. Though he was clean shaven, hair sprouted from his eyebrows, his ears, his nostrils and there were little tufts of it on his cheekbones. When standing he appeared to be leaning backwards and this effect was exaggerated by the fact that he tilted his head and looked down his nose. Everything about him proclaimed affluence and power. The Banco Lamberti had flourished under twenty years of Fascism. Now, of course, he was on friendly terms with the occupying Germans and in particular with the Consul, Dr Gerhard Wolf. Even Field Marshal Kesselring, Commander-in-Chief of the armies in Italy, had been entertained in this very *salone*.

The room had survived unchanged from the halcyon days of the Lamberti family. It was on a grand scale with a ceiling painted by Carracci, ornate walls replete with gilded mirrors and a parquet floor covered with Aubusson carpets. Every piece of furniture was an antique gem and the oil sketches hanging between the mirrors were by Tiepolo himself. Here in the days of peace, and even up till a few weeks ago, the Countess had been at home to the writers, musicians and artists of Florence. It was the ambition of many a foreign visitor to be invited to the *salone* of la Contessa de'Lamberti.

She spoke English fluently, for her mother had been a close friend of a Miss Gladys Elliot, whose grandfather had come to Florence with the Robert Louis Stephenson Company. Giulia de'Lamberti had a great admiration for Winston Churchill, which she made no attempt to conceal. Fortunately for her, the Count's influence was enough to provide her with an umbrella for this piece of privileged eccentricity.

Mario's eyes searching the room had found no sign of Caterina. He smiled at the young woman sitting reading by the window. Rosalba was twenty-four, the eldest of the family, and still unmarried. Just before the war she had become engaged to an Englishman and she was still faithfully waiting for him. Mario found it hard to establish a close relationship with her. She seemed withdrawn and sad, as if she had abandoned any hope of happiness.

'Ciao, Simonetta.' He always used the family nickname for Rosalba.

'Ciao, Mario,' she replied and went back to her book.

'You should have taken my advice,' the Count was saying, 'and moved in here. The English are already shelling Strada-in-Chianti. They have no regard for life or property. Caterina arrived this morning with only a suitcase – she was lucky to get through.'

'Will Caterina be staying here?' Mario tried not to let his voice betray his interest.

'She will have a room in the apartment of the Pedrotti. They will not return from Switzerland till the war is ended.' The count tugged at the hairs growing out of his left ear. 'There is plenty of room for you there too, Mario.'

'I will talk to Ornella about it,' Mario said. A little flicker of excitement had stirred in him at the thought of sharing the flat in the north wing with Caterina. 'There was something else I wanted to ask you, Papa. It is very urgent.'

The Count's brow darkened as Mario told him about the SD raid on the secret radio station.

'How can they be such fools?' he exclaimed angrily. 'Do they expect to escape justice when they defy regulations?'

'You must do something, Papa,' Mario insisted firmly.

But the Count had already made up his mind. He picked the tooled leather spectacle case off his desk and put his glasses away. 'I'll see. There may not be much time. Gerhard Wolf told me that he will shortly be leaving the city.'

'The German consul is leaving?' The Countess had sat down again and taken up her knitting. She was making gloves for the Italian soldiers on the eastern front in Russia. Her observant eyes had been flickering from the Count's face to Mario's, searching beyond their words for the real meaning. 'That's bad news. He has done so much for us Florentines.'

'Yes.' The Count opened the door and called for his hat and walking stick. 'The City is to be handed over to a parachute regiment. They will have the responsibility of defending it.'

'Then God help us all,' the Countess said as the door closed.

When the head of the family had gone the atmosphere in the room changed immediately. Rosalba put her book down and came away from the window. She was always very quiet in her father's presence. Her refusal to renounce her betrothal to an Englishman who was now fighting for an enemy army had put a barrier between them.

'Do come, Mario. Who knows what may happen? It'll be better if we are all together.'

Mario avoided her eyes. 'It depends on Ornella. We'll see what she thinks.'

The door leading to the servants' quarters opened and the plump, pink face of Susanna appeared.

'Il signore has gone?' she whispered.

'Yes, Susanna. What is it?'

'Il signorino is here, signora contessa.'

The Countess put down her knitting. Her face had lit up. 'Then tell him to come in. And Susanna. Go across to the apartment please and tell la signorina Caterina to come over.'

Susanna was withdrawing when she was jostled aside by the young man who burst in. He was nineteen years of age with a shock of curly hair. He had the same pale cheeks as all the others who were hiding from the security police. He was wearing a camouflaged combat jacket over the knicker-bockers of an old shooting suit. His manner, as volatile as quicksilver, brought an electric atmosphere into the room.

'Guido!' the Countess stood up and stretched her arms towards her son. He rushed into them, hugged her so tightly that she was lifted off the ground. 'Guido! My ribs! You'll crack them.'

Guido released his mother and embraced Rosalba with equal affection, only this time the hug was accompanied by a brotherly smack.

Guido had grown up under Mussolini's regime. He had

followed his father's lead and been an enthusiastic Fascist. Only a year earlier he had become an Officer in a Bersaglieri regiment, and had been happy to serve under the flag of the government which Mussolini had set up at Salò after his rescue by the Germans. Then two things had happened which completely changed his outlook. During the winter of 1943–44 the SS had been rounding up Jews and deporting them to Germany. Guido had seen a thousand men, women and children being crammed into cattle trucks in the Florence railway marshalling yard. Later, in the spring of 1944 he had seen the village of Civitella in Valdichiana after German troops had killed 400 of the inhabitants on their Saint's Day. With typical impetuosity he had at once deserted from the army and joined the partisans.

Of course that had placed him in direct opposition to his father. The Count condemned his desertion as a disgrace to the family and forbade him ever to enter his house again. But Guido was a Florentine and internecine strife was in his blood. Back in the 1300s Florence had been a Guelf city, supporting the Pope against the Ghibellines, who fought for the Emperor. Even the Guelfs however were divided between the Black and White factions, and many a family was split down the middle. The Lamberti were in the thick of it in those days when the hand of brother was raised against brother and the streets had become so dangerous that the conspirators moved across the roof tops or used plank bridges erected between the upper storeys. The bitterness engendered then had lasted for hundreds of years.

'Darling, how pale you are!' The Countess put a hand up to pinch Guido's cheek. 'And so thin! Are you getting enough to eat?'

'Mamma.' Guido swept these maternal concerns aside. 'I have an English prisoner with me. Is there room for him in the attic?'

'An English prisoner!' For a moment the Countess was shocked into fear. The Germans shot whole families when they found British POWs being sheltered by Italians. She quickly recovered herself to face this new challenge. 'Where is he?'

'In the kitchen. I didn't want to bring him in till I was sure Papa had gone.'

'Yes, all right, Guido. I am sure we can make room for him.'

A small trap-door in the library ceiling gave access to an attic which extended over all four sides of the palazzo. There was ample space up there under the roof timbers.

Mario stayed in the background when the British POW was brought in. He was thin and pale, and the exhaustion showed in his eyes. His uniform was hanging in tatters and he had not shaved for days. He had escaped from a camp near Bologna and made his way south through the Appenines, moving from farm to farm. A family near San Godenzo had sheltered him for a month but he'd left them when the Germans began house searches.

Guido had hardly taken the POW out to the kitchen for a meal when the door from the main stairway opened and a woman in her mid-twenties came in. Mario felt as if unseen fingers had jabbed him in the Adam's apple.

Caterina's eyes found his almost immediately. They rested on him for about as long as it takes a swallow to swoop for a fly. Mario could not take his eyes off her as she came into the room. Her waist was small, her hips and breasts lusciously full. She contrived to make the mere act of walking more seductive than the most erotic ballet.

'I wanted to tell you, Caterina,' the Countess said, 'that Mario and Ornella may be moving into the apartment with the children. But I'm sure there's room for you all. In time of war, you know, we must accept inconvenience.'

'Non ti preoccupare,' Caterina answered pleasantly. 'I can take the small bedroom. I'll be able to help Ornella with the children.'

Caterina gave Mario another brief glance. He hoped the Countess did not see the hint of conspiracy in it. Caterina had guessed that for Ornellla the duties of the mother outweighed those of the wife. She had conveyed to Mario by various glances and allusions that she would not be averse to filling the vacuum. Mario had up till now resisted the temptation. He genuinely loved Ornella and was a devoted father. But he was also a man and a Florentine at that. Now, force of circumstances was conspiring to throw him into close daily contact with Caterina. The prospect both alarmed and excited him.

He was relieved when Guido returned. The atmosphere in the salone had been full of unspoken words.

'Mamma you must not worry. I may not see you for some time now.'

'Oh, my darling!' The Countess went to put her arms on Guido's shoulders. 'You're going in montagna?'

Guido laughed. 'Not to the mountains, the fight will be here in Florence. The partisans are waiting for the signal to rise. It may be any minute now.'

'Oh, caro.' She stroked his face, tears in her eyes. 'Is that wise? The Germans are capable of taking such horrible reprisals. Remember the Ardeatine caves. Three hundred Italians murdered because thirty Germans were killed by that bomb.'

'The honour of Italy is at stake, Mamma.' Guido's eyes took on a stern look. 'We have to participate in our own liberation, not leave it all to the Anglo-Americans. The future shape of Europe depends on this. Federico says we must be prepared to turn Florence into a second Stalingrad if necessary.'

'Federico is a Communist!' the Countess flashed. 'Why should you listen to him?'

'He's also a patriot,' Guido came back with equal anger. 'He does not sing the praises of Italy's enemies.'

'Careful, Guido,' the Countess warned him. 'Do not quarrel with me. Remember I have protected you from your father all this time. If he knew . . . .'

There was an urgent knock on the door leading to the servants' quarters. The scared face of Susanna appeared.

'Il signore!' she hissed.

'Go, Guido! Hurry!'

Guido gave his mother a quick embrace. All the enmity had suddenly vanished. He blew a kiss at Rosalba and vanished through the door after Susanna.

'God go with you!' the Countess called after him.

There was a change in the Count's manner when he returned. He kept bracing his shoulders back and firming up the line of his mouth. Mario knew that this was a sign that his pride had suffered some reverse.

'The Consul is leaving,' he announced abruptly. His eyes met Mario's briefly then switched away. 'He was already closing his office down. There is nothing he can do.'

'But surely someone will be in charge of . . . .'

'Tomorrow all responsibility for Florence will be in the hands of the officer commanding the Parachute Regiment.'

'Have you met him, Lorenzo?' the Countess asked. 'Is it anyone we know?'

'I met him, yes.' It was obvious from his tone that the meeting had not been a comfortable one. He moved heavily behind his desk and sat down. That position gave him a greater sense of authority and confidence. 'His name is Fuchs. Colonel Fuchs. He has the reputation of being a hard man but an efficient soldier.'

'A hard man?'

'I am told that his wife and children were killed when the English bombed Hamburg.'

3

Edmund spent the night of 25 July in the outhouse of a Tuscan farm a quarter of a mile from Tac HQ of an Eighth Army infantry brigade. The aromatic hay provided a soft cushion for his bed-roll. He could see the stars through a hole blown in the roof by a shell from an American Long Tom. He fell asleep watching the Great Bear wheel across the jagged patch of sky. Not till 1a.m. did he discover that a battery of 25-pounders had sited themselves two hundred yards behind him. They chose that ungodly hour to start firing a programme at Monte San Michele, which the Grenadier Guards were to attack at dawn. The din was scalp-moving and almost continuous. But during the brief intervals between the salvoes he heard a glorious and most improbable sound. From a nearby copse a company of nightingales defying the cacophony of war were pouring their hearts out in a chorus of sublime song.

The artillery bombardment ended at dawn and so did the protest of the nightingales. In the uncanny silence, as his hearing readjusted itself, he became aware of more distant sounds to the north – the ugly crump of bursting shells and mortar bombs, the obscene blare of machine guns. The attack on Monte Michele was going in. He sat up and slid out of his sleeping-bag.

It took him five minutes to wash and shave at the pump in the farmyard. He polished his shoes and put on the clothes he had carefully folded over a spar in the barn – shirt, shorts, long socks and a pullover against the early-morning chill. Then he loaded his gear on to the Jeep and drove the few hundred yards to the larger farm where brigade headquarters had set themselves up. He had left his batman-driver back at Lake Bolsena. Scroope had gone into a blue funk when Edmund told him they were going to be the first into Florence. Edmund decided he'd be better off without him.

The Intelligence Officer on duty was an affable young Gurkha captain, obviously an Indian Army regular.

'No,' he said, in reply to Edmund's query. 'Florence hasn't fallen yet. Jerry is being remarkably unhelpful and we're up against our old friends the paratroopers. The Grenadiers have been invited to see them off Monte San Michele and we're just waiting to see how bloody-minded the Krauts are this morning. What's your interest? You're from Army Group, aren't you?'

'Yes.' Edmund nodded but did not offer any further explanation.

'Something hush-hush, eh?' The IO had been on the point of calling Edmund 'sir'. He had the air more of a colonel than a captain. There were some strange bods swanning around these days and with everyone in shirt-sleeve-order you could easily be wrong about rank.

'Well, not exactly hush-hush,' Edmund hedged. As a former infantry officer he knew how fighting units felt about staff officers from the rear area. 'As a matter of fact it's the pictures I'm interested in.'

'Pictures?'

'Yes. You know, the Florentine painters.'

'Oh, *pictures*. Works of art, you mean.'

'That's right.'

The IO surveyed his visitor with a puzzled expression.

'The pictures won't run away, will they? Why the great hurry to get into Florence?'

Edmund did not want to strain the Gurkha's credulity by telling him about that extraordinary meeting. He had taken Alex's comment as a personal directive. His mission was to restore the King's Madonna to its rightful owner.

'The C in C is very concerned that they should come to no harm. If I can ascertain where they are we may be able to prevent them being damaged.'

The Gurkha still found it hard to understand why Army Group were concerned about a few pictures when Eighth Army were encountering the stiffest resistance since the capture of Rome. 'I suppose you'd better come and have a look at the situation map.'

He led Edmund to a room where a large map had been set up on an easel. Several officers and clerks working at trestle tables glanced up curiously at the tall newcomer with his careful, deliberate gait and fresh-looking uniform. They noted that he carried a pipe in the turn-down of one sock but no revolver on his belt.

The enemy order of battle was marked up as well as the disposition of the allied forces. It showed that the Germans were standing firm in a crescent south of the Arno. With the Nazi obsession for Wagner they had named their defensive positions after the Valkyries and other heroic women. The Gurkhas, Punjabis and Mahrattas of the Indian Division, were pitting themselves against the Olga line, the South Africans and New Zealanders were sparring with Paula and Lydia, whilst the British were assaulting the Mädchen.

'4th Para are putting up a stiff resistance here – on the Chianti mountains.' The Intelligence Officer moved his pointer to a spot ten miles south of Florence. 'Here on the Corps' west flank the Germans are thinner on the ground. It's Kiwis versus Springboks over there. The South Africans and New Zealanders are vying to be first into Florence.'

'Shades of Twickenham.' Edmund commented.

The IO smiled at the hint that this cryptic base-wallah had his human side. 'Could be today, could be a week. Personally my money's on the South Africans. They have 24th Guards Brigade under command.'

Edmund stared at the map, committing it to memory. He

was interested in a dent in the German line on Highway 2, the direct route into Florence.

'You can see Florence from Grenadier Ridge,' the Gurkha said. 'It's that feature just to the north of us. I haven't been up myself but the Grenadier IO got quite excited about it.' He turned away from the map. A wireless had began to crackle in the 15-cwt signals truck beside the tent. 'Have you had breakfast?'

'No.'

'Stay and have some with us. You'll have to excuse me as I'm on duty here.' He signalled to a huge Indian wearing NCO's stripes. 'This is Havildar Singh. He'll take you down to the Mess.'

The opportunity to catch a glimpse of Florence even from a distance was more than Edmund could resist.

As he climbed the lower slopes the sun was well clear of the horizon, shining from a blue sky. He could feel its heat already on his face. It was going to be another scorching day, but here the dew still glistened on the grass and the air was fresh. The dark hump of the Prato Magno, the mountain range on the eastern side of the Val d'Arno, was still veiled in shadow. Only the vaguest outlines of the foothills could be distinguished. Smudges of light-grey smoke curled against the hazy purple background. Far away on the valley floor a patch of water gleamed, reflecting sunlight. On this side of the valley the vines stood in well-regimented rows like soldiers on parade. Every hillock between here and the Arno was crowned by a farmstead, each with its entourage of dark evergreens and a line of cypresses marching down the avenue. On one of the higher hills a flattish gable pierced by a round window over a canopied porch was the signature of a small church.

This whole countryside was in a sense a work of art. Here order had been brought out of chaos. At one time this must all have been swamp and forest, without form or shape. Over the centuries it had been fashioned by men's hands into this wonderfully cohesive harmony. The dark, vertical brush-strokes of the cypresses, the fields of bushy olives, the neat terraces of vines gave an impression of timeless order. This was the landscape that the Florentine painters, following the example of Van Eyck, had used as background for their religious subjects. Peeping past the madonnas, saints and martyrs of Piero della Francesca, Giovanni Bellini, Andrea del Sarto, you could glimpse these same stalwart farm houses, rocky escarpments and cultivated pastures. The small intimate fields had been the nurseries where Beato Angelico and Botticelli had plucked the flowers that so deliciously embellished their paintings. But now the companionable figures of peasants bending to the scythe or carrying baskets loaded with fruit on their heads were absent. Most of the country-folk had fled at the approach of battle, forsaking their homes to seek precarious safety where they had always sought it since the time of Hannibal and Lars Porsena – *in montagna*. Their empty farms had been taken over by gunner batteries and the service units that follow an advance, their fields invaded by drab camouflaged vehicles that rolled uncaringly through the standing corn. From the supply routes assigned to the different formations – often no more than a narrow lane for a whole division – clouds of choking dust rose from the baked earth. Tanks, personnel carriers and three-tonners were moving forward, yielding way occasionally to the ambulances that crawled painfully back from the battle areas.

Tuscany had become a very over-crowded place but the traces of rustic occupation were still there. On the balcony of a house the scarlet carnations in food tins were brilliantly alive. Poppies sparkled from a craftsman-built dry-stone wall. In one field the mown hay lay in bands where it had fallen. Each swathe was like a bouquet, the grasses interleaved with the yellow, scarlet and blue of buttercup, poppy or wild iris.

He passed a group of buildings clustering together in a hollow. The tones of chrome yellow, saffron and burnt siena had been blended and softened by centuries of sunshine. The advance headquarters of an armoured division was just moving in. With that instinct for dispersal which was a relic of the desert campaigns their big vehicles had blundered all over the crops, destroying a season's toil. The officers were taking over the house itself for their mess and quarters. The departing Germans had stripped it of every movable article of value, even down to the bed-linen and crockery. Sappers were checking the rooms for booby traps and orderlies were cleaning up the turds which had been deposited on the floors of all the rooms. A gesture from the departing enemy.

On the terrace of the house the dispossessed family, one of the first to return, stood staring dumbly at the devastation. Only the old grandmother keened softly. 'Hanno rubato tutto hanno rubato.'

Edmund was climbing more slowly now. The old pain in his right knee was beginning to make itself felt. The small enclosures of fields and vineyards were giving way to the cork and pine forest that covered the upper slopes of the hill. A whiff of stale cordite warned him that he was approaching the scene of the battle the Grenadiers had fought a few days ago. The meadows that had provided flowers for the foregrounds of Botticelli were giving way to a scene more appropriate to Dante in his most infernal mood. This was the place where the German paratroopers had made one of their fanatical stands. The trees had been stripped of leaves and small branches by the bombardment preceding the attack. The refuse of war was scattered about – neatly carpentered German ammunition boxes, metal mortar-bomb cases, ejected machine-gun cartridges glinting brassily in the sunlight, here and there a British or German helmet whose usefulness had outlived its owner. Mingled with the cordite was that other sickly sweet smell; there were still unlocated corpses decomposing among the undergrowth and boulders. He even came upon a burnt-out tank, though how it had got up here was hard to imagine. A jagged hole in its side showed where the AP shell had gone in. It was easy to picture its crew, or any who had survived, baling out through the open turret.

He trod carefully, and not only because of the throbbing in his knee. As well as unexpected bombs or shells there could be mines. Not the round Teller mines used against vehicles but anti-personnel mines, like the S-mine which popped six feet into the air before discharging a hail of ball-bearings in a 360 degree arc. Or the vicious little wooden Schu-mine that simply blew your foot off. If he trod on one of those he could lie here till kingdom come. This hill for a few hours had been to anonymous soldiers a place of heightened experience, terrible and glorious. But now the war had passed on, relegating it to oblivion until the regimental histories were written.

Ten more minutes, laborious climbing brought him to the top. He was glad that there was no one to see how badly he was limping. That medico who had refused to pass him as fit to rejoin his regiment had been right. He could never have taken a fighting unit into battle. Even before he reached the summit he had a clear view northwards through a dip in the hills. With a thrill of excitement he saw a pinkish dome and the square outline of a bell-tower rising from the flat plain ten miles away. He had no difficulty in recognising Brunelleschi's cathedral and Giotto's *campanile*.

Florence! Within its ancient walls Petrarch had written his *Canzoniere*, imitated by English poets from Chaucer to Keats, Amerigo Vespucci had proved that Columbus's discovery was a whole new continent, Galileo had laid the foundations of modern physics. More than any other city it could claim to be the art centre of the world, birthplace of artists so numerous that their pictures over-flowed the galleries. There it lay in the morning mist as helpless as a trussed child in the path of the brawling armies.

On Monte Michele nearer at hand the sounds of battle had died away. The Grenadiers had won their objective and were pushing on towards Strada-in-Chianti on the road to Florence. With a sudden sense of urgency he took one last look at that distant dome then turned and started skippety-hop back down the hill.

He was collecting his Jeep from the car park at Brigade HQ when a Regimental Policeman called over to him. 'Captain Vernon wants to see you before you go, sir.'

'Captain Vernon?'

'The IO, sir.'

Edmund found his Gurkha friend at the situation map marking up some changes in the enemy order of battle.

'Ah,' he said. 'The art collector. Have you hurt your leg?'

'I – bruised my ankle on that hill.'

'Bad luck. Report came in might interest you. Hang on just a sec.'

He rubbed out 29 Panzer Grenadier Division and marked in Herman Goering Division with a green chinagraph pencil.

'Right,' turning to Edmund and putting the pencil down. 'I thought I'd better let my G3 at Div HQ know about you.' Vernon smiled. 'He says you're harmless.'

'Oh, thanks a lot!'

'In fact he had something that might be of interest to you. A company of Mahratta Light Infantry captured some castle this morning which was chock full of pictures. Old stuff, apparently. Mostly religious subjects.'

'Where was this?'

'Place called Castle Something. Here, I've got it on this bit of paper.'

The Gurkha handed Edmund a sheet torn off a signals pad.

'Castello Acciaioli,' Edmund read. 'Good lord! Isn't that the Sitwell villa?'

'Search me, old boy. I never can get my tongue round these Italian names.'

'I didn't think they had anything much in the way of pictures,' Edmund mused and then, to the Gurkha: 'Can you show me where it is on the map?'

'It's right out of our sector, just about on the dividing line between 8th Indian and 2nd New Zealand division.' The IO's finger wavered for a moment and then stabbed down on a point twenty kilometres south-west of Florence. 'The map references are – Hang on.'

As the IO read them out, Edmund jotted down the co-ordinates on the pad stuck into his map case.

'You may have to wait some time before you can get up there,' the Gurkha warned him. 'It's still in the front line and the latest report is that Jerry's counter-attacking.'

'Sorry, sir. Only authorised vehicles beyond this point. Round that corner is under enemy observation.'

It had taken Edmund a couple of hours to work his way westward onto the axis of 8th Indian Division. He had pin-pointed the map references and was moving north on a road that led from Montespertoli towards Florence. The cross-roads where he had been stopped had the battered and omin-ously expectant aspect of a place that was regularly shelled. The intrepid military policeman on traffic-control duty was wearing a steel helmet. No other human being was in sight. There had been fierce fighting the previous night on both the New Zealanders' and Indians' front. A Maori battallion had taken Foltignano, forcing the enemy to fall back a couple of

31

thousand yards. As the front moved forward the roads and lanes running through the verdant hill country became choked with traffic. Edmund found himself swerving on the verges to avoid trucks driven by dark-faced Indians with flashing eyes and teeth. The Indians were splendid fighters and absolutely terrifying drivers.

'I *am* authorised.' Edmund had to shout to make himself heard. The thunder-claps of a battery of 17-pounders firing from a nearby vineyard were deafening and Beaufighters were swooping low overhead to attack German positions on the other side of the hills. He pulled out the cellophane-covered pass that Colonel Parkinson had obtained for him. It bore a passport photograph and was signed by Alexander himself. *Captain E V R Brudanell is authorised to be in any place at any time in the execution of his duties.*

The military policeman read the words slowly and shook his head with what might have been despair or pity. His eyes took in the unscathed paintwork of the almost new Jeep and its 15 Army Group HQ markings.

'Very good, sir.' If this tourist from the rear area wanted to get himself shot up that was his own funeral. 'But watch out for mines. The road's not been cleared yet.'

Edmund stuck his pipe in the sock of his right leg and engaged four-wheel drive. Once round the bend he put his foot down, the Jeep bucking on the dusty pot-holed track. For half a mile it curved round the flank of a hill. The whole of Tuscany seemed to be out there on his right. The wooded slope of a hill loomed up a mile away. It was under attack. Tufts of earth and smoke rose from the continuous shell-bursts. He knew that the Germans must still be up there and kept his foot hard down. He was passing through that eerie and frightening zone between the gun area and the front line where you feel that you are the only creature above ground. Once you've crossed it you enter another world – the more dangerous but more companionable world of the fighting troops.

Haven was the spot where the track curved under the lee of a hill and entered a forest. As he reached it he heard the first shell crump down on the road behind him. The vehicles and personnel of a battalion HQ were dispersed among the pine trees lining the track. The men dived for cover as the shells began to rain down. Edmund skidded to a halt with locked wheels and baled out of the Jeep. He joined a small group crouching in a roadside ditch. It was four years since he had been under fire but the animal instinct to go to ground had not lost its edge.

'What are you, then? Pony express?' A sardonic and lined but still humorous face looked up at him from under a steel helmet. The accent was Cockney. Edmund realised that he had fetched up with the one British battalion in the Indian Brigade. 'RSM's not goin' to be best pleased with *you*.'

The Castello Acciaioli stood on a hill above the small hamlet of Montegufoni. Clear cut against the sky it looked like a small replica of the Palazzo Signoria in Florence, and remained virtually as it had appeared in Zocchi's eighteenth-century painting. The elliptical-shaped cypresses crowding round it were new since then, though the formal box hedges dated from much earlier. There was a lull in the fighting as Edmund drove up the hill to the castle. He was accompanied now by an Indian NCO detailed by the Commanding Officer of the Mahratta Light Infantry.

The Indian combat troops round the big building were resting on the southern side of its massive walls. A few New Zealanders had heard of the find and come over to see for themselves. Edmund parked the Jeep near a small church on the south-facing slope and walked up to the castle. A flight of steps led through a massive wooden door to a small inner courtyard. There was the usual smell that pervaded all buildings vacated by the enemy. From this first *cortile* a door led through to a much bigger courtyard enclosed by the four sections of the house. Here a solitary Italian stood facing a dozen or more soldiers with his back to a doorway that led to the principal living rooms. He was about thirty years of age with a strong, squat body and the craggy features of a Tuscan peasant. When he realised that Edmund spoke Italian the dogged, protective expression on his face relaxed.

'Thank God, Colonello!' he said, elevating Edmund in rank. 'It's not right for too many to go in there. But how can I explain to them?'

'What have you got here, signore?'

The Italian gave Edmund a long, intent look. Then he put

a key in the massive lock and flung open the door. 'See for yourself, Colonello.'

Edmund stepped out of the real world into pure fantasy. The interior was gloomy. Until his eyes adjusted themselves he could not see much. He was in a long room decorated in an ornate rococo style. The coffered ceiling was intricately carved and the walls were embellished with mirrors and escutcheons. The furniture, all of it high quality antiques, had been stacked at the far end of the room. The centre appeared to be full of square-shaped objects.

Then the custodian opened a pair of shutters and the sunlight streamed in. Its rays fell straight onto a large canvas in a gilt frame about twelve feet long by eight feet high. Edmund stopped dead, as dumbounded as the previous morning when he had met the King by the shores of Lake Bolseno.

'It's the Primavera! Botticelli's Primavera!'

The custodian beamed from ear to ear. 'Si. La Primavera di Botticelli.'

It was on the ground, leaning against the wall opposite the door. Slowly he walked towards it, still unable to believe that here in the front line of battle he was in the presence of one of the three most famous pictures in the world. How often he had gazed up in reverence at this canvas as it hung on the walls of the Uffizi Gallery. But now his face was almost on a level with that of Spring herself.

'Of course, I'm looking at it from the wrong angle,' he muttered, forgetting that the custodian could not understand a word of English. 'Lorenzo di Pierfrancesco had it painted for the wall of his bedroom. That's why it's designed on a rising plane.'

As he walked towards it the picture grew until he could almost believe that he was actually walking into the Garden of the Hesperides. The provocative face of Flora gazed out at him with parted lips. Her suggestive conspiratorial expression seemed to say, 'You've been a long time.' A smile like that was rare in neo-classical art. Her hand was poised ready to throw rose petals over him from the bundle she held in a fold of her dress. Further to the left the three Graces were absorbed in their joyful dance. The diaphanous draperies blown against their bodies by a Zephyr emphasised their sensuous curves.

Over their heads a blindfolded Cupid aimed his arrow at the most nubile of the three – she whose glance rested on the god Mercury. In the centre of the picture Venus herself stood with her belly thrust forward in that posture which in the fifteenth century was thought to be attractive. She was sumptuously clothed, unlike the figure in Botticelli's other great painting, the *Birth of Venus*. If his model for both pictures had indeed been Simonetta Vespucci he could not very well have presented her naked in *Primavera* when she represented the future wife of Lorenzo di Pierfrancesco. By contrast the nymph Chloris was shamelessly immodest, the flimsy veil doing nothing to conceal her pointed breasts and her 'apple of sweetness'.

From as close as this he could distinguish plants that he had not noticed before, not only the spruce, laurel, myrtle and orange trees of the background but the profusion of flowers in the foreground. Botticelli must have spent whole days during the summer of 1478 studying the very same flowers that Edmund had seen in the Tuscan landscape that morning. He was able to identify grape-hyacinth, pink, dandelion, anemone, periwinkle, cornflower, daisy, love-in-a-mist, forget-me-not. There was always something new to discover in this intriguing and fascinating picture, so different from the carefully grouped compositions of most Renaissance paintings. The figures seemed to be inviting you to take part in nuptial celebrations, which contrived to be at the same time decorous and bawdy.

He resisted a temptation to stroke the left buttock of the central Grace, but could not pass up this opportunity to bestow a kiss on the seductive mouth of Flora. He was actually approaching the canvas to press his lips on it when another pair of shutters crashed open behind him and more sunlight came flooding in. He looked round and could not believe his eyes. The entire *salone* was filled with paintings. They were stacked along the walls one behind another or leaning against a wooden rack in the centre of the room. In one incredulous sweep of his eye he took in half a dozen paintings that were milestones in the history of art. Half way along one wall Giotto's *Madonna enthroned* sat on her marble throne, the gilded background reflecting the sunlight. Beyond the tops of three other pictures rose another *Madonna* by Cimabue. At the end of the room the spears of Paolo Uccello's *Battle of San Romano* slanted upwards. Near the door stood Andrea del Sarto's *Annunciation*, the angel gazing at Mary against a background of Florentine architecture and Tuscan landscape. He recognised in quick succession the *Supper at Emmaus* by Pontorno, Rubens' *Nymphs and Satyres* and Filippo Lippi's *John the Baptist*.

There must have been a hundred canvases in the *salone*, but the custodian was beckoning him through another door.

'Venga, Colonello. Venga, venga.'

In room after room were stacked crucifixions, madonnas, saints, huge altar pieces. On a table in one room that had obviously been used as a canteen, Ghirlandaio's circular *Adoration of the Virgin* lay face upwards on a table. It was covered with coffee stains and had been ripped by a knife. In a chamber off the *cortile* stood the immense *Madonna* by Ruccelai from the church of Santa Maria Novella. Its impact in the dimly lit room was awe-inspiring. Nearby was a dark corridor where eight of Fra Angelico's chaste pictures were stacked; it exuded unmistakeable evidence that it had been used as a *pissort*.

'But how – how on earth did all these pictures come to be here?' This time Edmund remembered to speak in Italian.

'It's all official,' the custodian answered him. 'I signed for everything. Come, I'll show you the papers.'

He led Edmund back through the main *salone*, shutting the doors behind them. It was with difficulty that they persuaded the soldiers who had drifted in to leave the room. They were gazing at the pictures with reverence, awed by the contrast between these beautiful religious objects and the carnage of the battlefield they had come from. A couple of tough New Zealanders had knelt down in front of the *Primavera*, oblivious of its pagan imagery.

Edmund followed his guide to a small room where he kept his few papers in a drawer. He produced a bottle of *vin santo* and insisted on Edmund joining him in a drink.

'But I still can't believe it. You've got most of the great pictures from the Uffizi here.'

'Eh, Colonello!' The *custode* hunched his shoulders and spread his hands. 'E incredibile ma è vero.'

The Italian spoke with the rough Tuscan accent but slowly enough for Edmund to understand the gist of what he said. As the story unfolded he stared at this small man with growing amazement.

His name was Guido Masti. He had been employed by the Sitwells as a general factotum and his daughter Elia had been their cook. Masti's job included driving Osbert to see various art collections and he had picked up some of his employer's taste for beautiful things. At the outbreak of war the Sitwells had departed leaving him in charge of the premises. There had been no problems until November 1942 when one fine day a lorry arrived from Florence. Its cargo included half a dozen of the most valuable paintings from the Uffizi. To his astonishment Masti learnt that the *castello* was to become a *deposito* and that he was to have sole responsibility for these treasures.

'Look, Colonello.' The custodian handed Edmund a sheaf of typewritten sheets listing the paintings. 'My name is on them, they made me sign for everything.'

'November 18,' Edmund read out. He leafed through the sheets. 'November 20, 23, 24, 25 – '

'Si, Colonello! For one week they kept coming. Not till every room was full did they stop. And each time I had to sign for them.'

Their total value, he was told, was three hundred and twenty million dollars and he was paid the sum of seventeen lire a day for looking after them. In July, as the Germans fell back before the advancing Allies, the refugees who had crowded the basement were driven out by a detachment of the Waffen SS. Masti had no illusions about what that meant, but he was not cowed.

The crisis came when British shells began to fall nearby and the SS prepared to pull out. Masti heard the officer in command give orders for the paintings to be taken out and burned in accordance with Himmler's orders. Small as he was, Masti squared up to him and told him he could not do that.

'What did you say to him?' Edmund asked curiously.

'I told him these paintings were the heritage not just of Italy but of the whole world.'

Masti had evidently acquired some of his employer's eloquence as well as his appreciation of art. Astonishingly the SS officer had not shot him. He had glowered but had taken his men away, leaving the doors of the castle wide open and the customary noxious reminders of German occupation.

Listening to this account, told in the matter-of-fact tones of the *contadino*, Edmund knew that every word of it was true. To this humble man the world owed the survival of the *Primavera* and three hundred of Florence's greatest masterpieces.

'And are there other deposits like this one?'

'Sisignore. Not five kilometres away. At the Villa Guicciardini in Poppiano, and the Villa Bossi-Pucci at Montagnana.'

Poppiano was still inaccessible but Montagnana a few miles to the north had been absorbed by the advance of eighth Indian Division. After suggesting to the Commanding Officer of the Mahrattas that a guard should be put on the *castello*, Edmund set off in search of the Villa Bossi-Pucci. Was it too much to hope that all the paintings would survive as miraculously as those housed in the Castello Acciaioli?

Thanks to his Indian escort he was able to make the dangerous drive to Montagnana up a road that was still under enemy fire. The village was still very much in the front line. There was no problem in identifying the Villa. It was the only large building in the place. Outside the gates an Army chaplain in white surplice was conducting a burial service over a form wrapped in a khaki blanket. The earth was piled beside the temporary grave. Three of the dead man's friends were standing by with bared heads.

Edmund was thankful to get within the shelter of the building's thick walls, but he saw at once that things were very different here. The first sign was the picture in a broken frame lying abandoned in the hall. He ran up the stairs to the first floor. There was no sign of pictures in any of the rooms. On the floor lay several frames from which the canvasses had been cut. All the furniture left behind had been smashed to smithereens.

As he descended the staircase again he saw a forlorn figure coming out of one of the ground-floor rooms. The man was dressed in a dusty and crumpled civilian suit. His sagging shoulders showed that he was absolutely exhausted. He halted when he saw Edmund and waited for him to reach the hall.

'Santissima Madonna! Che desolazione!' He flapped his hands despairingly, appealing to this stranger to witness his mortification. 'They have taken away everything.'

'Are you the *custode*?'

'The custode and his family were driven out by the Germans. I am Professor Bussola from the Soprintendenza in Florence.'

'Professore! You remember me. Edmund Brudanell.' Edmund had not at first recognised the Professor behind the mask of dust and sweat on his face. 'I came out the summer before the war for the auction of the Monterosa Collection.'

'Edmundo!' Recognition had come. The professor opened his arms. 'Ma come mai? Che coincidenza!'

Edmund had spent long enough in Italy not to be embarrassed by sharing an affectionate hug.

'Not really such a coincidence, Professore. We're both interested in the same thing. How long have you been here?'

He had walked out from Florence, Bussola told Edmund, using those ancient sunken lanes that snake between the modern roads. He had slipped through the lines by night, regardless of bombs and bullets, to tell the British where the precious deposits were located so that they would not bomb or shell them. He had arrived at Montagnana an hour ago to find this desolation.

'How many pictures were here?'

'Three hundred at least. One eighth of the most valuable paintings in the Pitti and the Uffizi, gone at one stroke!' He pointed to the broken frame lying against the wall. 'You see? They just abandoned the *Presentation* of Lorenzetti. That shows the place was sacked by common troops. They did not know what they were doing. God help the pictures!'

Not even a chair had been spared. Edmund and the professor sat down on the bottom step of the staircase. Edmund offered the packet of cigarettes he carried for such occasions. Bussola accepted gratefully, inspecting the Lucky Strike with appreciation before Edmund struck a match for him.

'You will not smoke yourself?'

Edmund pulled the Dunhill pipe from the turn-down of his sock and reached for his tobacco pouch.

'Ah! La pipa. Very English.'

Bussola cheered up a little when he heard that the deposit at Montegufoni was intact.

'And Poppiano? The Villa Guicciardini? Have you been there?'

'Not yet. We still haven't captured it. But, Professore, can you tell me what the situation in Florence is? Are there no paintings in the city?'

'Many, many!' The professor seized Edmund's shirt button to emphasise the point. 'We managed to bring a few hundred back before the fighting came close. But even there they are not safe. The Kuntschutz wants to take them all back to Germany. And we heard that Himmler has given orders for those they could not take away to be burnt.'

'Himmler's orders?' Edmund took the pipe from his mouth.

The professor released the button and raised his hands, palms turned towards Edmund. 'You cannot believe what they are doing in Florence, Edmundo. They're looting, taking everything. Your troops *must* get there quickly or all will be lost. Povera Firenze! Povera Italia!' He clapped his hands over his ears as a shell exploded against one of the outside walls. The detonation echoed through the building.

'What about the Mostra del Rinascimento?' Edmund asked when the sound of falling plaster had stopped.

'The Mostra del Rinascimento? For us, that has been a great responsibility. All those paintings – they were from many countries, you know – were taken to Casa Gamberaia at San Donato in Collina, but we were able to bring them back to the Uffizi to a room on the ground floor . . . .'

'And the Botticelli Madonna?' Edmund had struck two matches but had still not put a light to his pipe. 'The picture lent by King Edward – '.

'Ah, your King's Madonna! Che bellezza!' A smile of sheer pleasure came over the professor's face. He put the fingers of his right hand together and kissed their tips. 'The most beautiful painting in the exhibiton. I wish it were ours.'

'Professore', Edmund persisted, 'is it still there?'

The enthusiasm died rapidly from Bussola's face and he became very serious again. 'When I left Florence it was still there, yes. But the Kunstschutz will do anything to get those pictures back to Germany. Hitler wants the entire collection for Linz.' His eyes widened dramatically. 'And you know that Goering has his own looting squads. One of our spies told us that he is determined to possess the King of England's Madonna.'

4

In his youth Adolf Hitler had been something of an artist. His pictures were usually of buildings and towns, with exaggerated perspective. They were agreeable to look at but lacking in originality and imagination. In 1907 he presented his portfolio to the Academy of Fine Arts in Vienna. He was refused admission. The reason given for his rejection was interesting; it was found that his pictures were too lacking in human figures. Had he been accepted and achieved his ambition to become an architect, the history of Europe would have been different. As it was he sought other outlets for his energy.

All his life he was inspired by a picture called *The Wild Huntsman*, by Franz von Stuck. It portrays a madman personifying death and destruction who rides forth at night leaving devastation and horror in his wake. The madman bears a close resemblance to Hitler for the very good reason that the founder of Nazism modelled his own appearance on the artist's terrifying image.

When he strode jack-booted to power through a welter of blood and tortured flesh he took with him a dream. It was to rebuild his birthplace Linz and make it the art centre of the world. Thanks to the good offices of his henchman Martin Bormann that dream came close to realisation. Plans for the new Linz reached the stage of architect's models and, as Hitler's armies swept over Europe, the occupied countries were ransacked and the pictures that would stock the galleries of Linz flowed back to Germany. To store them in safety Bormann adapted a disused salt mine at Alt Aussee near Bad Ischl in Austria. By 1944 he had amassed in the shored-up vault of this secret repository an international collection that exceeded in scope and value both the National Gallery in London and the Louvre in Paris.

The official German organisation for safeguarding art treasures from the ravages of war was the Kunstschutz, a branch of the Army. This comparatively respectable organisation was merely a smokescreen for the official Nazi looting agency, the Einstab Rosenberg. Through the activities of Alfred Rosenberg and his minions Poland, was stripped bare within a few weeks of its invasion in 1939. The Low Countries, France, Russia, in turn received his attention, but the best was yet to come. When Hitler's Italian allies defected there were no longer any fraternal treaties to prevent him seizing all he could lay his hands on. And the cream of Italian art was in Florence. The order had gone forth – a Führerbefehl – that Italian art treasures were to be brought back to the Reich 'to save them from the Anglo-American criminals and thieves'. Himmler, acting independently, had added his corollary. Any that could not be brought back were to be destroyed.

In his aspirations as an art collector Hitler had a rival. Hermann Goering was a genuine connoisseur of beautiful things and in his own quiet way he too was amassing a collection to surpass that of any multi-millionaire. But whereas Hitler went for quantity, Goering chose selectively. It was well known that the best way to curry favour with the Reichsmarschal was to make him a present of some masterpiece, preferably featuring a nubile nude. Mad Ludwig of Bavaria's fairy castle of Neuschwanstein and the mansion on his estate at Karinhall were soon overflowing with the best statues, pictures and other objets d'art that European genius had created.

Hitler's real intentions with regard to Florence were obscured by the event which took place on 20 July. He had received Field Marshal Kesselring on 19 July and had then given orders that Florence itself was not to be defended; 1st Parachute Division would stand on a line twelve kilometres south of the Arno. If Alexander was prepared to declare it an open city the bridges would be spared. This decision was to be communicated to the Allied high command through the Vatican. On the 20th Hitler had a miraculous escape when the bomb planted by von Stauffenberg and his conspirators failed to kill him. Il Duce del Fascismo, visiting him a few hours later, was able to congratulate him on his escape. When Mussolini took his leave Hitler was concerned not so much about the fate of Florence but that his visitor might feel cold without a coat. 'A Duce does not catch cold,' was the valiant reply.

Hitler however had caught something more than a cold. The effects of the bomb were mental as much as physical. During the next few weeks it was hazardous to approach him on any difficult question. The mystery and confusion surrounding German intentions and orders on Florence is due to the macabre twilight into which the Nazi hierarchy sank during those days.

Enemies are seldom on speaking terms. Whilst both Kesselring and Alexander expressed a virtuous intention to regard Florence as an open city there was no communication between them. It is not clear whether the Vatican ever passed on any messages. After the bombing of Montecassino, Kesselring was not prepared to trust Alexander. And after the massacre in the Ardeatine caves and countless other atrocities, Alexander was not prepared to trust Kesselring. Florence was an important centre of communication. Alexander suspected that Kesselring wanted to continue to use it himself but to deny its use to his enemy. And if negotiations failed, the Allies could be blamed for the destruction of the city.

So the population of Florence, swollen to half a million, could only wait – and pray. Their faith in the humanity of the Allies had been shaken when Impruneta, a gem of a township ten kilometres to the south, was hit by American bombers on the night of the 26th.

Since Fuchs and his paratroopers had taken over control of the city, life had become very different for the Florentines. The Prefect and the diplomats had gone. The German Consul, Gerhard Wolf, who had done so much to protect Florence and its citizens, had departed. Even the detestable Carità had packed up his hell's kitchen on the Via Bolognese and sped northwards in the comfort of a looted ambulance. The partisans who raided the house to free the operators of the secret radio station found it unguarded. All they had to do was unlock the cellars where their maimed and bleeding comrades lay. The Germans had destroyed the city's telephone exchange beyond repair by pouring acid over the terminals. Only a few essential lines had been left open. Now they were blowing up the bakeries in the outskirts of the town. The SS had gone, but these new occupiers were even worse. The paratroopers were tough and disillusioned campaigners, the same troops as had fought with such fanatical ferocity at Cassino. All over Florence they were going into shops and homes, looting watches, jewellery and valuables. Most sinister of all, they were building defensive positions. To the Florentines this could only mean one thing: they were going to fight for Florence as they had fought for Cassino. The thunder of the guns was even closer now. On Monte Scalari and the heights south of Florence 4th Parachute Division was fighting with a savagery not seen since the battles in the Liri Valley. But the advance of the Allies was irresistible. They would be on the Arno in a matter of days. The whole city was in a state of terror and apprehension.

Mario, coming across the Ponte Santa Trinità that morning, had seen cabalistic signs painted on the roadway. There were pink, yellow and blue arrows, obviously intended as guide lines for a retreating army. 1st Parachute Corps were going to withdraw *through* Florence. Already, he noted, motorised and horse-drawn German vehicles were moving out of the city.

Before going to the Soprintendenza he had gone round to Palazzo Lamberti to tell the Countess that Ornella had decided she did not wish to leave her apartment. She had been afraid that the move would upset the children even more.

'Besides,' she'd added, 'if the Arno is to be the front line we shall be on the Anglo-American side.'

'Ornella is foolish,' the Countess had said. 'You didn't try to dissuade her, Mario?'

'No! Per carità!'

In fact Mario had found himself arguing in favour of the move.

At the Soprintendenza he found Pantano engaged in bitter argument with a smartly dressed officer of the Kunstschutz. The 'art protectors' had not left the city with the diplomats and administration units.

'They must have broken in last night!' Pantano was protesting. 'It is a disgrace, a violation of all your undertakings.'

'I can assure you,' the German said stiffly, 'the Kunstschutz knows nothing of this. We shall investigate it with the utmost vigour. If you will let me have a list of the stolen paintings . . . .'

'Well, to begin with there is a *Deposizione* by Leonardo, one of his finest paintings . . . .'

'In writing, Professore.' The officer picked up his gloves

and cap. 'If you could send it to my office by mid-day. And from now on there will be a German guard on this gallery.'

When the officer had gone, Fabio mopped the top of his head. 'You know, Mario, it's a strange thing, I had the impression he was as angry as me that those paintings have been stolen.'

'Yes,' Mario agreed. 'I was watching him. I'm sure he was telling the truth. Of course, the Kunstschutz is acting under Hitler's orders but there are other unofficial looting agencies and I suspect that one of them was responsible for last night's theft. Have any of the Mostra paintings gone?'

'Not so far as I can tell. But I have not been able to inspect the collections yet.' Fabio opened a drawer and brought out a typewritten list. 'Now, if you will help me, I would like to make a thorough check.'

Mario was typing out a list of the missing paintings in triplicate when he heard a woman's light step on the stair. He finished the line before he looked up.

'Rosalba!'

'Mario, you must come at once!' She was frightened and breathless. 'Mamma sent me.'

'But what's happened? You look . . . .'

'We are all to be evacuated! Oh, Dio! What is to become of us?' Rosalba was near to tears. 'Colonel Fuchs has issued a proclamation . . . .'

'Evacuated? You mean everyone in Florence?'

'The whole centre of the city. Your house as well as ours. You must come at once.'

Hurrying back to the Palazzo with Rosalba, Mario saw for himself the proclamation that had been put up all over the centre of the city. On Colonel Fuch's orders an area was to be evacuated on either side of the Arno in the vicinity of the bridges. In length it was about two kilometres, stretching back to a depth of one or two hundred yards from the river. In all, some hundred thousand people were ordered to leave their homes. They were to take only hand luggage and the evacuation had to be complete by noon the following day. After that, the order stated bluntly, anyone found within the zone would be shot.

At the *palazzo* Mario found the family gathering in the *salone*. The Count, the Countess and Caterina were already there. The old Countess, Lorenzo's mother, had come over from her own house bringing her faithful attendant, Alessio. She looked angry and defiant in her black clothes, with her grey hair drawn back into a bun so tightly that it pulled the skin of her face into even deeper wrinkles. The servants looked to *Il Conte* with pathetic trustfulness to tell them what to do in this bewildering crisis. Caterina threw Mario a look which he interpreted as meaning some kind of reassurance. Lorenzo's brother Carlo had come over from his house facing the old Countess's. He was a small and ineffective man who had lived his life in the shadow of Lorenzo. He preserved what he considered to be his aristocratic dignity by always wearing dark suits.

'This can only mean one thing,' the Countess said. 'They are going to defend Florence. They intend to blow up the bridges.'

'It is not yet desided, tesoro. The Cardinal is still trying to have it declared an open city. He is taking a delegation to see the Commandante della Piazza at one o'clock and has asked me to accompany him. You see,' the Count added pointedly, 'there is something to be said for being on good terms with the Germans.'

'I have no intention of moving,' the old Countess was declaring. 'I have lived in the palazzo since I was married. Even if the devil himself came with his fork and tongs I would – I would tell him to go to the devil.'

Caterina crossed the room to her grandmother's side. She had always been the favourite. Her own mother and father had been killed in a car crash when she was a baby and the old lady had taken her into her own home and brought her up. Caterina put her arms round the old Countess's shoulders, began to kiss her cheek and stroke her head with her long fingers. There was something almost incestuously sexual about it. Mario wondered if she was giving a demonstration of what she could do when it came to kissing and caressing. Each time her right arm lifted it drew the silky material of her blouse across her breast so that it rippled to her movement.

'Don't worry, Nonna,' she purred. 'Your Caterina will not let any harm come to you.'

'There's no need to fuss,' the Count declared. 'Do you not understand what I am trying to tell you? It's a mistake, the line should have been drawn to the south side of the palazzo, not the north. That means it's not included in the evacuation zone.'

'How much did that cost you, Uncle?' Caterina asked shrewdly.

Lorenzo did not answer. He merely exchanged a glance with his wife, who nodded her approval. The Count turned to his son-in-law.

'Your flat is within the zone, Mario. That settles the question. You and Ornella and the children will have to move into the top flat with Caterina.'

Mario firmly kept his eyes away from Caterina's face.

Cardinal Elia Della Costa was the only person remaining in the city who had the authority to speak for its population. At one o'clock his seven-man delegation made its way on foot to the Piazza San Marco, where Colonel Fuchs had his Kommandantur. Fuchs was a tough professional soldier of about fifty with a square jaw and gimlet eyes. He wore the battlefield uniform of a paratrooper and on his chest the campaign medal for Crete. His cold and aloof manner made it clear that he had little use for Italians. His adjutant, the handsome young Baron von Münchhausen, stood by to act as interpreter.

The Cardinal's main request was that he should be allowed to send two emissaries with a safe-conduct through the German lines to the Allied high command 'to inform them of the situation in order that the responsibility for acts which could bring great harm to a city of such importance, not only for the Florentines but for all Italians and for the whole civilised world, should remain clearly determined before the judgement of history'.

Fuchs did not attempt to hide his irritation at the Italian's lack of obsequiousness and the pedantic wording of the statement. Its implications were not lost on him.

He replied tersely that as General Alexander had refused to declare Florence an open city his own commander, Kesselring, was under no obligation to exercise any restraint. He silenced the Cardinal's objections by reaching in his pocket and producing his trump card. It was a copy of a leaflet dropped over Florence by the RAF that morning. In it, Alex-

47

ander appealed to the Florentines to defend the bridges and prevent their destruction. 'It is vital,' the leaflet went on, 'for Allied troops to cross Florence without delay to complete the destruction of the German forces in their retreat northwards.'

'This proves,' Fuchs told the Cardinal 'that the Allies do not consider Florence an open city.'

On this note the meeting ended. The delegation walked back to the archbishop's palace and the Count returned to Palazzo Lamberti. There he locked himself in his private study and began systematically to destroy his correspondence with Il Duce del Fascismo.

On Sunday 30th Mario's thoughts were too occupied with his own problems for him to worry about the fate of paintings. The orthopaedic hospital of San Giovanni was within the evacuation zone and he could not find it in him to refuse the appeal for help in moving the patients. There were harrowing scenes as the aged and crippled were turned out of their beds and put on carts to be taken to the Pitti Palace or wherever they could find refuge.

It was eleven o'clock before he got back to his own flat, with a handcart no longer needed by the hospital. That left just one hour before the deadline. The streets were already full of pathetic little groups of people carrying bedding and as much of their belongings as they could. The lucky ones had handcarts, others were using prams, bicycles, trollies and, when all else failed, the tops of their heads.

Ornella had been incapable of deciding what to take and what to leave behind. The children had picked up her mood. They were tearful and fretful. Mario had to be ruthless in cutting down the clothes and toys they would take.

'It will only be for a few days,' he reminded them. 'It's for our own safety. The Kommandantur has said that we needn't worry about leaving things behind, even valuables. The Germans will ensure that there is no looting.'

He said it more to calm Ornella than because he believed the reassurances of Colonel Fuchs. A small truck would have been needed to carry the stuff she wanted to take.

It was eleven forty-five, only fifteen minutes before the deadline, by the time he chivvied them out of the flat and triple-locked the door. The streets had become ominously empty and hardly anybody was moving across the Ponte Vecchio. All the inhabitants on the south bank were being directed to the Pitti Palace, those on the north to the Campo di Marte, a sports park at the western end of the town.

They were in the middle of the bridge when Ornella stopped dead. The impetus of the handcart carried Mario several yards past her.

'My pills!' Mario turned on her furiously. 'I put them on the table in the hall and then with Anna being so upset about her doll's house I – I forgot all about them.'

She was so dumpy and dejected standing there that Mario's anger and exasperation evaporated. He looked at his watch. It was five minutes to mid-day.

'We can't go back now. Even as it is we'll have to hurry to get out of the zone in time. Come, let's get the children to the palazzo, then we can think.'

They hurried up the empty Via Por S Maria and turned right along the Via SS Apostoli. Detachments of paratroopers were already forming up to move into the evacuated zone and enforce the total ban on all civilian movement. Some of them found light relief in the spectacle of the scared Italian trundling his handcart with his plump wife and two kids trotting to keep up with him.

As the big bells of the Duomo led the chorus of all the clocks striking mid-day an unearthly silence fell on the area either side of the Arno. Nothing moved in the streets where Ghibelline had once hunted Guelf. From beyond the hills the thump and rumble of gunfire gave proof that the battle for Florence was raging as fiercely as ever.

The flat of the absent Pedrottis was on the top floor and gave a fine view over the city's roof-tops. Caterina had moved her own things into the small bedroom, leaving the big double room free for Mario, Ornella and the children. Now she was making *pasta asciuta* on a camping-gas stove in the kitchen. Before they ate, she insisted on helping Ornella to make up the beds. Mario, ostensibly unpacking the children's toys, was able to see through the bedroom door. Caterina had her back to him as she bent over the bed smoothing the sheets. Feeling his eyes on her she glanced round and he averted them just in time.

'I don't want to be a nuisance,' she assured Ornella as the five of them sat at the kitchen table, winding the long strands of spaghetti round their forks. 'After today I can have my meals in my room. You and Mario will want your privacy.'

'No, no, Caterina, per carità!' Ornella protested. 'For as long as we are here you are part of the family. Non è vero, Mario?'

Mario kept his eyes on his plate. Caterina could make even the act of eating spaghetti sexually provocative. The stories he had heard made her if anything more fascinating. It was whispered that living alone out at Poggio Imperiale she had found consolation in the arms of a German SS officer, and perhaps more than one.

To cover the flush he felt come over his cheeks he said, 'Ornella left her pills in the flat.'

'No!' Caterina was shocked. 'How long can you go without them?'

'I have enough in my handbag to last me till tomorrow, but then . . . .'

'What will you do?'

Ornella glanced helplessly at Mario. 'I don't know. Try to get some more, I suppose. But my doctor is in the Oltrearno and he told me already that supplies are very short.'

'How could you, Ornella?' Caterina chided. 'Forget them like that?'

'It wasn't my fault!' Ornella cried. 'Mario left everything to me – the children and tidying up the flat and all the packing.' Her face crumpled and as the children gaped she put her napkin to her face, pushed her chair back and stumbled sobbing out of the kitchen.

Mario and Caterina were left staring at each other across the table.

Lunch had scarcely been cleared away when a boy arrived from the Soprintendenza. Fabio Pantano had sent him round to say that Mario was urgently required at the Uffizi.

Piazza Signoria was just outside the forbidden zone but it was no longer the place where the Florentines loved to stroll under the gaze of the statues of David and Hercules or to loiter by the fountains of Neptune. For some reason Mario did not want to cross the wide open space. He hurried past the Loggia dei Lanzi and slipped down the Via della Nina to the door of the Soprintendenza.

Fabio had shrunk further inside his grey suit. The lines in his cheeks were deeper than ever.

'Un disastro!' he announced as soon as he saw Mario. 'All gone! All looted!'

Mario stopped, appalled. 'Everything from the Uffizi?'

'The Mostra del Rinascimento. That's bad enough, is it not? And no sign of the guard the captain promised.' Fabio was cruising round the room like a caged animal that knows all too well there is no escape. 'All of them priceless masterpieces – a Leonardo, a Cimabue, a Michelangelo, a Verrocchio, a Baldovinetti, a Fra Angelico . . . .' His voice broke as he recollected in his mind the works that had vanished. 'What can we say to the owners? What are we to say to the Louvre, the Prado, the Metropolitan, the King of Britain . . . .'

'Has the Botticelli Madonna gone?'

'I told you, Mario. Everything!' Fabio was almost shouting, his anger focussing on Mario, who appeared slow to comprehend the magnitude of the loss. 'And the final insult. They used our own lorry that they commandeered from us. S'immagini! The Soprintendenza's own lorry!'

Fabio put his handkerchief away and fastened all the buttons on his jacket. Of another man it might have been said that he squared his shoulders, but of Fabio it would be true to say that he leaned back as if determined not to let his paunch weigh him down.

'I am going straight to the Kommandantur. I want you to come with me as a witness.'

They could have saved themselves the trouble of the kilometre walk to Piazza San Marco. They were kept waiting for two hours before being called in to the office of the Commandante della Piazza's sauve assistant. Major the Baron von Münchhausen told them that it was quite impossible for them to see Colonel Fuchs but if they made a complaint in writing the matter would be investigated.

As they left the Kommandantur, Mario noticed an Opel truck parked in the square. It bore the markings of a German engineer battalion. A detail of soldiers was unloading boxes of explosives and transferring them carefully to a smaller Kübelwagen utility. It confirmed his suspicion that the reason

51

for moving the inhabitants out of the forbidden zone had not been their own safety. His own military service had been done in the engineers and he knew TNT when he saw it.

During the next three days the standard of living in Florence steadily declined. Even in the tight-knit little community within the *palazzo* the deprivation bit deep. All the electric cookers were out of action. Ornella and Caterina were still using the little camping-gas stove to prepare the children's meals, praying that the cylinder would not run out.

Ornella's supply of pills was exhausted and the symptoms of rising blood pressure were beginning to show. As the days went by she became more and more fretful, subject to fits of breathlessness and irrational bouts of weeping. Caterina took over more and more of the responsibility for the children.

'I enjoy doing it.' She smiled at Mario when he tried to thank her. 'Jacopo and I have no children of our own. But I must be careful. Ornella may not like it. I think she is a little jealous.'

'Jealous?'

Caterina looked up at him under her long eyelashes. Her expression was all innocence.'

'Jealous in case the children become too fond of me.'

On Monday 31 August the water supply was cut off. It was a worse blow than the loss of electricity. Fortunately there was the ancient well in the courtyard. The Count decreed that its water was to be rationed to one bucket a day for each person. Mario spent much of his time labouring up the long flights of stairs with the four buckets allocated daily to the flat. He also had the less pleasant task of carrying the slops down for disposal in the pit laboriously dug by old Alessio. He was secretly glad to have this chore. It got him out of the flat and made it easier for him to avoid being left alone with Caterina.

Caterina had insisted that they must share their food with the old Countess. After they had eaten, she would always take a dish over to the old lady and the faithful Alessio.

'Nonna looked after me when my parents were killed,' she reminded Mario. 'So I must look after her now.'

The normal hygienic services of the city had broken down and refuse was beginning to pile up. A new black market, this time in drinking water, had come into being. A litre bottle fetched 100 lire. Such trading was carried out in the street, for the shops had all closed. Only necessity now brought the people out of their houses. The sun still shone from blue skies but the shadow of fear fell over everyone. Families closed their shutters and clung to the refuge of their houses. From the forbidden zone came the occasional sound of a shot as the patrols spotted some luckless civilian trying to creep back to his home. The smell of cordite drifted down from the battlefields, mingling with the stink of sewage and rotting food.

Now that his sister was occupying a flat in the *palazzo* Guido had made the apartment his base. He had Federico constantly in tow. Neither Ornella nor Mario liked the foxy-faced young Communist with his sneering references to the Lamberti's wealth, and the arrogant way he propounded his Marxist philosophy. Ornella agreed to feed them on condition they made some contribution. But she refused to let them sleep in the flat. The two partisans had to doss down in a room in the basement.

On Wednesday 2 August Guido and Federico turned up just as Ornella, Mario, Caterina and the children were sitting down to their mid-day meal. Guido was excited. Federico wore his usual sour expression.

'Got them!' Guido announced triumphantly as he strode into the kitchen.

'Oh, Guido,' Ornella protested petulantly. 'What is that supposed to mean? Got what?'

'Pills. One of our doctors had a supply of something in the house and he agreed to let me have a few.' He handed her a cardboard cylindrical box. 'Don't lose them. I may not be able to get any more.'

'Guido! You're a good brother!' Ornella stood up and put her arms round him. 'Grazie mille.'

'It's nothing,' said Guido, accepting her kiss. 'You may be able to do me a good turn some time. What's for lunch?'

'Pasta asciuta.'

'Pasta asciuta again!'

'You're lucky to have anything, Guido. If Papa had not laid in a reserve of flour . . . .'

'It's the Allies bombing everything on the roads,' Federico

remarked. He had sat down without invitation and poured himself a glass of wine from the Chianti bottle. 'That's why the food convoys can't get through.'

As the two partisans started on their plates of *tagliatelle* Mario glanced at Caterina. Her face was closed and hostile. She seldom spoke when Federico was present. The antipathy between them was almost tangible, though that did not prevent Federico from sliding his eyes over every part of her body except her face. She sat down at the table as far from him as possible.

Guido put his fork down when he had wolfed a few mouthfuls.

'It's as we thought, the Germans are going to blow up the bridges. It's called Fall Feuerzauber – Operation Firewizard.'

'How do you know this?' Mario demanded.

'From our agents in the SD. The Germans made an air photo survey of the whole area along the Arno and their official photographers have been taking pictures of the historic buildings. Why would they do that unless they mean to destroy them?'

'But surely Kesselring wants to have Florence declared an open city?' Caterina said, breaking her silence.

'It's orders from Hitler. All the bridges are to be blown up . . . .'

'*All* the bridges?' Mario echoed. 'Even the Ponte Santa Trinità?'

'All the bridges except the Ponte Vecchio.'

'I can't believe it. The Ponte Vecchio is not to be compared with the Ponte Santa Trinità.'

'I know.' Guido nodded. 'But apparently Hitler has a soft spot for the Ponto Vecchio. The Germans say it's his Lieblingsbrücke – his darling little bridge.'

Federico laughed.

'That shows how much Hitler knows about art,' Mario exclaimed angrily. 'That bridge is the finest in Europe, perhaps the world. Michelangelo himself drew the design for Ammanati and . . . .'

'It's all right, Mario,' Guido cut in with a smile. 'The Ponte Sante Trinità will not be blown up.'

'How can you say that?'

Guido exchanged a look with Federico. 'Because we're

going to remove the charges. That's how you can do us a favour, Ornella.'

Federuco leant back in his chair and stared across the table at Mario. His minatory expression contrasted with Guido's persuasive manner.

'The Anglo-Americans will almost certainly enter the city the day after tomorrow so we will have to do it tonight. We need somewhere to assemble close to the forbidden zone and the palazzo is right on the edge of it . . . .'

'Guido, you don't mean this apartment . . . .'

'Wait. We'll disperse after the raid so we won't be coming back here. But if any of our people are wounded we shall need a place to bring them. Rosalba is trained as a nurse . . . .'

'No, Guido.' Ornella's breathing had speeded up and her colour had heightened. 'I will not allow it. I have the children to think of . . . .'

'Guido,' Mario put a hand on Ornella's arm. 'I don't think it is fair to ask . . . .'

'Bear in mind,' Federico interrupted in his grating voice, 'that in a few days the partisans will be in control of the city and the Committee of Liberation will have taken over. Things could be difficult for people who refused to support the movement.'

From eleven o'clock that night young men were slipping into the *palazzo* through the tunnel that had been made in the old days of the Guelf-Ghibelline factions. Its opening was in a cellar near the basement being used by Guido and Federico. They made their way in ones and twos to the flat on the third floor. When all ten of them had arrived there was not much room in the small *salotto* for Mario, Ornella and Caterina. Rosalba brought the number of the *squadra* up to eleven. She was pale and apprehensive.

The partisans had smuggled their weapons concealed under their coats or stuffed down their trouser-legs – old rifles, shot-guns, pistols, a couple of Sten guns dropped in the Appenines by the RAF, and half a dozen Italian army Red Devil hand grenades. The oldest of the group was twenty-one. Most of them wore fierce expressions to hide their fear.

Federico made them sit on chairs or squat on the floor

while he remained standing. In that way he was able to dominate the meeting.

'You are all volunteers,' he told them. 'If anyone wants to back out, say so now.' Eight pairs of eyes stared back at him unblinkingly. No one spoke and Federico did not wait long. 'All right. Now, I'm keeping the plan simple so there will be no excuse for not remembering your orders. Listen carefully.'

The plan certainly was simple. Mario shivered as he thought of these raw youths going out to tacke the battle-hardened paratroopers.

'When the job is done we disperse as arranged. If we can preserve silence there need be no shooting. At the worst we can jump in the river and swim for it. Is that clear?'

'Wounded, Federico?' Guido prompted.

'Oh, yes. Any wounded can be brought back here. Rosalba over there is a trained nurse.'

Eight apprehensive young faces swung towards Rosalba standing in the doorway. They must have found reassurance there for when they faced Federico again they had the dedicated look of men who have found a cause worthy of the big sacrifice.

They were silent as they filed out, Guido and Federico the last. Guido did not look even at his sisters, much less at Mario and Caterina.

The waiting was long. The children had been put to bed hours before but they had caught the atmosphere and would not go to sleep. The three women passed the time reminiscing about their childhood: how Ornella had always been the pretty one admired by all the boys, how Rosalba had fallen in love with the Englishman she met when she'd gone over to do the London Season, how they had both been jealous of Caterina because she was the favourite of Grandmamma and was always being held up as a shining example of how little girls ought to behave.

When the hands of the clock moved round to ten-past-one they all fell silent. Ornella's lips were moving and her eyes were closed. Rosalba, though pale, was impassive, with that ethereal look which fascinated Mario but at the same time estranged him.

A few minutes passed and then they heard a fusillade of shots from the direction of the river. That was followed by three staccato explosions. Then came the harsh blare of an automatic weapon.

'Oh, Dio!' Rosalba put a hand to her throat.

For the next five minutes sudden bursts of machine-gun fire were interspersed with single shots. From the street below came the quick tramp of booted feet, a detachment of soldiers running towards the river.

'Non ne posso piu!' Ornella had gone down on her knees and was audibly praying. Rosalba quickly went to check up on the first aid equipment she had prepared.

It was half-an-hour before they heard steps on the stairs and a dragging sound. Mario rushed to open the front door. The light of the candles fell on Guido and another young partisan. Their faces were haggard and they were dripping wet. Between them they supported the drooping form of Federico. His head and face were covered with blood. Mario checked that the staircase was empty and closed the door.

'What happened?' Caterina demanded. She was staring in fascination at Federico's contorted features.

Guido and his comrade put the wounded hero down on the sofa. Rosalba knelt swiftly beside him and began to wipe the blood away so that she could locate the wounds.

'It was a massacre,' Guido said, straightening up. He was still in a state of shock. 'They must have known we were coming.'

'The others?' Mario hardly dared to ask the question.

'Two were shot on the bridge, three taken prisoner. The rest of us jumped into the water but the Germans were shooting at us from the bridge. They hit everyone except Cesare and me. The only one we could get to was Federico.' Guido nodded at the wounded man. 'We let ourselves be carried down by the current and got ashore just below the Ponte alla Carraia before the patrol came along.'

'The explosive charges. Did you have time to remove them?'

On the sofa Federico raised his head and found his voice. 'That damned bridge!' he screamed. 'Five men killed and you are worrying about the blasted bridge.'

His injuries were not as bad as they appeared. He had hit the pointed buttress of one of the piers as he jumped into the water. His left ankle was broken or at least sprained and he had cuts on his head. No bullets had hit him. When Rosalba had stopped the bleeding and put dressings on, Guido agreed to take him down to the basement.

By the time the morning sun woke the children the flat had been cleaned up and there was no trace of the partisans' visitation.

That day, Thursday 3 August, the sound of battle was at the very gates of the city. Vehicles, horse-drawn and motorised, were pouring across the bridges, following the coloured signs Mario had seen painted on the roadway. The Germans had become very edgy. A total curfew had been imposed on the entire city. The order stated that anyone seen on the streets or even at the window of a house would be shot.

What could this mean unless a deed of darkness was to be perpetrated in broad daylight?

Marshal Kesselring was at the headquarters of OK Sud in Recoaro that evening. Since his meeting with his Führer on 19 July he had received no very clear directive other than that the bridges of Florence, with the exception of the Ponte Vecchio, were to be blown up. Kesselring was one of the few generals who had not sent Hitler congratulations on his escape from the bomb plot of 20 July. He had been in bad odour for sparing the bridges of Rome and he was not about to commit the same mistake again. At 6.15 his Chief of Staff authorised 14th Army to carry out the demolition 'as envisaged'.

At 7.30 a signal relaying this order was despatched from 14th Army to General Schlemm, the Commander of 1st Parachute Corps. In due course the order was passed on to the Kommandantur in Florence, where a Corps Engineer Battalion was standing by in readiness.

The matter was now in the hands of Colonel Fuchs.

At ten o'clock that evening there was still plenty of light in the sky. A small Auster monoplane was cruising high above the Arno. It was piloted by a gunner who had learnt to fly an aircraft. He was an Air Observation Officer of the South African artillery and he was spotting for a programme they were firing in support of the New Zealand division. The air was still and the enemy guns were silent, waiting for him to buzz off before they opened up again. Suddenly he felt the Auster buck as if an invisible fist had punched it from below . . . .

Down in Palazzo Lamberti Ornella was trying to soothe the children to sleep with an old Tuscan lullaby. Shells were falling near the Ponte della Vittoria, their ugly crump-crump echoing through the streets. Caterina was in the kitchen washing the dishes used for the evening meal. Mario had just brought up two buckets of water in readiness for the morning.

'Grazie, Mario.' She turned to smile at him. 'Sei bravo. Why are you looking so nervous?'

Over her shoulder he could just see the roofs of the houses on the Ponte Vecchio. From the direction of the Piazza Signoria came the sound of a clock chiming the quarters prior to striking ten.

Before it had time to strike the hour the guts of Florence were torn out by a gigantic explosion. It shook the earth and the blast was so colossal that human ears could hardly register it. The very foundations of the *palazzo* trembled. Mario felt his scalp move. The cutlery on the draining-board danced.

Caterina's eyes widened. Her mouth opened to scream but no sound came out. She spun round, and, as if impelled by the shock-wave rushed into Mario's arms. She pressed her body against him like a child seeking refuge at her mother's breast. But this was no child. He put his arms round her and held her tight.

As the reverberations died away the children began screaming with terror. Looking over Caterina's head Mario saw a column of thick smoke rising from the area of the Via de' Guicciardini, just beyond the Ponte Vecchio. Somewhere in the *palazzo* a man was shouting. Running feet pounded in the street below. And still he held her. Even in the moment of fear he felt the softness of her breasts and the suppleness of her waist.

It was the sound of Ornella's desperate movements and the continuous crying of the children that brought him back to his senses.

'Mario! Mario! Where are you? It's an air raid.'

'They're blowing up the bridges.'

'No, it's an air-raid, like Berlin and Hamburg! I'm going to take the children down to the basement.'

'There's no point,' he shouted. 'That's why they cleared the zone. We're safe here.'

'We could all be killed. Dio mio, è un finimondo!'

Mario tried to free himself from Caterina but she held him. 'Stay,' she whispered. 'I need you more.'

There was a minute of frenzied movement from the other room as Ornella grabbed for blankets, pillows and candles for the children to carry. Given something to do, they had stopped crying. Muttering prayers, Ornella hurried them through the hall, her slippers flapping. She was so obsessed with the instinct to get below ground that she knocked over the hall table and sent a Faenza vase flying. The sound of their footsteps receded down the stairs. She had left the door of the flat open.

'Leave it.' Caterina still spoke in a whisper. 'No one will come.'

Mario had wanted to go and help Ornella but he was like a man half asleep who cannot make the effort to get up. Caterina was pressing herself against him. Her face was turned up, her eyelids drooping, her lips parted. 'Kiss me.'

Gently at first he put his mouth to hers. Her tongue flickered out and the shock of it went through his whole body. Ornella, good Catholic that she was, had never made so bold. He crushed her to him, mouth to mouth, pelvis to pelvis, as they tried to blend their bodies into one unit.

He glanced up wildly in a desperate attempt to hold onto reality. Through the window he saw the great cloud of dust rising over the Arno, tinted an unearthly orange in the afterglow of sunet.

'Oh, amore!' Caterina breathed. 'Ti voglio tanto bene.'

Her tongue explored his ear as his hand slipped to the strong curve below her waist.

'Do you want me, Mario?' Her voice was more urgent now. 'Do you?'

'Yes. Dio mio, I want you!'

Abruptly she pushed him away from her and with one violent movement pulled the front of her dress apart. The buttons, ripped from their moorings, skittered across the tiles of the kitchen floor. Under the dress she was naked. He stooped, put a hand behind her legs and swung her off her

60

feet. As he carried her into the hall towards the double bedroom she said, 'No! My room.'

Caterina's bed was narrow but firm. As he dumped her on it, she never took her eyes from his face. The sight of her struggling to free herself from the sleeves of her dress enflamed him. He somehow managed to shed his own clothes.

'Sei bello, Mario.' She was staring at him with frank interest. Ornello had been too prudish ever to do that. He found it very exciting. His aching for her became unbearable.

They were both too aroused to spare time for preliminary caresses. As they coupled she gave a gasp and a cry, rolling her head from side to side in a frenzy that could have been agony or ecstasy.

The second explosion, ten minutes after the first, was even louder. It was as if the heart was being torn out of Florence.

Caterina's body convulsed, gripped him tighter. 'Don't go! Stay here! It's the end of the world.'

Even if we are to die in the next minute, Mario thought, I will have experienced this consummation. As fragments of stone pattered down on the roof overhead and a second column of smoke rose to obscure the last of the daylight, he clung to her, ready to perish with her, made one flesh.

'The third,' he murmured.

'What did you say?'

'The third. It's the third of August.'

After that second explosion there was silence for two hours. Silence, that is, exept for the murmurings of terror that came from the houses nearest the forbidden zone.

'How long is it since you made love?' Caterina asked, lying back relaxed now, her fingers teasing his chest.

'Two years. Maybe three.'

She laughed, a deep laugh that had a touch of possessiveness in it. 'You have a lot of time to make up.'

She rolled over onto her stomach, supporting her chin on her elbows so that her back dipped to the curve, pliant as a withy.

'Ti piace la mia schiena?'

From midnight onwards the explosions followed each other at intervals of about two hours, and each explosion goaded them into a fresh passion of love-making. Florence was being

61

torn in two and Mario knew that the same thing was happening to his heart and his life.

During one of the longer lulls he got up to fetch a glass of water from the jug in the kitchen. The outer door of the flat was still open. He knew that he ought to go down and find Ornella but all he did was close it. From the kitchen window he looked out towards the Arno. The light of a nearly full moon was struggling to pierce the great cloud of black smoke that hung over the city.

'Mario,' Caterina called from the dark bedroom, 'What are you doing?'

'Just getting a glass of water,' he said, the sadness already starting to seep through him.

'Don't be long. I'm frightened of being alone.'

And Ornella? Was she not frightened too, huddling down there in the basement with his two children? All the same, he went back to the bedroom where Caterina reached out towards him as if he had been gone a month.

The last of the explosions, at five o'clock, came from the direction of the Ponte Santa Trinità. Ammanati's creation was as strong as it was beautiful. Three sets of charges had been needed to destroy it. From the kitchen window Mario could not see the houses in ruins all along the river, but he knew all too well that the bridges of Florence had gone. The ironic beauty of the sunrise sharpened the double agony in his heart.

Caterina had at last fallen asleep under a crumpled sheet. He crept into her room like a thief, found his clothes and went into the double bedroom to put them on. Then, already tormented by remorse, he started down the stairs to look for his wife.

5

In the end it was the South Africans who won the race to the Arno. One of their patrols pushed forward as far as the river at 4.30 a.m. on 4 August. They were fired on from the northern bank and pulled back to report that the Oltrearno was clear of enemy.

The Florentines still cowered in their houses terrified by the explosions, far heavier than bombs, that had punctuated the night. Even the small wagtails that frequent the Arno had fled from their haunts. The sluggish river, a breeding ground for mosquitoes, lazily nudged its way past the débris of the blown bridges. Overhead the little Auster was already circ-ling, its pilot peering down through the cloud of smoke tinted red by the rising sun. The city had been sliced in two, a dismembered and eviscerated body but still breathing. The historic centre, once the haunt of the proud Medici, was in ruins. Ancient palaces had been reduced to rubble and dust, mediaeval towers toppled. The parish priest of Santo Stefano had seen the destruction of his church and lay dead of a broken heart.

Edmund had spent the night at Tac HQ of 6th South African Armoured Division. He was roused at 5.30 by the Intelligence Officer.

'One of our patrols has reached the Arno. Tanks of the Imperial Light Horse and a company of the Scots Guards are at the Porta Romana. They report no enemy south of the river.'

Edmund dressed quickly and hitched a lift with a liaison officer who was going forward in a Daimler Scout Car. The main Siena-Florence road was littered with the junk of recent fighting – burnt-out tanks, corpses in the gutters, masonry and dirt on the road. The sappers had put up white tapes to mark the route cleared of mines. A company of tin-hatted infantry sat on a grassy bank, resting before moving on to the city. They paid little attention to the familiar spectacle of a burial party in a roadside field.

It was seven o'clock when the Scout Car reached the Porta Romana. The Eighth Army troops, experienced in capturing towns and cities, had already imposed their casual but efficient patina on the scene. A large notice had been put up at the end of Via Romana: 'Under enemy observation'. A couple of tanks with open turrets were parked at the side of the square. An MP was preventing any vehicles from moving into the city.

Edmund climbed out of the Scout Car with the haversack into which he had stuffed his gear and some iron rations. He watched the Daimler move off up the hill towards Piazzale Michelangelo, then turned towards the Porta Romana. The gateway to Florence was only a hundred yards away from him. Through that arch Dante had passed on the mission to Rome from which he never returned, and through it the Emperor Charles V had ridden when he came to instal his son-in-law on the throne of Florence. The sun was high enough now to shine on the ancient stones. The savage battles for Florence were over and already the war seemed far away. The Germans had vanished, but the high peaks of the Appenines looming mistily to the north were a reminder that they lived to fight another day – in the Gothic Line.

He strolled towards a YMCA tea van that had pulled up near the two tanks. The driver was a girl in a grey hat and uniform. She was just opening up the side of the van. She had ash-blonde hair and the kind of face you saw on the first page of *The Tatler*. Edmund took his place in the queue of other ranks that had already formed. There had not been time to snatch even a cup of tea before he left Tac HQ.

When his turn came, he said, 'Cup of tea and a wodge, please.'

The eyes of the girl in grey flickered briefly, but she was careful to make no distinction of rank.

'With or without?'

'Oh. With, please.' His mind had flashed back to London. He had just realised why Helen considered it so important to be on the scene of an 'incident' promptly. There was something immensely comforting about receiving a cup of hot tea from an attractive young woman. Her voice was Mayfair but without any trace of snobbishness. The soldiers munching wodges and sipping tea were feasting their eyes unashamedly on this unexpected vision of home and beauty.

A trooper of the Special Service battalion who'd been

behind him in the queue was able to give Edmund a quick run-down of the situation in the southern part of the city. 'Jerry's pulled out, sir, but it's a bloody shambles down there. He's blown up everything and the streets is full of rubble, mines everywhere and snipers taking pot shots from the roof-tops.' He nodded at the YMCA girl. 'Nice bit o'crumpet, sir. Wish I was in the Guards Brigade. Goes everywhere with them, she does, right up in the front line.'

To avoid the MPs on the Via Romana, Edmund made a detour through the Boboli gardens and came out at the Piazza Pitti. From the direction of the Palace came the babble of a thousand voices. The vast building had once been occupied by the Grand Dukes of Tuscany. Until 1943 it had been a residence of the Italian Royal Family. Now it was crammed with evicted families. Bed-clothes had been hung out to air at the windows. Under the arches at either end smoke rose from dozens of fires and improvised cookers. In the square, every Allied soldier was surrounded by an eager crowd, largely of women.

He spotted in the crowd a young Italian with an ancient rifle slung over his shoulder. He was in civilian dress except for a peaked cap and a green, red and white arm-band. His face was alert and intelligent but he had the lost look of a man who returns to his own home only to find that some stranger has organised a party there. As he saw Edmund coming towards him, he moved to meet him. His face lit up with pleasure when he heard this *Inglese* addressing him in Italian.

His name was Corrado, he explained, and he was a member of the Giustizia e Libertà partisan brigade. He had been cut off from his unit when the bridges were blown.

Edmund nodded towards the Pitti Palace. 'Any pictures left in there?'

The Italian shook his head. 'It's chock full of refugees. The Germans drove out everybody from their houses – sick old men, dying women, suckling babies, everyone.'

'Any way of getting across the Arno?'

'Impossible!' Corrado annihilated the idea by wagging his index finger to and fro. 'The Ponte Vecchio is blocked and mined, the other bridges blown up. If I could cross I wouldn't be here, I promise you.'

He swelled with pride when Edmund talked to him as one fighting man to another. Yes, he knew a way down to the river without going through the mined area. Had he not lived here all his life?

He led Edmund through a corner of the Boboli gardens and then by a circular route through narrow streets and alleys to the Piazza S Maria Sopr'Arno. This was the spot where Florentine swains liked to bring their sweethearts but now it was deserted.

Corrado stopped aghast as they emerged from an archway. Between this small square and the Ponte Vecchio a hundred yards away, not a house was standing. The Via de'Bardi and the *palazzi* along it had become so many heaps of rubble.

Edmund could not speak. He walked to the balustrade overlooking the river and leant his elbows on it. He had been moved enough by the ruins of the Monastery of Montecassino, but in a way the Monastery, however sacrosanct, could be seen as a fortress standing on its lofty hill. This was different. This was a city where people lived, a city prized by its inhabitants more than any other. What made the destruction seem so pointless was that no battle had been fought here. The din of war which for weeks had been a constant background had ceased. There was silence on the Arno broken only by the occasional crack of a rifle or a burst of Spandau fire or the thud when some unwary person stepped on a mine.

'Capitano!' He felt Corrado tugging at his belt. 'Take care! The Germans are still on the other side.'

He did not heed the Italian. He was staring towards the Ponte Vecchio. Often he had stood at this very spot taking in the famous view of the bridge with the ancient palaces reflected in the water. Now they were slag heaps spilling into the river. Nothing moved on the opposite bank, no vehicles, no bicycles, no people. The only sign of life came from the window of a house further down where a solitary old woman waved a white handkerchief.

He still found it hard to take in the extent of the damage. From the Mercato Nuovo on the north side, to the Palazzo Pitti on the south was a clean sweep of destruction. Here and there wierdly-shaped fragments of buildings rose like phantoms. It was possible to see straight through to the square block of Orsanmichele and the Cathedral, so little was left of the buildings between. As if to emphasise the point, a nauseating stink wafted from the wreckage. The sewers had been smashed, for the Germans had placed their charges deep so as to blow the buildings upwards.

Gradually he had become aware that the rifle shots he was hearing had come from one particular spot, just at the edge of the demolished zone. With Corrado tagging him he moved round and saw slightly below him a man lying in the marksman's position, legs spread in a V shape and the barrel of his .303 rifle steadied on a fallen block of masonry. He was wearing British uniform, but with long trousers rather than short. A service-dress cap was pushed onto the back of his head. As they watched he squeezed the trigger, a round went off and his shoulder jerked. He slid quickly back behind cover. From across the river came the reply – a long burst of Spandau fire spraying the rubble fifty yards away. The Germans had not pin-pointed the source of the fire. The marksman worked the bolt to eject the spent cartridge. Then he picked up a stone and scratched a mark on a smooth slab of masonry. There were three marks on it already. He rolled over to take another clip of ammunition from his haversack and saw the two men watching him.

'A couple of brace. That'll do for now.'

He applied the safety catch and squirmed back. When he was under cover of the same wall as Edmund and Corrado he stood up. 'Would you ask your friend not to point his rifle in my direction?'

Edmund gently pushed the barrel of Corrado's old rifle round till it was pointing across the river. 'Where's the rest of your unit? You're not Scots Guards.'

'My battalion was pulled back to a rest area near Siena. I decided to apply for some leave.'

He was wearing a Major's crown on the shoulder of his tropical shirt, but he was seven or eight years younger than Edmund. Battle fatigue had etched shallow lines on his face. His manner was deliberately casual and languid. The blue eyes were hard and bitter. That easy smile was no more than a gesture.

A second burst of machine-gun fire spattered the tottering wall of the house behind them. By common consent the three men moved back into what was left of the Via de'Bardi.

'Odd way to spend your leave,' Edmund suggested.

The Major brushed the dust off his uniform and corrected the angle of his peaked cap. He too carried a bulging haversack slung from his shoulder.

'Well, I have my reasons.'

One of the reasons, he explained in his off-hand way, was that his battalion had taken a real pasting in their attack on a feature in the Chianti hills called Monte Piccolo. The Commanding Officer had been killed by a mortar bomb and his own Company Sergeant Major had been shot dead right beside him.

'One in a million, my CSM was.' He stared across the river. 'Saved my bacon I don't know how many times. Want to get even with those bastards – 4th Para.'

Corrado was gazing with open-mouthed admiration at the Major. The meaning of the four marks on the stone had not escaped him. He was soldier enough to recognise a real fighter who has just come out of battle, but he found it hard to understand the relaxed manner and casual drawl.

'Besides,' the Major added with his faint smile. 'I have a fiancée in Florence. Been looking forward to this since El Alamein. Always sworn I'd get in as soon as Florence was captured – even if it meant deserting.'

'Is she – English or Italian?'

'Italian. We got engaged before the war. Haven't seen her since 1939.'

'So you know Florence?'

'We met in England. She did the London Season in 1939 when I was a Deb's Delight.' Suddenly he held out his hand. 'By the way, I'm Jason Fitzgerald. Royal Ulster Fusiliers, familiarly known as the Roughs.'

Edmund introduced himself and explained how he'd picked up Corrado. 'Corrado and I were going to try and get over to the other side. Do you feel like joining us?'

'Perchè no?' Jason gave Corrado a grin. 'Are you confident that Jerry won't raise any objections?'

'I think there might be a way. Through the Vasari Corridor.'

'Say again.'

'It's a corridor from the Pitti Palace to the Uffizi. There's a chance they don't know about it.'

Although the Ponte Vecchio was only a couple of hundred yards away they were separated from it by mounds of rubble. The explosions they had heard showed that the area had been sown with mines. Corrado led them back to Piazza Pitti. From there the sappers had now cleared a taped lane through to the southern end of the Ponte Vecchio. Negotiating it was like walking along a mountain pathway.

'Watch out!' A Sapper yelled, as a rash Italian strayed beyond the tapes. 'This whole area's mined.'

At the Ponte Vecchio a Military Policeman was stopping anyone who tried to cross. A little knot of Italians who had been trapped on this side were waiting patiently in the hope that the liberators would by some magic enable them to rejoin their families.

'It doesn't matter how many passes you have, sir,' the MP was explaining to a lieutenant wearing an Intelligence Corps badge. 'The GOC has given orders no one is to be allowed across. In any case Jerry has a machine gun post at the other end of the bridge so you wouldn't get far.'

'Hello, Ken!' Jason hailed the I Corps man as he turned away. 'Still on the track of Mata Hari? Edmund, this is Ken Formby, our Field Security Officer. He tells us whether our Italian girl-friends are spies or not.'

Formby looked reproachfully at Jason as he heard this flippant description of his role. He was a stocky man of about twenty-eight with a neat moustache and a square, slightly angry face. He listened intently as Jason explained why Edmund wanted to get across to the main part of Florence.

'Pictures? Why the urgency? They won't run away.'

'The Germans are looting the galleries and Himmler has given orders that what they can't take away is to be destroyed.'

'You plan to stop them?'

'Well . . . .' Edmund did not want to admit that he was interested in one particular picture. 'I want to find out what the situation is.'

'You'll never get across,' Formby stated in his blunt way. 'I have a pass signed by the DMI and that's no good.'

'How badly do you want to get into Florence?' Edmund asked him.

'Very badly.' Formby said, and left it at that.

Edmund gave Jason an inquiring glance. Jason nodded, though he obviously thought Formby a bit uppish for a mere Subaltern.

'We're going to try and get through the Vasari Corridor. If you'd like to make a fourth we'd be glad to have you.'

The demolitions that had destroyed the Via de'Guicciardini, where the Macchiavelli had their palaces, had also chopped a section out of the Vasari Corridor. The graceful little Piazza Santa Felicità was an oasis in a desert of shattered masonry, splintered beams, bricks, tiles, plaster, metal. Here and there a fireplace, a bed, a fragment of statuary jutted from the wreckage of fourteenth century houses.

Edmund persuaded a Sapper with a mine detector to sweep a passage for them to the northern side of the little Piazza, where the demolitions had cut the corridor. Its opening had been blocked by masonry fallen from the high buildings around. Edmund had to work out its position by following the line of the surviving portion. At this point, he calculated, it must be twenty feet above ground level.

The four men worked for an hour lifting blocks of masonry out of the way and clearing dust with a spade Corrado had found. There was constant danger that they would touch off a mine, so they had no attention to spare for the books, old parchments, and personal belongings that were embedded in the rubble. At last a heap of stones slithered down and there before them was a dark opening.

Corrado, scrabbling away at the top, cleared a space big enough for a man to squeeze through. He dived into the hole, his legs kicking in the air before they vanished.

'It's all right.' His voice came back after a minute, echoing as from a tomb.

'I'll go next,' Edmund said. 'You can pass the rifles to me.'

He peered in through the opening but the sun was now high overhead and he could see only darkness. He had to squirm on his belly to get through the short tunnel. As he emerged he realised he was level with the ceiling of the corridor.

Jason's and Corrado's rifles were passed through, then Jason and Ken Formby followed. They all slithered down the pile of rubble to the floor. The corridor stretched ahead of them, sloping upwards and curving slightly to the left.

'We're still a hundred yards from the bridge,' Edmund whispered.

'I'll go first.' Jason worked the bolt of his rifle to put a round in the breach. The rattle was loud in the eerie silence. Every sound from outside was muted. 'Follow at intervals. Don't bunch.'

Holding his rifle at waist level ready to fire from the hip he walked forward. The others followed in a zig-zag pattern, hugging the walls. Corrado was imitating Jason's posture. Ken had drawn his revolver. Edmund was the only one who carred no weapon.

The corridor straightened out as it came onto the bridge. Now it stretched straight ahead of them for a hundred yards. Jason silently signalled the others to wait while he went forward to the point where the corridor turned right. It was a scary moment, for this hundred yards of bridge was the No-Man's Land between two armies. Standing on tip-toe Edmund could look through the rounded window. The Ponte Santa Trinità was a short distance downstream. The two piers still parted the water like ship's bows but the arches were gone. Those subtle elliptical curves, at the same time graceful and tense, now lay in smashed fragments at the bottom of the Arno, along with the statues of the four seasons that had graced its balustrades.

Ken nudged him. Jason had reached the far end and was beckoning them to follow. He put his finger to his lips and pointed to the ground. When they reached him, treading carefully on the broken glass, Edmund understood why. From below came the voices of the paratroopers manning the machine-gun post. At that moment they loosed off a burst. The sound was deafening in that enclosed space. Corrado jumped and dropped his rifle with a clatter. All four of them froze.

Down below the paratroopers were talking excitedly. They had heard the sound but could not locate it.

Jason hissed, 'Come on!'

Shame-faced Corrado picked up his rifle. Jason gave him a reassuring pat on the shoulder and made a life-long friend. Not bothering so much about noise now, they moved fast along the section supported on the arches flanking the river. Ahead a long flight of stairs led upwards. Jason, out-pacing the others, reached the door first. It was locked. He stepped

71

back, raised his right leg and kicked hard with his heel at a point level with the lock. The door burst inward.

As they crowded through Edmund got his bearings. They were in the Loggia on the second floor of the Uffizi gallery, just beside Room 25. From the nearby window swarms of tourists had once goggled out over the Arno, drinking in one of the most evocative views in Europe. Looking at it now was like seeing one of Canaletto's canvases slashed by a madman. Across the water those heaps that cast fuzzy reflections on the water had once been the palaces of the Bardi, the Carrigiani and the Menelli. From this vantage point he could see the crew of the machine-gun post beside the Ponte Vecchio, with their pot-shaped paratrooper helmets. They were peering up at the windows of the corridor.

Still not speaking the four went round the corners to the east corridor of the Loggia, Edmund now leading the way. All the windows had been blown in. There was glass everywhere. It was impossible to walk silently. In the rooms they passed the walls were bare, the lighter rectangles showing where the pictures had been. He could not resist stopping to look into Room 10. An unusually large patch showed where the *Primavera* had hung and where, thanks to Guido Masti, it would one day hang again. But what about its companion the *Birth of Venus*, which Botticelli had also painted for Lorenzo di Pierfrancesco de'Medici? Where was it now?

'Come on, Edmund!' Jason called impatiently.

They were near the grand staircase, where the Hermaphrodite once reclined to baffle the innocent visitor, when the sound of feet crunching on glass made them take refuge in the Cimabue and Giotto room. Jason posted himself behind the doorway out of sight, his rifle at waist level, finger on the trigger.

The crunching footsteps gave Edmund no sense of danger. They did not sound like jackboots. He was not surprised when into the room walked an Italian in civilian dress.

The man stopped, turned to stone, when he saw the four intruders. Surprise rather than fear made his extaordinarily intense eyes even more vivid. What struck Edmund was his brow, a very protruberant brow, as if the brain inside was pushing at the skull.

'Chi siete voi?' he challenged. 'Cosa fate qui?'

72

'Sono ufficiali Inglesi,' Corrado explained.

Mario Benvenuti switched his extraordinarily intense stare to Jason. Jason lowered his rifle.

'And who are you?' Edmund asked, still in Italian.

'An official of the gallery. How did you get here? Through the Vasari Corridor?'

Another burst of fire from the machine gun at the bridge echoed through the smashed windows and along the corridor.

'The Germans are still hunting for pictures,' Mario said. 'Come, I will take you down to the Soprintendenza.'

As they hurried down the staircase Edmund told Mario how he had met Bussola at Montagnana.

'Ah! He got through then. Meno male.'

'He told me that the Mostra del Rinascimento paintings were still safe. Are they . . . .'

'No longer,' Mario said bitterly. 'Four days ago they were still here. But on 30 July they all vanished.'

'All? The Botticelli Madonna? The King . . . .'

'Gone like the others. From what we hear Goering himself is determined to have it.' Mario opened a door at the bottom of the stairs. 'Through here.'

The Soprintendenza offices were empty. Mario took Corrado and the three British officers into the Director's room. He was nervous, as if he expected Germans to jump out from behind every door. The paratroopers, he explained, still controlled the centre of the city. Civilians were confined to their houses. Anyone seen on the streets was shot. Here on the edge of the demolition zone it was particularly dangerous.

'Then how did you get here?'

Mario shrugged and made a gesture implying that his own life was of no importance. 'Have you come to contact the partisans? They are ready to rise when you give the word. The situation here is desperate. We have no food, no water, no sanitation, no electricity. When will your troops come?'

'We each have a special mission,' Edmund began.

'Careful,' Ken Formby warned. 'Don't tell him too much. We don't know yet if we can trust this chap.'

'Nothing hush-hush about me,' Edmund told Ken. He turned to Mario and went back into Italian. 'I'm with the Commission for the Protection of Art Treasures. Our job is to do what we can to safeguard . . . .'

'Ah!' Mario's smile banished the frown from his brow. 'You've come to help save our pictures!'

The Italian seized Edmund's hand and began to shake it vigorously. Suddenly he froze. From the street came the tramp of marching feet. As they passed the door leading into the Via della Nina they sounded loud enough to be in the room. Then they faded as the patrol moved into the Piazza Signoria.

'It's not safe for you to stay here.' Mario had instinctively dropped his voice. 'These paratroopers are worse than the SS. You must come to my flat. There we can talk and decide how to protect what is left.'

'How far away is it?'

'Not far. It's in a big palazzo. We close the main door to keep strange people out. Much safer there.'

Edmund turned to Jason and Ken.

'What do you people want to do?'

'Stick together,' said Ken.

'You said a palazzo?' Jason was evidently intrigued.

'Yes,' Mario said proudly. 'Palazzo Lamberti. One of the oldest in Florence.'

'Small world. All right if I come too?'

'But of course! Three is a good number. We shall be the first to welcome our liberators.'

At Mario's suggestion Corrado slipped round to the clandestine partisan report centre in the old post office next to the Uffizi. When he came back after a quarter of an hour he was accompanied by two other young men. They stared back at the three officers with a hint of defiance, anxious to make the point that they too were fighting men. Jason and his rifle got the longest look. It was obvious that Corrado had been recounting his feats of marksmanship.

'God protect us from our friends,' Ken murmured.

As it turned out these young braves knew what they were doing. The partisans' intelligence service, based on the Café Porcellino, kept tabs on the efficient and punctual Germans and knew where their patrols would be at any given moment. Corrado took charge of the little posse, sending one partisan ahead and using the other as rear guard. In this order they ventured out into the Via della Nina, through Piazza Firenze and past the Bargello. The chosen route zig-zagged through narrow streets in a wide semi-circle north of the Duomo and finally turned back towards the river.

The journey ended in the basement of a house which gave access to a low tunnel. At this point they dropped their partisan escort. Mario led them through the tunnel. After a hundred yards they came to a flight of stone steps leading up into another cellar.

'This is how I came out this morning.' Mario shut the door after them. 'Now I must leave you here while I warn my wife and make sure it is safe for you to come up. Pazienza.'

The three were left in the dark. Their only illumination was Jason's lighter and Edmund's box of matches, which he wanted to save for his pipe. They squatted down on the bare floor with their backs to the wall like prisoners in a cell. The luminous hands of Ken's watch showed that it was past three o'clock. They were all feeling very hungry.

'Glad I brought some rations,' Ken said, 'though I don't fancy eating in the dark. If there's a shortage we can't expect any food from these people. What makes you think this girl of yours is still in Florence, Jason?'

'I had a message through Switzerland a few weeks ago. She said she'd be waiting for me.'

'Lucky sod. A nice bit of Italian crumpet waiting for you with open arms – or legs.'

Jason did not join in Ken's laughter. 'She might have changed her mind. You've been very cagey, Ken. What's so hush-hush about you wanting to come in with us?'

'Didn't want to talk about it in front of the Wops but no harm in you chaps knowing, I suppose. We picked up an Italian spy in Arezzo, stay-behind agent. He decided to talk, told us among other things that they were going to leave an agent in Florence with a radio-set and a bevy of beautiful signorinas to milk information from the troops. You know our chaps are sex-starved and it's a piece of cake for anyone with a hole in their ass to persuade them to talk. Did you know that half the casualties in the hospital ships going back to North Africa were VD cases?'

Jason remained silent and Edmund was busy filling his pipe.

'The G3 at Corps promised he'd get a gong for whoever picked him up. When I realised that Florence was on our axis I decided it was going to be me. I thought an MC would go very nicely with my Africa Star.'

In the silence that followed this statement Edmund guessed what Jason was thinking.

'Can you give me a light, Ed? My briquet ist kaput. Anyone else for a cigarette?'

'Not for me, thanks,' Ken said, and laughed again to himself.

The flame of the match was dazzling after the darkness. It surprised on Jason's features as he bent forward a feral, Mephistophelian intensity of expression.

'It's a funny old war, isn't it?' he said as the match went out. Edmund thought how strongly one's opinion of someone is influenced by their voice. He wondered how much of his real self Jason concealed behind his casual way of talking. 'Ed is only interested in pictures, Ken's after a gong and I'm here to find my girl. I'd give a lot to hear what my old Sergeant-Major would have to say about it.' The tip of his cigarette glowed as he drew hard on it. 'When somebody like that goes you begin to wonder.'

'Wonder what?' Ken asked sharply.

'Whether it's worth it. All those chaps killed. For some reason it's always the best ones that cop it. What I can't stomach is the padre's line. You know, that killing Germans is all done with God's approval.'

'The doctrine of the just war . . . .'

'How can war ever be just, Ken? If you're a Christian you've got to believe it's wrong to kill, whatever your reasons. A just war is a contradiction in terms.'

'According to St Augustine it is justifiable for soldiers, who are fighting not for themselves but for a cause, to kill people in battle.'

'The pacifists,' Edmund said, 'maintain that a Christian should let himself be killed rather than take the life . . . .'

'Is that why you don't carry a revolver, Ed?' Jason asked. 'It's against your principles to kill anyone – even a German?'

'No.' Edmund smiled in the darkness, remembering the carnage he and his platoon had inflicted on the enemy at Dunkirk before they were over-run. 'It's for very practical reasons. It's no good carrying a gun unless you mean to shoot first. As soon as someone sees that you're armed the situation changes – it becomes a shooting match. Being unarmed gives you a moral advantage.'

Jason grunted, unconvinced.

'Under the Emperor Theodosius,' Ken said, reverting to an argument that obviously fascinated him, 'you had to be a Christian to serve in the Roman army at all.'

Jason laughed. 'Some of my chaps would have been kicked out pretty smartly. They weren't interested in religious theories. With them it was kill or be killed.'

'One thing you have to admit, though,' Edmund said. 'Even if war can never be regarded as just it's possible to wage it justly – I mean, with humanity. That's where we differ from the Germans.'

'Oh, come *on*, Edmund.' Jason protested. 'What about those thousand-bomber raids? Let's face it, once a war gets under way humanity goes out the window . . . .'

The door opened and a shaft of brighter light flooded the room. Mario was standing there with a candle.

'It's all right for you to come up now. The Conte is having his siesta.'

'The who?'

'The Conte. He owns this palazzo. Very important fascist.'

'Jesus Christ!'

'The rifle, capitano. You had better leave it here.' Mario had watched with alarm as Jason slung his .303 over his shoulder.

'The rifle stays with me.

'Please, capitano. My wife. She's very nervous. I'll lock the door. No one will come here.'

'All right then. For the time being.'

They followed Mario up a flight of steps which emerged in a corner of the *cortile*. Edmund blinked in the sudden sunlight. The flowers and plants were dazzling after the grey streets and dark cellar. Mario hurried them towards the stairs which led up to his flat. The great main doors of the *palazzo* were shut.

Ornella was waiting at the door of the flat, the two children peering out with apprehensive eyes from behind her skirts. Fascist propaganda had depicted the English as barbarians.

'S'accomodino, s'accomodino.' She urged them in, holding the door wide.

'Quick,' Mario fussed. 'Close the door quickly.'

Edmund could not help smiling at the incongruousness of the scene in the small hall as everyone was introduced and solemnly shook hands.

'Jeepers!' Edmund felt Ken nudge him. 'What about that?'

A woman had appeared at the doorway of the *salotto*. Edmund was puzzled by the expression on Mario's face as he turned towards her. It showed a mixture of panic and tenderness.

'May I present the cousin of my wife, la signora de Angeli?'

Caterina came forward smiling to exchange a handshake with each of the three men. She gave off a faint but very subtle perfume. Bracelets jingled on her wrists. Ken was last and he could not stop his eyes dipping to the cleavage between her breasts.

'S'accomodino.' Ornella was still trying to shepherd them into the sitting-room. 'I am afraid we have not much to offer but I know you must be hungry.'

Edmund was first into the room. At once he felt embarrassed. The table was laid for three. A dish heaped with spaghetti was steaming in the middle. Two bottles of the best Chianti Gallo Nero had been uncorked. The family must have scraped the barrel to provide this meal but to refuse would have been an insult. The three newcomers sat down to eat while the Italians stood round watching. Caterina stayed at the end of the room opposite Ken. His eyes kept straying back to her.

To break the awkward silence, Edmund said, 'I hear you have been having a bad time.'

That was enough to unleash an eloquent catalogue of the tribulations of the Florentines – culminating in the terrible night Ornella and the children had passed shivering in the basement while the world rocked under their feet.

'They say it took them three attempts to blow up the Ponte Santa Trinità,' Ornella told them. 'Not till five o'clock this morning was the last arch destroyed. Mario saw it. Didn't you, Mario?'

Their plates had been cleared away and they were well into the second bottle of Chianti when there came a sharp knock on the front door. All the Italians instantly turned to stone. The letter-box flapped. A strong male voice boomed through the hall.

'Ornella! Sono io.'

'Oh, my God!' Caterina laid a hand on her left breast. That's the Count!'

'He mustn't come in.' Ornella stared round wildly. 'Mario, what shall we do?'

Jason leant back in his chair and tapped the ash off his cigarette.

'This Count. Is his name Lamberti?'

'Yes, yes. Il Conte Lorenzo de' Lamberti.'

'Let him come in,' Jason said calmly.

'But, maggiore . . . .'

'Let him in.'

Edmund and Ken were watching Jason with curiosity but he gave no sign.

Reluctantly Mario went out to the hall. Jason stubbed his cigarette in an ashtray, got up from his chair and came out from behind the table.

'Ciao, Mario.' The Count's resonant voice echoed in the hall. 'The doctor told me that he may be able to provide some pills for Ornella . . . .'

He stopped dead on the threshold of the room. For the first time in his life Mario saw his father-in-law's jaw drop. For a few seconds the tableau froze, the big man facing the three officers and the little family staring from one face to another.

6

'I am sorry I cannot offer you Scotch whisky, gentlemen. We Italians have to be grateful for what we can get.'

The Count was the embodiment of affability. His wife watched with amusement as he fussed over the British officers. He had insisted on bringing them up to his own house and now the whole family was assembling to welcome the 'liberators'. The inevitable *Vin Santo* had been produced and Susanna was handing round a tray of glasses. No one seemed to consider that they might have come into Florence for other than social reasons. Edmund had been astonished at the change in Mario's manner since they had been in the *palazzo*. He seemed unsure of himself, almost cowed, whereas at the Soprintendenza he had been so positive.

'But Rosalba?' the Count demanded. 'Why is she not here?'

'She's with Nonna,' Caterina explained.

'Susanna, go over and tell her to come at once. But do not say why. Let it be a surprise.'

'I am sorry my son Guido is not here,' the Countess said to Edmund in a low voice. 'He is a partisan and does not see eye to eye with my husband. But now that the Allies have come . . . .'

'We are not out of the woods yet, Contessa. It may be some days before the Army enters the town.'

At the other side of the room the Count was bemoaning the fate of Italy, and at the same time trying to ingratiate himself with Ken and Jason.

'You understand, a person of my rank had no alternative but to support Mussolini. Italy is a new nation. We have not a thousand years of history behind us like you English. Whatever its faults, Fascism has welded us into one nation . . . .'

During the next few minutes the Count lost whatever respect he still held in the eyes of his family. In embarrassed silence they listened as he catalogued the achievements of Fascism and whitewashed the role he had played in the Tuscan and Florentine hierarchy of the movement.

'Signor Lamberti,' Edmund cut in on him impatiently. 'Do you still have contact with the Germans?'

The Count swung to face this new challenge. The question had sounded like an accusation.

'Yes, of course. It is necessary in my capacity as . . . .'

'Can you find out what has happened to the Mostra paintings? The Mostra del Rinascimento. . . .'

Before he could say more the door opened. As he looked towards it, the words died on his lips. Everyone else in the room was suddenly silent.

Rosalba had halted after a few paces, quickly searching the ring of faces. When her eyes came to Jason her expression changed. The tense, almost monastic set of her features softened. For a few seconds she could not say anything. Then her face lit up with a smile.

'Jason! Is it really you?'

'Yes, Rosalba, it is me.'

Self-consciously before all those watching eyes they went to meet each other. Rosalba offered her cheek to be kissed.

'I knew you would come. Let me look at you.' She took his elbows and held him at arm's length. 'Yes. You are Jason all right.'

The silence in the room was broken as the family, sharing Rosalba's pleasure, broke into excited chatter and laughter.

'Let me introduce my friends.' Jason was embarrassed under Rosalba's intense scrutiny. 'This is Ken Formby. You'd better be careful what you say in front of him. He's in the Intelligence Service.'

'How do you do?' Rosalba shook hands.

'And this is Edmund Brudanell. Edmund is a man of peace.' Jason's self-consciousness had made him adopt a bantering tone. 'He's here in pursuit of a Madonna – one of Botticelli's.'

She turned to Edmund and the cool, slim hand rested in his. Ever since she had entered the room he had been studying her, trying not to stare. Her face was familiar, but he could not place it. Somewhere before he had seen that straight-bridged nose, the upward-curving brows, the auburn hair. The mouth was particularly memorable with its full lower, and bow-shaped upper lip.

'A glass of *Vin Santo*, signorina.' Susanna had appeared at Rosalba's side. 'Il signor Conte is going to propose a toast.'

It was another ten minutes before Edmund could button-hole the Count again. At last he cornered him in the window embrasure.

'You said you still had contact with the German occupying forces, signore.' Edmund's brusque tone belied the politeness of his words. 'In that case you can help us to find out what happened to the Mostra paintings.'

'I'm not sure.' The Count's eyes were shifty. 'If the German Consul Wolf were still here it would be simple. But the city is now under the command of Colonel Fuchs, a paratrooper and – what can I say? – a rather rough kind of soldier.'

A silence had fallen in the room and everyone was now listening to the exchange.

'I thought you were on friendly terms with him, Lorenzo,' the Countess said sweetly. 'Were you not able to persuade him to change the boundary of the demolition zone?'

The Count gave her a furious look. 'But all movement in the streets is forbidden, tesoro.'

'I am sure you can find a way,' she said, still smiling. 'Since when has a Lamberti been unable to move about Florence without using the streets?'

'Aren't you running a big risk, Ed?' Ken muttered when the door had closed on their host. 'He's only got to drop a hint to the Jerries . . . .'

'He won't. We've got his family, haven't we? He knows which side his bread is buttered.'

The Countess had not heard their words but she had guessed what was in Ken's mind. She signalled Susanna to fill Edmund's glass. 'I'm sure that you can count on my husband's full co-operation, capitano. He's very realistic, able to adapt quickly to new situations.'

Edmund exchanged a glance with her. They understood each other perfectly. He was fascinated by the silent dialogue of the Italian women's eyes. The sudden irruption of three young officers had disturbed the calm pool of their life, sending ripples over its surface and bringing currents up from its depths. Edmund had to discipline himself not to stare at Rosalba. He had surprised on her face a shadow almost of apprehension when Jason had snaked an arm round her shoulder. And what of the Countess herself? Judging by the age of her children she must be well into her forties, but she was still crisp and vibrant. Anyone in search of an accomplished bed-fellow could do a lot worse than *la Contessa*. He caught her smiling at him again in an almost conspiratorial way. He wondered if she had read his thoughts.

It was the Countess who brought a little reality back into the situation. Experienced hostess that she was, she had been considering how to accommodate these unexpected guests. 'I am afraid I haven't room for you all in this house. But of course Jason must have the guest room so that he and Rosalba can be near each other.'

'It's like a bloody house-party,' Ken muttered. 'She'll be suggesting croquet next.'

Mario was quick to say that he and Ornella would look after Edmund, and perhaps Caterina could move in with her grandmother. Caterina flashed him an angry look. Carlo, the Count's vapid brother, invited Ken, but he refused to commit himself. Edmund could tell by the way he kept glancing at Caterina that he had plans to move in with her and the old Countess.

To forestall some forthright remark, Edmund stepped in. 'It is very considerate of you but you are forgetting that for us this is still enemy territory. Until the Count returns we would like you all to remain in this house.'

The Countess nodded, looking at Edmund with a new eye. 'I understand. We are your insurance policy.'

'You could put it like that.'

'You mean . . . .' Carlo was staring from Edmund to Ken. He was particularly fascinated by the revolver on Ken's belt. 'We are sequestered?'

'Until the Count returns, yes.'

Carlo's hands darted up to cover his mouth. He shrank back, gripping Mario's arm. Held hostage! It was the fulfilment of a dream. He had not lived in vain.

Edmund passed the time of waiting discussing with the Countess the cultural links between England and Italy. The Countess had evolved the interesting theory that being allies in the 1914–1918 war had destroyed the long association and being enemies in this one might renew it. Rosalba had taken Jason away to show him the guest room. Ken's impatience had got the better of him and he had gone off with Mario to find Guido or Corrado. There was no danger of the 'hostages' dispersing. No-one wanted to miss a moment of the drama. Wild horses could not have dragged Carlo away.

When the Count returned he was holding onto the remnants of his dignity with difficulty. The realisation had gradually come over him that he had been humiliated in the sight of his women folk. He sat down and poured himself a cup of the ersatz coffee that had succeeded the *Vin Santo*.

'It is no longer possible to make contact with the Kommandantur. But I managed to find a member of the Kunstschutz who is still in the city. The situation is confused.'

'Yes?' Edmund was standing over him.

The Count sipped his coffee, made a face and put the cup down again. 'You know the Kunstschutz is the official German organisation for safeguarding art treasures in war zones. But the Führer has his own agency for collecting *objets d'art* . . . .'

'Looting.'

'. . . he instructed Colonel Bauman to make sure that the Mostra paintings were removed to the safety of the Southern Tyrol. However . . . .' The Count realised that one arm of his jacket was covered with mould and dust. He began to brush it as he talked. 'Another German Officer, acting for a different agency, was also anxious to gain possession of them . . . .'

'He was acting for Goering?'

'Lo credo, si. You know he has a very fine collection on his estate at Karinhall. He particularly wanted the Botticelli Madonna.'

'Yes.' Edmund sat down on a chair facing the Count. He had tasted the coffee and been unable to finish his cup. 'I suppose the fact of it belonging to the King of England would have given it a special interest for him.'

'My information – and I hope you appreciate, capitano, that such things are not easily found out – my information is that this officer, Major Kurtsdorf, was successful in obtaining the Botticelli and a number of other paintings, but he may have difficulty in getting them back to Germany.'

'Why?'

'Well, you see, the Führer has become suspicious about what the Reichsmarschal's squads are doing.' The Count had not shed the habit of referring to Hitler and Goering by their high-sounding titles. 'The Feldsicherheitspolizei have been instructed by OKW to recover these paintings for the Führer's personal collection.'

Edmund was watching the Count carefully, searching for any sign that he was not being frank. The Countess was studying her husband with equal intensity and it was the look of reassurance which the Count gave his wife that convinced him he had not betrayed his guests. Like Marshal Badoglio before him Lorenzo Lamberti had decided where his future interests lay.

'Do we know where they are now?'

'No.' Lorenzo shook his head. 'All I can ascertain is that they were removed from the Uffizi five days ago. That was all I could find out, capitano. If I had asked too many questions he would have become suspicious. As it is I took great risks to get this information for you.'

Emund did not offer the Italian the thanks or assurance he wanted. He despised the man's toadying manner and was still very far from trusting him.

'I hope what you have told me is correct, signore. Can I have your assurance that you will have no further contact with the Germans?'

'Of course, capitano! And anything more that I can do . . . .'

His voice trailed away as Edmund turned his back. Rosalba had come into the room followed by Jason. Jason's face was dead-pan and his manner more deliberately off-hand than ever. Rosalba was flushed and a little breathless. She crossed the room quickly and sat down on an upright chair beside one of the low tables. The book she had been reading lay open on it. Feeling that several pairs of eyes were on her she bent her head and idly stretched out one hand to turn a page. Her mouth had a pensive, almost sad look.

In that moment Edmund saw the resemblance. It was the modern hair style that had confused him. He'd had similar experiences before. Often, coming out of the Uffizi or Pitti Gallery, he had noticed girls in the streets whose features were strangely familiar. The explanation, of course, was that he had seen them an hour or so before in the framed pictures of the Florentine masters. It was not surprising when you considered that they were the direct descendants of the girls who had posed for the Renaissance artists. But never before had he seen such a striking resemblance as this. Put a veil round Rosalba's head and she was the living image of the Madonna in the King's *tondo*.

Edmund did not feel secure enough that night to take his clothes off and go to bed. He was isolated in enemy territory and had gambled his safety on his reading of the Count's state of mind. He and Mario sat up late arguing passionately about the rival merits of the Venetian, Sienese and Florentine schools. Niether Ken nor Jason availed themselves of the clean sheets and comfortable beds that had been prepared for them. Ken had managed to link up again with Corrado and had gone off to set up a raid on the Pensione Matilda. Jason had paired up with Guido and left the *palazzo* on some unspecified errand of his own – accompanied by his rifle.

Not long after midnight the city was again shaken by a series of heavy explosions, this time further away. After calming Ornella and the children, Mario took Edmund up onto the roof. It was an eerie spectacle. The artilleries of both sides were duelling across the city, the flash of their guns outlining roofs and spires for an instant of time. Shells passed through the sky overhead with a brief furtive swish like a whiplash. From the streets came the rumble of tracked vehicles patrolling the city centre, and the occasional crack of a rifle shot. The thud and flash of heavy explosions were coming from the northern suburbs. The Germans were blowing the bridges over the Mugnone, the river that ran from east to west encircling Florence before it swung south to join the Arno. More than ever the city had become an island sandwiched between the two armies.

Ken returned at four, tired and disappointed. His raid on the Pensione Matilda had produced nothing more than a suitcase radio-set.

'At least that's proof our information was correct. Christ, I'm hungry!' He sat down at the kitchen table and poured himself a glass of wine. 'They usually have a number of alternative addresses they can use, with a radio in each. I've got to catch up with the bastard before Eighth Army take over.'

'Better keep your voice down, Ken. Those kids are trying to sleep.'

Jason returned with the dawn. He had been out hunting Germans, using Guido as a loader.

'Got three more and winged a couple,' he said with a thin smile, as if he were reporting the day's bag on some Scottish grouse moor.

The three of them felt safer sticking together, despite the Countess's solicitous arrangements. Ken stretched out on the sofa in the living-room. Jason dropped into a deep arm-chair and was asleep on the instant.

Caterina's bed had been remade but her perfume still clung to it. Edmund lay for a long time with his hands behind his head, watching the light grow beyond the curtains. The sparrows which had colonized Palazzo Lamberti had already started their impertinent chatter. Of the three who had crossed the Arno the previous day he was the furthest from his objective. Jason had found his fiancée and Ken was hot on the scent of his stay-behind agent, but the Palace Madonna had slipped from his grasp.

He eventually fell asleep and dreamed voluptuous dreams fuelled by the traces of Caterina's scent.

It was Caterina's real voice that awakened him. She had come over to find out why Ken had not slept in the bed that had been prepared for him. Edmund went into the sitting-room to find Ken rubbing his eyes and Jason lowering his legs from the chair he had pulled up to support them. Mrio, Ornella and the children had been whispering over their frugal breakfast in the kithen. Caterina was very fresh and appetising in a white dress.

'We have some breakfast for you,' she was telling Ken. 'Nonna is very hurt that you did not accept her hospitality.'

'Go on, old son,' Jason advised him, obviously referring to Caterina rather than breakfast. 'Don't refuse your greens when they're offered to you on a plate.'

Ken gave him a grin. 'Might as well. There's nothing I can do till dark anyway.'

Caterina smiled. She had not understood the words but she had caught their drift. Edmund saw her fling Mario a glance in which there was both triumph and defiance. Mario winced as if he had been slapped.

If Caterina had intended to hurt Mario by appropriating the overtly lascivious Ken, she had succeeded. The gnawing remorse which had attacked him at dawn the previous day had not lessened, but the night he had spent with her had enflamed his passion and already he desperately wanted her again. The thought of her sharing those same delights with another man was unbearable. And yet at the same time he shivered when he remembered his infidelity to Ornella, his desertion of her in a moment of extreme need. More than ever reckless of his own safety he went to Piazza Strozzi through the streets instead of using the tunnel and the clandestine route. He almost hoped that he would run into a German patrol or one of the Fascist gangs which were roaming the city in search of violence and loot.

Conditions were if anything worse on this Friday 5 August. The stench of rotting refuse had thickened and the rats were gorging themselves. The state of emergency was still in force and few people ventured from their houses. Florence had now been without electricity for seven days and without water for six. The CTLN, the Tuscan Committee for National Liberation, had set up their headquarters in Piazza Strozzi. They had prepared plans to assume control as soon as the paratroopers withdrew. Though they were not now to be seen in the centre the Germans were not far away. Their tanks and self-propelled guns were on the Viale, that wide boulevard which describes a half-circle round the old city . The partisans still bided their time, hesitating to turn Florence into a battlefield. They knew that the paratroopers could storm down to the Arno in a matter of minutes. The Germans had withdrawn only because they did not want to have any responsibility for the desperate plight of the population.

Armed with a pass from the CTLN headquarters Mario made his way to the Soprintendenza. The gangs left him alone. He did not have the furtive manner of most civilians. He walked straight across the middle of a deserted Piazza Signoria, past the brass plaque marking the spot where Savonarola had been gibbeted over a tall bonfire 444 years before. Fabio Pantano had not ventured to the Soprintendenza that morning, but the entrance to the Uffizi was guarded by several partisans.

'What is going on?' Mario asked a tall fellow with a beard.

'We're running a telephone line through the Vasari corridor, so that we can talk to our people in the Pitti. Come in, dottore, it is not safe to stand here.'

Mario slipped inside and the door was shut again. 'Is Corrado here?'

'He's somewhere about.' The partisan cupped his hands round his mouth to bellow, 'CORRADO!'

'Eccomi,' came a voice from the landing upstairs.

'C'è il dottor Benvenuti.'

'Vengo subito.'

Corrado came bounding down the stairs. The passing of the telephone line, literally over the heads of the Germans, was a small triumph but it meant a great deal to the Italians. It was a symbol of their coming resurgence and their capacity to help themselves. Corrado's face showed his elation.

'The Inglesi are not with you?'

'No, they asked me to come and thank you,' Mario invented, 'for helping them yesterday.'

'We have some news for the capitano. The tall fair one with the pipe. You must come with me to see Bacio. He's in the old post office.'

Bacio Ferrato was a quiet, gentle man with a sad face. Formerly a member of Italian Military Intelligence in Bologna he had allowed himself to be recruited to the Italian SS as a penetration agent. Harmless though he appeared, he was a very brave man. If captured, he would almost certainly be hanged against a wall with a meat-hook through his jaw.

He relayed his information in a level, unemotional voice. The Uffizi lorry requisitioned by the Germans had been seen outside the gallery on the morning of 30 July. A party of German soldiers had loaded it with pictures, mostly in small frames.

Mario nodded eagerly. 'Yes. The Mostra paintings are nearly all small.'

The lorry had driven north up the Via Calzaiuoli and past the Duomo towards San Lorenzo. It had been located later hidden in the courtyard of a house in Via Landini, near the Piazza della Libertà. That part of the town was still in German hands but only lightly held.

'Do you know if it's still there?' Mario had a hand in his jacket pocket and was feeling for a cigarette. He did not want to let these people see the packet Jason had given him.

'It was there this morning, dottore. None of the pictures had been unloaded.'

'So they haven't got far.' Mario looked from Bacio to Corrado. The vivacity had come back to his face. Just for the moment he had forgotten the black cloud that had descended upon his spirit.

'Dottore!' Corrado's eyes were shining with enthusiasm.

'We, members of the Giustizia e Libertà brigades, will mount a raid tonight to recapture the lorry. What do you say?'

'Benissimo.' Mario put the cigarette between his lips. 'And I will come with you.'

It was early afternoon when Edmund went over to the south block of the *palazzo*. The crisis had not prevented the Count from taking his customary siesta. When Susanna opened the door she spoke in a whisper. The interior of the house was dark. The shutters had been closed to keep out the sun.

No, Susanna told him, Major Jason was not there. He had been, but he had gone out again.

'Is that you, Jason?' Rosalba's voice called from the upper landing.

'No. It's me, Edmund.'

'Oh, Edmund. Please come up.'

Jason, she explained, had gone off with Guido again. The partisans were planning a raid that night and they had asked Jason to help. She led him past the *salone* to a smaller sitting room furnished with more compact but equally elegant eighteenth century pieces.

'I found the album of photographs I took during that summer I was in England. Would you like to see it? The photographs might remind you of home.'

To look at the album he had to sit beside her on an upright sofa with bandy legs and gilded arms. She quickly turned half a dozen pages of Italian scenes before stopping at a photograph of an obviously English country house. A group had posed in front of the French windows.

'This is the country house of the family I stayed with. That's Mr and Mrs Vincent and their three children.'

He nodded politely as she took him through half a dozen pages of fading snapshots. Sitting so close to her he felt as nervous as a schoolboy. Since that moment when he had seen the resemblance he could not help identifying her with Botticelli's Madonna. And here she was, alive and breathing beside him. He had always considered that the face in the *tondo* was too sensuously attractive for a Virgin.

Realising that the photos were not arousing much interest, she closed the album but kept her finger in it to mark the place. 'You have known Jason for a long time, he is an old friend of yours?'

'No. Only a few days. We teamed up when we found we both wanted to get into Florence.'

'I'd forgotten. You Englishmen have this trick of seeming to have known each other all your lives. I suppose it's because you were all at the same kind of school.'

He laughed. 'He might have been at Borstal for all I know.'

She did not understand the illusion but his laugh had brought a smile. 'Radley. You know it?'

'I've heard of it.'

'He used to talk about it a lot, almost as if he was still there as a schoolboy.' She watched her index finger slide along the edge of the album cover. 'He has changed a lot since I last saw him.'

'That must be – what? Five years?'

'It will be five years on September the 10th. It's a long time to wait, non è vero. But we fell very much in love and we made a promise to each other, that we would not let anything, not even the war, come between us. We never guessed it would last so long, but I kept that promise – even though at times it was very hard. I'm twenty-four now, you know. All my friends are married.'

He smiled at her anxious look. Not a wrinkle marred her face except for the momentary puckering between her eyes.

'I wouldn't have blamed Jason if he had found someone else.' She had leant her back against the far end of the sofa so that she was facing him as she talked. It was hard to meet such an intense gaze, so he kept glancing away at the window, the clock on the mantelpiece, the Persian mat in front of the fireplace.' But I'd had letters, telling me that he was getting nearer. We have cousins in Switzerland, you know. Even so, when I walked into the room yesterday and saw him – it was an unbelievable moment.'

She was smiling now, her thoughts turned inward. Edmund waited. He could tell by the signs that she had something to confide.

'Of course, I knew that he would have changed. I had prepared myself for that. And he is different, but in a way that I had not expected.'

He still said nothing. Her long eyelashes were black against

91

her cheek. Her mouth had again taken on that downward curve.

'He used to be such a gentle person. I even remember him taking spiders out of the house rather than killing them. But now . . . . Do you know what he was doing last night?'

'Yes. He told me.'

She shook her head. 'This lust to kill. He talks of shooting Germans as if they were – wild boar.'

'His regiment has had a very bad time. They took a lot of punishment in the Chianti hills . . . .'

'I know, it's what I keep telling myself. But it's not only that . . . .'

She looked up at him again and put a hand out to touch his arm in that friendly way that Italians have. The eyes of the Palace Madonna are cast down so that one cannot tell their colour. Rosalba's eyes were a greeny golden, with sable irises and specks of blue and silver. 'I can talk to you, Edmund, can't I?'

'Yes.' He had to clear his throat. 'Yes, of course. Do you mind if I smoke my pipe?'

She had put the album down on a side-table, the photographs forgotten. Edmund found it settling to go through the familiar routine of unrolling his pouch and filling his pipe.

'Even if you haven't known Jason for long I was sure that you would understand. And there's no-one else I can talk to.'

Ten years can be a lot when you are only twenty-four. He hoped he did not appear old enough in her eyes to be a father figure. More like an elder brother, perhaps. He took refuge in the ritual of striking a match, sucking the flame into the bowl, placing the matchbox over the top to improve the draught.

'When I knew him in England he was always so considerate, so courteous. I respected him for that. But yesterday evening when we were alone . . . . Well, he was more like – like a certain kind of Italian.'

She was close enough for him to feel the fragrance of her breath on his face. He could sympathise with Jason if he had tried to rush his fences.

'You see, Edmund, I don't want to spoil it. Especially as we've waited so long. This war will soon pass and then we can get married.'

Could she possibly be telling him that she was still a virgin, that she had kept herself intact for Jason? He turned his head away so as not to blow smoke in her face.

'War has curious effects on men,' he said, thinking of the New Zealanders kneeling in front of the *Primavera*. 'After the fear and the violence and the disgust of battle they have a desperate need for tenderness and beauty.'

'Is that why you are so passionate to find your picture?'

So Jason had told her about that. 'I wasn't talking about myself. But I can see Jason's point of view. It's natural in a man who has experienced what he's been through. I don't have to tell you that you're a very attractive woman.'

'Am I?'

'Yes.' He steadied himself and decided to say it. 'You are the most beautiful woman I have ever seen.'

There was a moment of silence. She studied him intently then switched her eyes away.

'The family make fun of me. They call me la Simonetta because . . . .'

'I know. You are the living image of Botticelli's model. I saw the resemblance as soon as you came into the room yesterday. Particularly your mouth . . . .' He stopped, suddenly realising that he had been talking with passionate enthusiasm. 'I'm sorry. I shouldn't have been so personal.'

She reached out to touch his arm. 'No-one has ever said that to me before.'

'About the Botticelli Madonna?'

'That I'm the most beautiful woman they've ever seen.'

'Did you mind me telling you?'

'Now it is I who have embarrassed you.' She stood up and walked to the window. 'But who else can I talk to? Who else can help me see it from Jason's point of view?'

Edmund could see Jason's point of view. Very clearly from where he sat. He would be doing his friend a good turn by advising submission but somehow he could not bring himself to betray Rosalba's confidence.

'Give it time. Don't sacrifice your principles. To thine own self be true.'

'To thine own self be true.' She looked over her shoulder. 'Is that Shakespeare?'

'Yes. The much maligned Polonius. "To thine own self be true then canst thou not be false to any man".'

'I'll remember that.' She came back and stood looking down at him. He made to rise but she put a hand on his forearm and sat down beside him again. 'You don't know how much you have helped me, Edmund. I am very grateful.' She gave his forearm a little shake. 'Look, you've let your pipe go out.'

'You stay out of it, Ed. If they insist on getting themselves killed let them go.'

Jason had spread some old newspapers on the table in the *salotto* and was pulling a piece of 4 by 2 through the barrel of his rifle. The stub of his last cigarette was in the heaped ashtray. He and Mario had demolished four packets between them.

'I can't, Jason. If I could persuade Mario to stay behind I'd take your advice. But I can't budge him. He's dead set on going.'

'The whole idea is crazy. These paratroopers are professionals. The partisans are amateurs.'

'We're always saying that the Italians have no stomach for a fight, but these chaps are willing to risk their lives for the paintings. I can't stand back. You must see that, Jason.'

'Oh, well.' Jason sighed and held his rifle up towards the window to squint down the barrel. 'I suppose I'll have to come along and cover the pair of you. Pity we can't rope old Ken in, too.'

'Where is Ken?'

'Hasn't come back from breakfast yet.' Jason grinned. 'Nonna is up with the Conte creating merry hell about her water ration so our Ken has the field to himself. Can't say I blame him. Caterina certainly has it in the right places.'

Ken declined the invitation to join the raiding party. He left before darkness fell, accompanied by Guido, to follow up a fresh lead on his stay-behind agent. Jason, Edmund and Mario followed him through the tunnel a couple of hours later. A band of eight young men led by Corrado was waiting for them in the house at the other end. Like all partisan squads they were armed with an assortment of weapons ranging from a tommy-gun to an axe.

'Jesus!' Jason muttered.

'The Major will take command?' Corrado suggested politely, as if offering a friend a spell at the wheel of his car.

'Not on your life,' Jason replied. He tapped his rifle. 'I'm the support group.'

'You take command, Corrado,' Edmund confirmed. 'Or Bacio, as he knows the route.'

'Bacio is only a corporal. I'm a sergeant. Okay, ragazzi, you know your orders. Mario, you stay close to me.' Mario obediently moved to Corrado's side. His face was white and he was swallowing continually. 'We shall need you when we get to Via Landini.'

Edmund and Jason exchanged a glance. They would make it their business to safeguard Mario. For once Edmund was armed. He had accepted the loan of Jason's revolver.

The raid confirmed Jason's gloomy predictions. It turned out that Via Landini was north of the Mugnone in an area still occupied by the Germans. The assault on the villa was hair-raising. The Soprintendenza lorry had vanished and the house was now the headquarters of a machine-gun company. It was only thanks to Jason's rapid and deadly covering fire that Mario, Edmund and six others were able to extricate themselves. They had to leave Bacio and another partisan dead on the ground. The timely arrival of an RAF plane overhead had forced the Germans to douse all their lights and enabled the survivors to double back round the railway station. Daylight was breaking by the time the three returned to the flat. An almost hysterical Ornella rushed to greet Mario and enfold him in her arms. He was still stiff with fear.

'Only just beat you to it.' A dejected looking Ken was sitting in an arm-chair, his arms dangling over the sides. 'Christ, what wouldn't I give for a double Scotch!'

'Catch your spy?'

'No. The bugger had flitted again but we'll get him tonight. We collared one of his girls and she's been persuaded to co-operate. Did you manage to steal your lorry?'

'Bloody shambles.' Jason said. 'Ed's friends are very heroic but their battle training is pathetic. Ah well, at least I've added another few Jerries to my bag.'

7

It was daylight before Jason and Ken finally went off to get some sleep in their respective beds. When Edmund woke at eleven they had still not reappeared. He went through to the kitchen. Mario was standing by the table. His face was abject in its misery. Stefano and Anna were crying with hunger. They could not get their small teeth into the hard stale bread which was all Ornella could supply.

Watching them, Edmund made up his mind. 'You people can't go on like this. I'm going back to report on the situation here. General Alexander can't know what it's like or he would have taken over the city.'

'Back over the Arno?' Mario had snatched at the suggestion. 'Then I'll come with you.'

'Mario, no!' Ornella protested.

'I don't need you, Mario,' Edmund assured him. 'Surely you had enough last night.'

'I have to find out what happened to my house. There is something I need to fetch.' Impulsively Mario took Ornella's hand and held it in both of his. 'Something very important.'

On that Saturday, 6 August, the iron fist that held Florence in its grasp was relaxed slightly. The citizens were allowed out of their houses for a few hours to collect water – if they could find any. It was the first time in a week that the ordinary people had dared to use the streets. They moved hurriedly and in fear. There were still Fascist snipers on the roof-tops, especially in the area of Via Tornabuoni. Every now and again a macabre little procession would pass by. The undertakers were out of action and the Brothers of Misericord in their white robes and black cowls had taken on the task of burying the dead. They used handcarts to trundle corpses to the burial ground of the Giardino dei Semplici in Via Lamora.

The area all round the northern end of the Ponte Vecchio was still deserted and the bridge itself inaccessible. The demolitions had effectively prevented any relief being brought in. Masonry was still liable to come crashing down from the toppling houses or towers. The mines had not been cleared, as more than one luckless person discovered when trying to identify the ruins of his home. The stench from the breached sewers was appalling.

Mario and Edmund followed the clandestine telephone line through the Vasari Corridor and emerged by the now enlarged hold at the other end. The area on the south side of the bridge was equally deserted. Casualties among the troops from roof-top snipers had been so heavy that they had been pulled back to the outskirts. Apart from the Town Major and a couple of AMGOT officers there was no military presence in the Oltrearno.

The building in which Mario had his flat was on the very edge of the demolished area. The block next door was half destroyed, a whole section having been torn away by the blast. Rooms were obscenely exposed showing fireplaces canted at an angle, beds balanced on sloping floors, pictures in smashed frames hanging askew on the walls, bathrooms and lavatories exposed shamelessly.

Mario gave a cry of relief when he saw that his own block had escaped. He hurried on ignoring the KEEP OUT notices put up by the Sappers. There were footsteps on the stairway above as he and Edmund entered the hall.

'What floor's your flat on?'

'The fourth.'

They were half way up when an explosion overhead shook the building. On the next landing a toothless old man was standing shaking his head.

'I told him but he wouldn't listen. He wouldn't listen.'

'What happened?'

'The Germans have left booby-traps. Even dead bodies are mined.' The old man had lost his glasses and his eyes were not focussing. 'My sister went back to her house to sleep and when she got into her bed it blew up. God forgive them! It is a week since they went and they are still murdering us.'

Edmund took Mario's arm to prevent him going further. 'You can't go up, Mario. It is too risky.'

'I have to,' Mario said fiercely. 'I have to.'

He tore himself free and dashed up the last two flights of stairs. The old man put his head on one side, listening for the explosion.

Edmund followed more slowly but he caught up with Mario

in the hall of his flat. He was standing there, staring dumbly. The door had been smashed open at the side opposite to the lock. The hinges had torn loose. The interior had been hit by some kind of tornado. In their search for valuables the looters had flung the contents of drawers to the floor, ripped open the covers of chairs and sofa, smashed the doors of cupboards.

'Even the children's room,' Mario muttered as he stared through the gaping doorways at the wreckage.

'Watch where you tread!' Edmund warned as Mario moved forward. 'Don't touch anything.'

But Mario was not interested in the rooms. He had seen the bottle of pills on the table where Ornella had left it in the panic of their departure.

'Thank God!' He scooped the little bottle up and rattled it.

'What on earth – ?'

'Ornella's pills. For her blood pressure.'

Mario was oblivious to Edmund's fury. Even the rifling of his flat was of secondary importance. He let Edmund lead him down the stairs and out of the building, still clutching the bottle to his breast.

It was Tuesday 9th August before Edmund was back in Florence. He had the unhappy feeling that he had achieved very little. It was not the journey back to 15 Army Group that had taken up the time. He was determined to avoid Parkinson, who was quite capable of ordering him out of Florence. He'd wasted a day in the hope of getting a personal interview with the C in C, or his Chief of Staff or even the Director of Military Intelligence. All of them were inaccessible. In this period between the visits of two VIPs they were trying to get on with their task of fighting the Germans. The King had spent ten days with Alexander, inspecting units and conferring decorations. He had departed on 4 August, the day Edmund entered Florence. Now Churchill was due in less than a week. The Prime Minister was bringing Sir Alan Brooke and the nucleus of his Private Office with him and would be spending a fortnight with 15 Army Group. He intended by this visit to show his support for Alexander.

This was the moment the Chiefs of Staff in London had chosen to deprive Alexander of the forces he needed most.

Since the Normandy landings on 6 June the Italian campaign had come to be regarded as a side-show, almost forgotten by the public at home. Now, under pressure from Papa Stalin, it had been decided to make a second landing in France, this time on the south coast. Naturally the forces for Operation Anvil would have to come from Italy, so 15 Army Group was about to be milked of four French and three US divisions as well as seventy per cent of its air support. This blow had not deflected Alexander in his resolve to smash the German armies in Italy and drive a sword into the under-belly of the Nazi Reich. But on 7 August 1944 the plight of Florence and its inhabitants was not his main problem.

As a last resort Edmund sought out James Fothergill, who was now a Lieutenant Colonel and a GSO I on Alex's staff. James belonged to the same regiment and they had been in the BEF together before Dunkirk.

James had been surprised and pleased to see an old friend. 'I've often wondered what happened to you. How come you're still a Captain? I'd have thought you'd be at least a Colonel by now.'

'I got wounded and put in the bag at Dunkirk.' Edmund was practised at summing up in telegraphese the hellish experience of his capture and escape. 'When I eventually got back to England I was Grade C so they buried me quietly in the War Office. I got dug out when Florence was about to fall.'

James listened patiently while Edmund described the situation in Florence and argued the case for sending troops in without delay.

'We have to re-group, Edmund. One can't lose seven divisions without feeling it.'

'Will you at least see that Alex gets this information I've brought back?'

'I'll talk to General Airey about it. He will decide whether to pass it on to the C in C.'

'But there are *half a million people* on the brink of starvation . . . .'

'Well, *we* didn't ask them to declare war on us, did we?'

Back in Florence, however, Edmund did see signs that the British Army was reaching out towards the northern part of the city. Quantities of flour were being stock-piled near the Ponte Vecchio ready to be moved across the river. There was some movement of civilians across the ruins of the Ponte alla Carraia where corpses still lay to remind the foolhardy of the danger from mines. The Sappers had started to build a Bailey Bridge, using the surviving piers of the Ponte Santa Trinità as a base. The route through the Vasari Corridor was still a secret. Only an acute observer could distinguish the thin telephone cable dangling from the opening.

Back at the flat, he was relieved when a composed-looking Mario opened the door. Edmund had to stand with his back to the kitchen table to ease the weight of the big pack off his shoulders. It contained flour, compo biscuits, assorted tins of food and chocolate for Stefano and Anna. There was a round tin of fifty State Express for Jason and at the bottom, wrapped in spare underwear, a bottle of whisky for Ken.

'He was here half an hour ago, inquiring if you were back,' Mario said in answer to his question. He was trying to decipher the label on a tin of steak and kidney pudding. Ornella had had three days to recover from the news that her home had been ransacked but her eyes were still red from weeping. 'We have some new information that will interest you. The Soprintendenza lorry has been located at Dicomano.'

'That's north of here?'

'North-east. About 35 kilometres out on the road to Forli. It is hidden in a garage in the centre of the town.'

'Pictures still on board?'

'According to our information, yes.'

At the old Countess's house Alessio opened the door and signalled Edmund that his mistress was asleep in the ground-floor room where she now spent all her time. She could not manage stairs without assistance.

He found Ken lying naked on his bed in the guest room on the third floor. It was wide enough for two at a pinch. The pillow beside Ken's was dented by the imprint of a head. Ken was reading *The Tailor of Gloucester*. He had found a complete set of Beatrix Potter in the bookshelf.

'Gosh, this takes me back!' He grinned as he put the book down. 'Caterina can't understand why it fascinates me so much.'

'Has she deserted you?'

'She's in the nursery, I expect,' Ken said casually.

'The nursery?'

'She still calls her room the nursery. She was brought up in this house by Nonna – you know, Grandma. I say, what have you got there?'

'Johnny Walker. Suit you all right?'

'Just the job.' Ken rolled off the bed. 'I need something to celebrate with. We caught the bugger last night.'

'Your spy?'

'You know, he had hide-outs in four different lodgings. They all thought he was dead respectable. *Dottor* Rossi! Doctor my ass.' Ken had found a couple of glasses, each with a pool of wine at the bottom. A smear of lipstick smudged the rim of one. 'Such an insignificant little chap too, knee high to a grasshopper, wouldn't say boo to a goose – you'd think. But he was all set for a long stay. Here's mud in your eye.'

'Cheers.' Edmund turned the glass round to avoid the lipstick.

'Know how the Abwehr were able to put the screws on him?'

Edmund shook his head, enjoying the tang of the neat whisky in his gullet.

'The bugger had syphilis. He couldn't get the medicine except from the Germans. You should have seen his suitcase. Full of the stuff, phials of it. I've got it now. No difficulty about making him talk, in fact it's hard to stop him. We'll be flushing out his squad of girls tonight.'

'Will he be shot?'

'Doubt it.' Ken was sitting on the edge of the bed, pulling his socks on. 'Too eager to talk. You see, by the Geneva Convention, you can only shoot a spy if you prove that he had the intention to spy. That's why the preliminary interrogation is so important. If he lies, feeds you a nice cover story, you've got him, you can argue that if he did not intend to spy he would have told the truth. Rossi spilled it all straight away, he was too scared, so unfortunately he may get away with his life. Might nobble some of his girls, though. It would help if we could get one of them executed.'

'I don't see what that would prove.'

'Oh, my dear Ed.' Ken looked up at him very seriously. He had detected the distaste in Edmunds' voice. 'The shooting of spies is the single biggest deterrent to spying. That's why we *have* to shoot one from time to time . . . .'

'But a girl . . . .'

'Girls can do more damage than anyone. A girl can cross the lines, let a few soldiers screw her and go back to report their position to enemy gunners. One girl's life against dozens of men? Which would you choose?'

Edmund hoped that was not a choice he'd ever have to make. 'Where have you got him?'

Ken winked and tapped his trouser pocket. 'Down in one of the cellars cooling off. I've got the key. Should be good for a gong if Bertie keeps his promise. Oh! I've got a message for you.' He unbuttoned his shirt pocket and took out a folded sheet. 'Jason asked me to give you this.'

Edmund unfolded the note.

Dear Ed,
Am going back to my regiment. Sod this for a lark. Hope to get some real fighting soon. Sorry to let you down. Best of luck with your Madonna!

Jason.

P.S. I'm leaving you my revolver. You may need it.

'When did he take off?'

'About three this morning, damn him!'

Rosalba was in the small sitting-room, standing at the window with her back to the door. She was watching the crowd round a couple of *contadini* who had somehow managed to bring a barrow of farm produce into the city. They were doing a brisk trade at astronomic prices. She turned listlessly when she heard him come in. Her eyes showed no signs of weeping, but they were hurt and bewildered.

'Oh, Edmund it's you.'

'I had a note from Jason. He left it with Ken.'

'He's gone.'

'Yes.'

She faced the window again, staring out over the reddish-brown roofs.

'It was my fault. I was selfish, thinking only of myself.'

The sunlight through the window caught the aura of her hair bringing out golden tints. The effect was as if she was wearing a lace veil.

'Perhaps the advice I gave you was bad'.

'No, Edmund, it was not. I've been repeating it to myself all night. "To thine own self be true." But I am afraid that I may have lost Jason. I was his *fidanzata*, he kept saying, as if that gave him the same rights as a husband.' She turned and came a few steps closer. 'What did he say to you?'

'In his note? Just that he was going back to his regiment.'

'To fight, to kill. And if he gets killed it will be my fault. Oh, Edmund! If that happens I do not know what I shall do.'

A fracas had broken out in the street below. A woman was accusing the *contadini* of profiteering. They were protesting that they had risked their lives to bring food to the starving citizens. Their voices rose to a hysterical pitch.

'You really love him?' Edmund said. 'Un vero grande amore?'

She was startled by the question. 'How can you ask? Have I not waited five years for him?'

Edmund was at the mantelpiece, watching her profile in the mirror above it. 'You've both been asking a lot of yourselves. All these years you've kept this dream of the moment when you'd meet again. It was hard for the reality to live up to your expectations. Neither of you is to blame. "Just such disparitie as is twixt Aire and Angels twixt women's love and men's will ever be." '

'That's Shakespeare.'

'No. It's Donne.'

'You are so wise, Edmund.' In a spontaneous movement she came and took his hands, one in each of hers. 'I could never talk to Papa and Mamma like this. Oh, I'm so glad you are back!'

The inhabitants of the *palazzo* had settled down to a life that was uncomfortable but not intolerable. In Italy a black market can flourish under the most unfavourable conditions and those who have the money can usually procure what they really need. The Countess herself would not stoop to bartering but she made sure that Susanna had enough to outbid most people for the produce that was somehow finding its way in from the surrounding country. Alessio had no scruples where *la vecchia contessa* was concerned. He was prepared even to filch food and water from her two sons.

The constant background of gunfire as the artillery of both sides duelled across the city had become so much a feature of everyday life that no-one any longer heeded it. The illusion that the war would wash past the walls of Palazzo Lamberti leaving it unscathed was abruptly shattered at twenty-three minutes to seven on the evening of Tuesday the 9th. A short shell fired by a 105 mm gun on the Fiesole hill struck the south west corner of the roof. The explosion sounded deafening in the enclosed courtyard. The blast blew out most of the inner windows and sent a shower of stones and débris into the courtyard.

Wednesday 10 August was the twelfth day of Florence's torment. In the northern district the paratroopers were still carrying on with their vendetta of rapine, looting, torturing and killing. Twenty Italians had been rounded up and shot as a punitive measure for the two Germans killed during the raid on Piazza Landini. But there was one sign that the ordeal was soon to end. The engineers building the Bailey bridge had already spanned the gap to the first pier of Ponte Santa Trinità.

At nine that morning Edmund was with Mario in the sitting-room of the flat. They had a map spread out on the table. Mario was pointing out the location of Dicomano. It was at the foot of the Appenines, just below the Passo del Muraglione.

'The partisans report that there are security checkpoints on all the passes. That's probably why they haven't risked taking the pictures any further north.'

'Can the partisans do anything about immobilising that lorry?'

'They're going to try. But after the raid on Piazza Landini . . . .'

Mario was interrupted by an unearthly scream, a ghastly throat-tearing sound that went on and on. It came from the interior of the *palazzo* and it was becoming louder. Both men rushed to the window of the children's room which overlooked the *cortile*. They were in time to see Susanna stagger out from Nonna's house.

Racing down the stairs Edmund collided with Carlo, who had emerged from his own part of the *palazzo*. Susanna tottered against him, bile dribbling from her mouth.

'Che c'é, che cé?' Carlo shook her. 'Per l'amor di Dio, cos'è successo?'

But Susanna was incapable of speech. Struggling for breath, she shook her head from side to side, her eyes staring.

'Stay here and look after her,' Edmund told Carlo.

He ran to the open door of the house. The old Contessa's boudoir-sitting room was on the right at the bottom of the staircase. The curtains were still drawn over the windows and the only light came from the door. A familiar smell drew Edmund inside. He pulled the curtains back from the nearest window. There was no feeling of presence in the room. As he turned, his eyes were drawn to the black-clad form slumped in the high-backed arm-chair beside the fireplace. The old Countess's head had nodded forward.

'Contessa! Nonna!'

The old lady was very still. Edmund went up to her, put his hand under her brow to raise her head, but she had stiffened in *rigor mortis*. Her forehead was icy cold, her face grey and bloodless. He let the head dip slowly into its nodding position, took a deep breath. There was a sound of running feet in the *cortile*. It could be Rosalba, she must not see this. He ran to the door and closed it in the face of the protesting Carlo.

'Alessio! Ken!'

His voice sounded hollow, bounced back emptily from the ceiling above. As he went up the stairs to the first floor he noticed a walking stick that had got hooked in the bannisters. The only room he knew was Ken's. It was empty, the bed neatly made up but not slept in. He guessed that the room across the landing was the 'nursery'. The door was closed.

When he opened it he got the same smell, only stronger. Here too the curtains were still drawn. His eyes had already adjusted themselves after the bright sunlight. As he crossed the room to the window he could see the body sprawled on the bed. He pulled the curtains back and forced himself to look.

Someone was hammering on the door below. Edmund let his eyes take in the atrocious scene. What was hard to believe was that this was the work of human hands. Experience of horror had taught him how to distance himself from the most mind-shattering sights, but it took him a moment to steady himself.

Then he went down the stairs to the front door. When he turned the key it was pushed open. He was knocked back against the wall. The Count thrust past him and rushed into his mother's room. Edmund slammed the door shut again, holding it by main force against Carlo. Lorenzo's shout of anguish came from the boudoir.

Edmund had seen Ken's face behind his besiegers. 'Ken, for Christ's sake! Help me keep these people out!'

Carlo had his foot in the doorway. Titillated by the scent of violence, he was determined to be in at the blooding. Ken pulled him away unceremoniously while he slipped in beside Edmund. Between them they got the door shut again.

From Nonna's room came the lamentation of the Count. Ken looked in, saw the distraught man kneeling in front of his mother's dead body.

'Jesus Christ! What the hell's happened here?' He spun round and stared at Edmund's face. 'Caterina?'

'She's upstairs.' Edmund grasped Ken's arm as he started to move. 'Don't go up there, Ken.'

'I bloody will!' Ken shook himself free and raced up the stairs two at a time. Edmund followed, caught up with him two paces into the room. The terrible thing on the bed had stopped Ken in his tracks.

'God!' Ken lowered his head and turned away, his face contorted. He gripped Edmund's arm so tightly that his fingers crushed the bone. He retched as his gorge rose, and vomited on to the carpet.

'Ken!' Edmund barked at him. 'Get a hold of yourself.'

Ken released Edmund's arm and wiped his chin. He stumbled towards the stairs and hung onto the bannisters.

'Who? Why? How could anyone – ? Ed, we've got to stop them touching anything.'

He was beginning to recover but the nausea of shock is catching. Ken's revulsion was making it harder for Edmund to control his own stomach.

'I want to get the Count out of there. Come and give me a hand. *Come on*, Ken!'

The command steadied Ken. The two men went down the stairs. To Edmund's surprise the Count, sobbing with total abandon, let himself be led like a child out of the room. Ken opened the front door. A circle of pale, frightened faces pressed forward. Mario was standing a little way behind the group. He looked like a man summoned by Torquemada's Inquisition.

'Papa!' Rosalba ran to her father, incredulous at this collapse of a monument. 'What has happened? Is it Nonna?'

The Count managed to choke out one word. 'Morta.'

'No!' Rosalba made a dash for the door. Moving quickly Edmund stepped in the way, seized her by the arm. 'No, Rosalba. Do not go in there. I forbid it.'

The Countess had been playing a 78 record of Beniamino Gigli on a wind-up cabinet gramophone with a huge horn. She had heard nothing of the commotion in the *cortile*. Her first intimation of the disaster was when her shattered husband was led into the room by Rosalba. When she grasped what had happened she immediately took charge. Mario had hurried up to the flat to prevent Ornella and the children from coming down. The others had all crowded up to the *salone*.

'First we must have a priest. Where's Alessio?'

'We cannot find him, signora.' With her peasant's fortitude Susanna had recovered.

'Well, you go, Susanna, and see if you can find Don Antonio. Tell him to come at once.'

'Sisignora.' Susanna nodded and vanished.

'Has anyone seen Guido?'

'He's on his way up,' said Ken.

The Countess shot him a glance but did not press the question. She turned to Edmund. 'I understand it was you who found the – who found them.'

'Well, it was really Susanna. I was up in the flat with Mario and we heard her screaming.'

'You said that they had been murdered. Why are you so sure?'

He was conscious that Rosalba was listening so he gave

107

only a brief and terse account of what he had seen, omitting the gruesome details.

'I am sorry I had to act in such a high-handed manner,' he finished, 'but in cases like that it is important not to disturb anything.'

'You did right, Edmund.' Since his return the Countess had been calling him by his first name. 'I am grateful. Ah, Guido. You have heard what happened?'

Guido took one look at his father and his lower lip trembled. 'Yes, Mamma. I cannot believe it. I was down in the basement with Federico. I did not see anything. It's appalling. Who would want to kill Nonna – or Caterina?'

'Susanna has gone to fetch Don Antonio. Your father has had a bad shock so I want you to go and fetch Doctor Salvi. Do not tell him what has happened. Just say he is needed very urgently.'

Guido hurried out, glad to be given a job to do.

Some of the colour had come back into Ken's cheeks. His instincts as a trained security officer were beginning to reassert themselves. 'I don't like to interfere, Contessa, but this is a police matter. We've got to have a representative of the civil authority here.'

'What about Tenente Ascari?' Carlo suggested. He had barely been able to control his excitement. 'He lives just down the street. A lieutenant in the Carabinieri.'

'He'll do. Just so long as he comes from outside the palazzo. This thing may have a personal basis.'

Ken's words sent a tremor through the assembly. Edmund felt an arm brush his elbow. Rosalba had moved round to stand beside him.

'I think it would be best if we all sat down,' the Countess suggested. 'Lorenzo . . . .'

'Yes, tesoro?'

'Ascari will come if you ask him personally.'

'You want me to go and fetch him?'

'Well, you can't telephone, can you, dear?' she said dryly. 'Corragio! It's only a hundred metres.'

The Count braced himself. It was unusual for him to be at the receiving end of such orders. He was accustomed to sending emissaries himself.

'Carlo. As the door closed on her husband, the Countess

turned to her brother-in-law, 'I think this is a good moment to open that bottle of cognac we were keeping for the Liberation.'

The priest was the first to turn up. He was a moon-faced man, surprisingly well-fed in this famine-struck community, clad in a black cassock and biretta. He carried a small case containing the oil and holy water for administering the last rites to the dead. For him this was a task of extreme urgency. Ken had difficulty in persuading him to wait till the Carabin-ieri lieutenant arrived. During the five minute delay he managed to convey the impression that the souls of the old Countess and Caterina were slipping away from his grasp into Purgatory or Hell.

Ascari was old for a lieutenant. Promotion had passed him by. Murder investigations were not his province, he explained, he was a traffic specialist.

'That doesn't matter,' Ken reassured him. 'All you have to do is represent the civil authority.'

'But the city is under military rule.'

'Whose? The Germans have abdicated responsibility. The Allies are in no hurry to take it on. The Geneva Convention requires police forces to remain *in situ* and carry on normal duties. You must at least make a preliminary investigation, establish the facts.'

The lieutenant's pencil-thin moustache and black eyebrows gave him a fierce appearance belied by his gentle manner. He looked to the Count for guidance.

'The capitano is right, tenente.' Lorenzo Lamberti momen-tarily recovered some of his dignity. 'You have your duty.'

With a shrug of his shoulders and an eloquent upturning of his hands, Ascari gave in.

'Hurry!' the priest was saying. 'Already we have lost much time.'

Edmund, Ken, Don Antonio and Ascari were crossing the *cortile* when Guido came through the archway with a small, dark man. He had been unable to find Doctor Salvi but had located his son, who was also a doctor. Warned by Ken not to touch anything, the priest went first into the ground-floor room to administer the rites to the old Countess. The rigidness of the body with its slumped head made it difficult for him to inscribe the sign of the cross with oil on her forehead. Only when that had been done would he make way for the doctor.

Upstairs the sight of Caterina's body stopped the priest as it had stopped Ken. He drew his breath in sharply, closed his eyes and stood there for a moment, praying. Then he steeled himself to go to her and perform the same little ceremony. When it was done he hurried away, neither looking at any of them nor speaking a word.

'I am a gynaecologist not a forensic specialist,' Doctor Salvi said when he had made a quick examination of the body. 'In a sense that is relevant because of the nature of the injuries. I do not have to tell you that there has been an element of sexuality, perverted sexuality, in the attack on the young woman.'

'Cause of death?'

'Oh, manual strangulation, almost certainly.'

'And the old lady?'

'She has a fractured wrist and some contusions on the head but I doubt if that would be enough to cause death. I would say that she died of heart failure — possibly as a consequence of a fall, or some shock.'

'So she could have been carried to the chair and placed in it?'

'To say so would be speculation on my part,' Salvi's way of talking, like all his movements, was quick and decisive. He had small eyes like buttons, and a neat triangular beard.

'Can you place the time, doctor?'

Salvi pursed his lips. 'As far as I can tell, death occurred between six and twelve hours ago.'

'That is the nearest you can get?'

'For the moment, yes. A forensic scientist would be able to give you more precise information.' He paused and for the first time showed that the veneer of professional detachment was only skin deep. 'If I may say so, what you need most is an expert undertaker. I bid you good-day.'

Ascari obviously envied the priest and the doctor for being able to make their escape so quickly. Watching him, Edmund realised that he was at a loss how to proceed.

'If I may suggest . . . .' Ken said, stepping in to take command.

'Yes, capitano?'

'You make a quick note now for your report and perhaps a sketch showing the position of the bodies. Then we can both go over the ground for any possible traces of the intruders. After that I think we should take a statement from everybody in the palazzo.'

'I noticed a walking stick on the stairs,' Ascari said, with some pride in his powers of observation.

'Yes. It's the old Countess's walking stick.'

'Perhaps,' the lieutenant suggested 'That is what they used to . . . .'

Edmund shook his head. 'No. You've seen her. That is not what they used.'

During the afternoon two of the Brothers of Misericord accompanied by a nun came to wash and lay out the corpses, restoring at last some semblance of dignity to Caterina's contorted body.

When Ken came up at about half-past-eight, dog-tired and famished with hunger, Edmund had just finished cooking up a concoction from his Compo rations for the two frightened children. He had washed their hands and faces and finally put them to bed.

'I'm going to kip up here.' Ken slumped down in a chair and covered his face with his hands. 'Even if they have taken the bodies away I can't sleep in that house. God!'

'Have a peg of whisky.' Edmund waved his pipe at the bottle. 'It'll do you good.'

Ken shook his head. 'Not on an empty stomach. Is there anything to eat?'

While he demolished a plateful of steak and kidney pudding, Ken gave Edmund a synopsis of all the statements he and Ascari had taken. If Doctor Salvi was correct the murder had been committed between ten the previous evening and four in the morning. For that period, four of the eighteen people in the *palazzo* had alibis only from their spouses. It was hard to believe that Caterina's injuries had been inflicted by a woman but, as this appeared to be a totally illogical crime, you could not exclude anyone.

'Ascari wants to pin it on Alessio. No-one's seen him since yesterday evening.'

'That faithful old man. I can't believe any of these people could do a thing like that.'

'Italian passions.' Ken managed to talk with his mouth

full. 'When they get really fired up. Seen a few rough old sights, I can tell you. Of course, the old lady had plenty of enemies. She was never one to mince words. Very pro-monarchy, pro-Fascist. Hadn't a good word for the Commies. But Caterina . . . .' He laid his knife and fork down and stared out of the window. 'Trouble with her was too many friends.' He wiped his lips and helped himself to a stiff measure of whisky. The level was going down rapidly. 'Well, at least we've got something down for the record. When things return to normal the police can take it from there. I'd better take some of these biscuits down to my prisoner. He must be getting hungry now. Want to come and have a look at him?'

Edmund nodded at the closed door of the *salotto*. 'I think I'll stay here. These two kids have taken it very hard.'

Five minutes later Ken was back in the flat.

'The bugger's gone! Someone sawed the padlock off the cellar door. And to think I was soft enough to let him have some of his bloody medicine.'

8

At 6.45 on the morning of Thursday 11 August Edmund was wakened by a new sound. Somewhere in the city a bell was ringing out with all the bloodthirsty vigour of a tocsin. A few minutes later he heard a thundering on the door of the flat and the footsteps of Mario going to open it. In the next room the children were chattering excitedly.

Guido burst in. He was arrayed for battle with a bandolier across his chest, two grenades at his belt, an Italian army helmet on his head and his rifle over his shoulder. All he needed to complete the picture was a knife between his teeth. His eyes were alight.

'Capitano, it's the signal! The partisans are rising!'

'That bell?'

'It's La Martinella, the bell of Il Bargello. Four years it has been silent. That's the signal of our liberation. The Germans have gone! My reparto is rallying at Piazza Strozzi. Come and join us. This is a glorious moment for Florence!'

'What about Federico? You're not leaving him in the basement?'

'Federico is coming with me.'

'But I thought he couldn't walk.'

'We'll help him. He'll be all right.'

Edmund got out of bed, and shaved and dressed in his own time. When he joined them, the little family were all up sitting round the breakfast table. Since Edmund had brought back his Compo rations they had become addicts of sweet tea laced with Libby's tinned milk. The streets were still echoing to the clamour of the great bell.

Mario elaborated on Guido's brief explanation. 'It's the signal for general insurrection. You know the Bargello was formerly the prison and the bell tolled to announce an execution.'

'Uncle Guido has gone to kill the Germans,' Stefano informed Edmund. 'Are you going to fight too 'Mundo?'

Edmund laughed. 'I'll leave that to the experts.'

'Where's Ken?' Ornella asked.

'His prisoner escaped and he went off to round up a partisan search party.' Edmund nodded in the direction of the Bargello. 'I'm afraid this will put the lid on that.'

'Do you think . . . .' Mario was lighting up yet another State Express. Edmund had given him the tin intended for Jason and he was getting through it as if there was no tomorrow. 'Could it have been the spy – what happened yesterday?'

'Hard to see what his motive would have been.'

The Germans had indeed withdrawn from Florence, but they had not gone very far. The paratroopers, supported by artillery and tanks, were entrenched on the line of the railway and the river Mugnone, whose bridges had been blown the night after those on the Arno. The main part of Florence was thus virtually an island, enclosed on the north, south and west by its two rivers. For the first time since the middle ages it had again become a city-state. There were no foreign troops.

The Germans had pulled back, the Allies had not yet advanced. Florence had its own army, its own government. Three formations of partisans – Brigate Sinigaglia, Brigate Giustizia e Libertà, Brigate Lanciotto Buozzi Caiano – were moving into position to attack the German lines. The Committee of Liberation was putting into operation its plan for taking over public order, health and hygiene, food distribution, the banks. The tricolore flag was hoisted on the tower of the Palazzo Vecchio in Piazza Signoria.

Now at last the people could flood out into their own streets. An atmosphere of festivity reigned. Ornella even dared to take her children out for their first walk in two weeks. Mario threw off his gloom and depression. 'At last our honour as a nation is restored,' he told Edmund. 'We are proving that we can fight for ourselves and govern ourselves. The future of Italy is being forged here!'

There were dark patches on this general picture of rejoicing and enthusiasm. Two attractive young girls were led into Piazza Signoria to have their heads ceremonially shaved in front of a jeering crowd. Their crime was that they had surrendered to the blandishments of the blond warriors of the Master Race. A cretinous, half dotty youth was dragged from a house in Via Calzaiuoli and made to run a gauntlet of fists and boots before he was tied up and driven away to cries of 'Spia!, Spia!' In the *piazza* in front of Santa Maria Novella eleven Fascists were lined up and shot in the morning sunlight. In many places, out of sight of human eyes, old scores were settled with the savagery of the ancient internecine factions. The Fascists had not all fled. In the Via Tornabuoni their snipers were still picking off targets from the roof tops.

In the northern part of the city a more tragic drama was unfolding. The din of battle had broken out again only a few streets away. The partisan brigades, armed only with rifles and other light weapons, were attacking the experienced paratroopers. The latter were well dug in; for months they had been defending themselves against a modern, mechanised army, they had artillery and tanks to back them. More insidiously they had the support of Fascist snipers who had taken up positions in houses behind the partisans and were now inflicting a fearful toll on them. The snipers were hard to winkle out. The partisans had pin-pointed fire coming from one particular fourth-floor window. Every time they rushed the room they found only a mother suckling her child. The firing continued. At last they surprised the sniper in action. It was the mother herself.

In the next two days of fighting, the partisans lost 190 dead, with 435 wounded.

The Committee of Liberation sent a message through to the Allied Command, begging them to come in and drive the Germans back. The reply was unhelpful. Not till the Florentines had dealt with the snipers in the city would the Allies cross the Arno.

Guido, who had come back to have a nick in his arm dressed by Rosalba, was desperate, grieving for his friends who had been killed.

'Why does your Army not come?' he demanded of Edmund. 'Don't they want to risk their own skins? You tell us to clear the city but we have only old rifles against tanks!'

The *palazzo* was more than ever an enclave. The Lambertis had folded themselves in with their own shock and grief. The Brothers of Misericord had come and taken the bodies away for burial and Nonna's house remained closed up. Ascari had completed his sketchy inquiries and gone home to write his report. No trace of Alessio had been found in any of his Florence haunts. To Ascari, that was as good as a confession of guilt. Ken had picked up a new lead on Rossi which lead back across the Arno, where the spy had yet another safe house. If he was operating a radio-set from the Oltrearno, now filled with British troops, he could be doing a lot of damage.

Not till the second day after the murders did Edmund venture to go over to the Count's house. Lorenzo had not left his room since the afternoon of the crime but the Countess agreed to receive Edmund. She was as always in full control of herself.

'It's the war, Edmund,' she said, when he muttered some condolence. 'We Florentines have strong emotions at the best of times, but the strains we have been living under these last weeks have brought everyone to breaking point. When will it end?'

'Can't be long now, Contessa. The bridge is nearly finished.'

'I want you to talk to Rosalba. Poor child, she has had a double blow. First Jason and then Nonna. None of us seem able to console her.'

The Sappers took five days to complete their bridge across the Arno. On Sunday 13th, just two weeks after the evacuation of the doomed zone, the two halves of the city were linked again. The snipers in Via Tornabuoni, into which the Ponte Santa Trinità had led, were gone. That morning, troops of 8th Indian Division headed by partisans of the Brigate Sinigaglia marched into the city. The fighting troops pushed on to make contact with the German positions. The partisans gratefully yielded pride of place to them but continued their fight under the direction of the British commander.

In the wake of the line regiments came the full panoply of Allied Military Government, the spick and span administrators who would move into cushy billets, take over the best offices and set out to impose their Anglo-Saxon order on this Italian chaos. There were AMGOT officers, a Town Major, engineers of 71 Garrison, Claims and Hirings, Military Police, Field Security, the Displaced Persons unit, even a YMCA tea van. It was all strictly controlled and only those with the requisite pass were allowed to enter the city.

Allied Military Government had brought with them not only food supplies but lists of notable liberals, Catholics, monarchists and aristocrats who would be invited to take responsible posts. To the amazement of Edmund and the disgust of his son, Il Conte Lamberti was on the list. There was even a nationally known monarchist who was to be City Commandant. To their discomfiture AMGOT found the Tuscan Committee of Liberation in full control of Florence. When the monarchist was informed in blunt terms that the partisan Marte Brigade was in command, he accepted the hint and retired as gracefully as possible. The Allied Military Governors had taken over the Palazzo Medici-Riccardi as their offices but at night abandoned it to withdraw to the Villa Torregiani across the Arno. This proved to be a wise decision, for during the night of the 13th a German tank rumbled into the city, and its commander reached up from his turret and removed the AMGOT sign from the front of the building. It reminded the more timorous spirits that the Germans had threatened to return and shoot anyone who collaborated with the Allies.

Edmund felt an odd sadness as he walked through Piazza della Republica, Piazza del Duomo and down to the Piazza Signoria. The city had been taken over by strangers who, he felt, had no right to be there. They bustled about with infuriating self-importance, preening themselves when groups of Italians began clapping at the sight of an Allied uniform.

In the Piazza Signoria the YMCA tea van was parked in front of the Loggia dei Lanzi, right by Giambologna's statue of the Rape of the Sabine. As he approached, Edmund recognised the fair-haired girl he had seen at Porta Romana on 4 August. Once again he joined the little queue.

'Cup of tea and wodge, please.' He could tell from her smile that she had recognised him. 'I thought you were with the Guards Brigade.'

'I usually am but they've been pulled back for a rest. I got permission to bring the van into Florence.'

'Good idea. My wife drives one of these.'

'Oh?' She was drawing a cup of tea from her cylindrical urn. Her hands had not shaken when a stray shell landed a few blocks away. 'For the YM?'

'No. She works for the rival firm. Salvation Army. In the East End.'

'Among all those flying bombs?' She handed him the tea and a thick cheese sandwich. 'Brave girl.'

He found Mario in the Director's office at the Soprintendenza. Fabio Pantano had shed more weight but his lugubrious features had become almost cheerful.

'The Mostra paintings haven't gone far,' Mario told Edmund. 'According to our agents the lorry is still at Dicomano, but closely guarded night and day.'

'There's nothing more we can do about it until the advance continues.' Edmund had been reminding himself sternly that the King's *tondo* was not the only *objet d'art* at risk. His obsession with the Madonna had tended to blind him to everything else. 'I have to be getting on with my report for COPAT. I wanted to ask you, Professore, if you could lend me Mario for a few days?'

For the next week the work kept them out from sunrise to sunset, and it was heart-breaking. Only now were they able to measure the true extent of the damage done by the demolitions.

The German plan had been to destroy the routes by which the Allies could enter Florence. To do this they had blown up seven bridges. The Ponte Vecchio had been spared at a great cost, for to block the approaches on *both* sides a large portion of the most historic part of the city had been taken out. To the south the buildings flanking the Via Guiciardini had been destroyed to a depth of 150 metres. To the north those on either side of the Via Por S Maria had been toppled into the street over an equal distance. Two churches, ten mediaeval towers and twenty-five historic palaces were gone.

The home of the Colombaria Society with its famous collection of manuscripts, diaries and letters was in ruins, but Mario found vestiges in the rubble. It seemed that something might be saved. But now it became apparent that a new danger threatened. The British engineers were bidding fair to complete the damage done by the Germans. Under the rubble of Via de'Bardi lay buried the broken gas and water mains essential for the continued existence of the inhabitants. Sappers of 71 Garrison were working with remarkable speed and efficiency to clear them. The Chief Engineer had authorised the use of a bulldozer. Edmund remonstrated. That rubble certainly concealed documents and objects of historic value, all of them irreplaceable. The engineers were not sympathetic. He had to stand helplessly by while the precious rubble was pushed by the bulldozer's blade into the Arno. The extent of the loss could be read on Mario's stricken face.

The Torre di Parte Guelfa had stood at the southern end of the Ponte Vecchio. Two of its ancient walls had survived the blast. When Edmund and Mario got to it one of these walls had already been pulled down. It was deemed unsafe. Surely, Edmund argued, the remaining wall could be shored up. Again his protest was over-ruled. The grapples had already been attached. When the cable was tightened the last vestige of the Torre collapsed in a cloud of dust. The most picturesque square in Old Florence had been needlessly destroyed.

Sickened by what was happening in the city but powerless

to prevent it, Edmund decided after two days that he'd had enough.

'If I can scrounge some transport we'll get out of here, Mario. I want to see what's happening in the country around and we can visit some of your deposits.'

'If the Germans have not taken it, my car may still be in the garage.'

Mario's car turned out to be a nice little Fiat 1100. Tucked away in an obscure, cave-like garage with a roll-down door, it had escaped the looters. With the authority of his special pass Edmund was able to fill the tank at a 71 Garrison petrol station.

Stories were coming in of the damage done by American bombers at Impruneta, the little town in the hills south of Florence. It was Wednesday 16th when they drove up the winding road. Eastward from the Val d'Arno came the sound of gunfire, but it was desultory. The Basilica of Santa Maria had been consecrated in 1054. The inhabitants had regarded it as a sanctuary, immune to the perils of war. On the night of 26 July, the day after King George VI arrived in Italy, the Allied air force had visited Impruneta. The attack was completely pointless, as all but a few Germans had departed. After the first raid the injured were carried for safety into the Basilica. It had been hit in a second attack and they had all perished, buried under the rubble.

So another scene of devastation greeted Mario and Edmund. Through what remained of the roof, light poured on shattered beams and mounds of wood and masonry. On top lay the remnants of the 13th century ceiling. The Renaissance tomb of Bishop Antonio degli Agli had been ripped open by the blast. Bones and shards of brown dried flesh had spilled out. The skull had fallen off its brocade cushion. As he stared down Edmund's mind reclothed the bones with flesh. He could almost see the face of the old prelate staring at him accusingly across the centuries.

When he looked round for Mario he saw that he had picked his way to where the high altar had been. Edmund followed him. He was shaking his head as his eyes searched the wreckage.

'Gone. The trecento altarpiece. Twenty-eight panels and fourteen golden pinnacles. One of the most important examples of the iconography of the Virgin.' Mario turned to Edmund in a rare outburst of bitterness. 'Why, Edmundo? Is this your Liberation? Is this the price we have to pay for your victory over the Germans?'

During the next three days the little Fiat carried Edmund and the chain-smoking Mario to most of the deposits south of Florence. They spent their nights in the houses of people with whom Mario had only the briefest acquaintance. After what he had seen Edmund was embarrassed by the hospitality and generosity of these ordinary Italians. By the time they returned to the city on the Saturday evening he had made a fairly thorough assessment of the depredations of the Germans.

What was interesting was that some of the biggest hauls had been made not by the Kunstschutz but by line regiments. In Florence itself the Finaly-Landau collection had been seized by the Trettner Parachute Division. 362 Infantry Division had removed 307 paintings from the Uffizi and Pitti. The looting at Montagnana had been carried out by 562nd Infantry Division.

Some of the losses had hurt Mario more deeply. From the Villa Medici at Caiano fifty eight crates of sculptures were missing. One of them contained Donatello's statue of *St George*, probably the single work of art most dear to the Florentines. It was some compensation that Michelangelo's *David*, in the Accademia, had been protected by its brick wall and was safe, and even Mario cheered up when they found that Michelangelo's great sculptures from the Medici Chapel – *Dawn, Dusk, Night* and *Day* – were intact in the Martini villa at San Donato.

In their tour of the region they verified another less quantifiable loss. Empoli and many of the lovely towns of the Arno valley had been destroyed by the retreating army.

'I can't understand why they do it Mario. They still behave as if they were going to win the war. Right up till the arrival of our armies rapine, demolition, plunder, mass murder. It's going on in the Casentino at this moment.'

The Casentino was east of the Arno beyond the Pratomagno, where German patrols were still marauding and plundering. Mario wanted to satisfy himself that the companion to *Primavera*, Botticelli's *Venus*, was safe. It had been sent to the castle at Poppi, in the heart of the region. Edmund marvelled at Mario's reckless readiness to take the risk but if the Italian was willing he would not hold back. By good fortune they reached Poppi without encountering any enemy. Two hundred pictures had been looted from the Castello but the *Birth of Venus* was safe. Opening a crate, Edmund had gazed on the same face as he had seen in the *Primavera* three weeks earlier at Montegufoni.

It had become clear that Florence had suffered robbery on a scale to dwarf the plunderings of Napoleon. Between 1 July and 15 August close on 600 paintings and over a hundred sculptures of major importance had vanished. This amounted to one quarter of the most valued possessions of the Florentine museums and galleries.

It was Sunday 20 August. A week had passed since the entry of British troops into Florence. An occasional shell landing on the city was a reminder that the Germans were still on the hills around Fiesole. But now there was food and water and the shops were opening again. That morning the church bells were ringing out, led by the deep tones of the cathedral, Santa Maria dei Fiori. Rich and poor were bringing out clothes that they had not worn for months and dressing up to attend this first real Mass since the Liberation. During the week that had elapsed the pall of shock and grief hanging over Palazzo Lamberti had lifted. Ken was still absent and Rosalba had received no word from Jason. The Count, dignified in his grief and still hopeful of finding a place in the Allied administration, was assembling his family to take them to High Mass at the church of San Lorenzo. They were all there in the big *salone*, attired in deepest black as befitted a bereaved family. The Count had donned a frock coat and his brother Carlo wore a black serge suit that was turning slightly green with age. Guido, back from the battle zone for this special occasion, had brought out his uniform of an officer in the Bersaglieri. By comparison Mario would have seemed almost festive in his grey suit had his closed and sombre expression not belied his dress.

Edmund was glad he had brought a pair of long trousers back with him. He wore a pullover over his tropical shirt.

Though not a Roman Catholic he had decided to accompany the family. Nonna and Caterina had had no proper funeral and in a way this was a memorial service for them. The Count and Countess seemed to take it as natural that he should be with them. Rosalba gave him a quick smile of gratitude.

'Allora, vogliamo andare?' the Count suggested and the procession of ten filed out in order of family seniority. Edmund at his own insistence, followed behind.

It was a bright sunny morning. The way to San Lorenzo took the party through the Piazza della Repubblica where girls in summer dresses were swinging their hips for the benefit of the lounging soldiers. All over Florence Christian folk were moving at a leisurely Italian gait towards their churches – to the Duomo where Savonarola had once arraigned the congregation for their luxury and vice, to Santa Croce, where Giotto's frescoes recalled the death of St Francis, to Santa Maria Novella with its paintings of Dante's *Inferno*, or to whichever one of Florence's seventy churches they frequented.

San Lorenzo had escaped damage. The Lambertis had two pews on the left side of the aisle. Edmund's place was at the end of the second one. From where he sat he could see Rosalba's veiled cheek. When the clergy processed in behind the Cross in their gold and scarlet robes, he allowed his thoughts to be borne away by the swelling chords of the organ and the chanting of the choir. He made no attempt to follow the service. He stood up when Rosalba stood, sat when she sat and knelt when she knelt. The Latin words, the ritual, the scent of incense, the music, the tinkling bell moved him to emotion that needed no expression in words. After the experience of the past weeks this seemed an affirmation that in the end good would triumph over evil, that the world would emerge from its long nightmare.

From time to time Rosalba would turn her head a little and he could see her profile. When the priest intoned the comfortable words he saw a tear slide slowly down her cheek. The only time their eyes met was when she gave him an inquiring look and he shook his head to indicate that he did not intend to accept the Sacrament.

When High Mass ended it seemed that a great weight had

been lifted from the Lambertis. The women put up their veils to wipe their eyes and the men blew their noses. With reluctance to leave the scene of a deeply moving experience, the congregation trickled slowly out into the sunlight. Families and friends gathered in groups smiling and chattering. Up on Monte Morello to the south, the crew of a 105mm gun rammed a shell into the breach and readjusted their aim to a new set of co-ordinates.

Edmund had moved away from the Lamberti group to greet Corrado. He had spotted the partisan coming out of the church. To catch him up he had to chase him round the north-west corner. This time he did not hear the familiar whistle of the falling shell for the good reason that his own number was on it. It landed in the road thirty yards behind him. He was bowled over by the blast and fetched up against the wall of the church, unconscious.

Twenty of the congregation of San Lorenzo were killed on that morning of 20 August. There were casualties outside other churches too. Whether it was pure chance or deliberate design that led the Germans to bombard Florence at that moment no-one ever knew.

Edmund recovered his senses to the sound of frenzied screaming. At once he knew he'd been hit again. It was the same leg as at Dunkirk but higher up this time. He struggled to a sitting position and got his back against the wall. The wound was in his thigh. His trouser leg was wet with blood. The pain had not hit him yet. He was still in a state of shock.

It was five minutes before anyone came to him. Round the corner of the church there had been carnage. The body of Corrado lay twenty yards away where he had fallen. Edmund was using his tie to make a tourniquet round his leg above the wound when a white-faced young woman found him. She had flung her hat off and rolled up the sleeves of her church-going dress. She knelt down beside him and ripped his trouser leg to expose the wound.

'Looks like a piece of shrapnel. It's deep. I'll have to stop the bleeding till we can get you to hospital.'

'Not hospital!' Edmund protested. He had visions of being evacuated to Rome, possibly even North Africa. 'Get me to the Palazzo Lamberti. I have friends there.'

The girl used the veil she had been wearing round her

shoulders to improvise a more efficient tourniquet. As she tightened it Guido came round the corner.

'Oh, thank God, capitano! We thought you'd been killed.'

'The others? Is Rosalba – has any of your family been hurt?'

'No, but only by a miracle. The corner of the church protected us.'

'Guido, can you get me back to the palazzo? This wound's not too bad and I don't want to wind up in military hospital.'

Guido fetched Carlo to help him support Edmund back to the Palazzo. Edmund had enough presence of mind to find out the name of the girl Samaritan but by the time they got him to the room that Jason had occupied he could only see a red mist in front of his eyes. The Countess with her usual decisiveness had already summoned a doctor. He was the father of the young Doctor Salvi who had examined the bodies of Nonna and Caterina.

He shook his head when he saw the wound. 'You ought to be in hospital. There's a piece of shrapnel which must be taken out. I can't give you an anaesthetic here.'

'Could you – could you dig it out without – ?'

'Without an anaesthetic?' The doctor stared at Edmund. 'I could, but the pain would be extreme.'

Edmund did not believe that the pain in his leg could be made any worse. 'Take that chance,' he grunted between his teeth. 'Please. Can't go to hospital.'

Doctor Salvi turned unhappily to the Countess. She was kneeling by the bed, gripping Edmund's hand. 'I'll need help. Your daughter was a nurse, wasn't she?'

'Rosalba's still at San Lorenzo, dealing with the wounded. I can help if you tell me what to do.'

'And we'll need someone to hold him down when I start to probe.'

'I'll fetch my son and husband.'

Edmund had been wrong when he thought that the pain could not become any worse.

The first of his senses to return was hearing. Someone near him was whispering words which his brain was still too dull to comprehend. There was a fragrance in the air, a perfume. He felt the touch of a cool cloth on his forehead. The terrible pain which had knocked him out had subsided. He lay still. His mind groped for recollection. Now he was able to make sense of the whispered words.

'Ti voglio bene, tanto tanto bene . . . .'

He opened his eyes. The face of La Simonetta was leaning over him. Her brow was furrowed with concern. The amazing eyes looked down at him, golden with a shading of green, a patina of moisture gleaming on the deep black irises. Her lips were parted and she had stopped in mid-sentence. A blush spread over her cheeks. Her hands had not stopped gently sponging his face with the perfumed cloth.

'Rosalba . . . .'

'Sh. Don't try to talk.'

'Where . . . ? The doctor.'

'He's gone. You fainted with the pain. He took the splinter out and put stitches in the wound. It's clean. You'll be all right if you rest.'

He was between sheets. The sun was slanting through the window, haloing her head. In spite of the pain he had a deep sense of repose. He closed his eyes again. She stopped sponging for a moment to push his hair back. He felt her long fingers combing against his scalp.

'Did you – did you hear what I was saying?'

He had heard, but in a way he had been eavesdropping. She'd let her secret out involuntarily and he needed time to adjust to such an unexpected admission. If ever the time came when she was ready to say openly, 'I love you – so much,' he wanted to be ready to respond in kind.

'No. What did you say?'

'Nothing.'

For the next five days Rosalba devoted herself to nursing Edmund. Jealously, she prevented anyone else from doing a hand's turn for him. He was very weak but this was due to loss of blood rather than the severity of his injury. She brought him his meals, made his bed, helped him wash, saw to all his needs.

The first time she dressed his wound she pointed to the scar below his knee. 'That was not a very professional job. What a mess!'

'I was lucky to get it done at all. I was a prisoner of war at the time.'

As entranced as Desdemona hearing the exploits of Othello, she listened while he told her about the prison camp, his escape, the long trail through France and into Spain.

'But you could not have done all that with your injury, over the Pyrenees!'

'It wasn't easy.'

She laughed. 'You English! Always the under statement. Now be careful with that pipe. We don't want to set the bed on fire, do we?'

When her duties were done the professional nurse became an occupational therapist. She had the wind-up cabinet gramophone brought into the room so that she could play him the symphonies of Beethoven, Rachmaninov, Brahms. So as not to interrupt the music, she forbade him to speak when she got up to turn each record over and recut the wooden needle. They talked for hours about the painters of Florence and especially about Botticelli.

'It was such a tragedy when La Simonetta died,' he said, as they were looking at a reproduction of the *Birth of Venus*. 'He never found such a beautiful model again. One feels he must have been in love with her.'

'He shouldn't have fallen in love with a married woman,' she said emphatically. 'Madonna Simonetta was faithful to her husband.'

Edmund turned the page. He had not yet been able to bring himself to tell her that he was himself married.

The life of the *palazzo* went on round the room where he lay in bed. From outside came the occasional crump of a shell landing. Since the 20th the Germans had taken to shelling the city in desultory fashion. Most of the casualties were civilians. Mario came daily to bring him the news. Santo Spirito, Santa Croce, Giotto's campanile, the Duomo, Palazzo Strozzi, all had been hit. Every morning personnel of the Soprintendenza patrolled the streets to recover the fragments knocked down during the night.

Mario wanted permission to hand the report, which he and Edmund had made, to the Monuments, Fine Arts and Archives Officer who had now opened an office in the *palazzo* of Princess Lucrezia Corsini. Edmund demurred when he heard he was American.

'He is a very good man, very brave,' Mario reassured him. 'He knows as much about Florentine art as you do. And,' Mario turned the palm of his right hand upward,' as you are out of action, capitano . . . .'

Ken returned on the 22nd and made his billet in the room Edmund had occupied in Mario's flat. He had finally caught up with Rossi in a villa near Piazzale Michelangelo and he had taken him back to Corps headquarters, where he would be interrogated by Scotland Yard Officers attached to the counter-intelligence unit.

'Guess who I met at Corps. Old Jason. Wearing a pip and crown.'

'He's a Lieutenant Colonel now?'

'Yes. The 2nd and 3rd battalions of the Roughs – what's left of them – have been amalgamated and he's their new commanding officer. So he's a dog with two tails. Asked me to tell Rosalba he's sorry.'

'Sorry?'

'She wouldn't let him have his greens, you know. Tough, since that's all he's been dreaming about since we landed in Sicily.'

'You think that really was . . . .'

'Nar, that wasn't the real reason, Ed. He's in love with his regiment, the poor sod, more than any woman. And the death of his Sergeant-Major really hurt him. That's why he has this mania for killing Jerries.'

Ken helped himself to a grape from the bowl beside Edmund's chair. He said casually, 'They've given him an MC – for that attack he led on Monte Piccolo.'

'And are you going to get your gong, Ken?'

Ken looked disgusted. 'Bertie said he'd try and get me a Mention in Despatches.'

He had brought in three NCOs from his own Field Security Section and they were engaged on more general security duties – winkling out Fascists, screening line-crossers, checking out Italians being employed by the Allies.

'How's the war going?'

'Not much happening at the moment. We're re-grouping before tackling the Gothic Line. XIII Corps have been switched from Eighth to Fifth Army. I think the show will start over on the Adriatic. That's where Churchill is now. The Generals are trying to keep him out of the front line bu of course he wants to fire something at the Krauts.'

The wound mended fast. On the fifth day Edmund was able to get out of bed and hobble about with the aid of a stick. Rosalba, at his request, was reading Dante's *Divine Comedy* to him in Italian. She had a good sense of rhythm. There was something hypnotic about the onward march of the *terza rima* with its interlinking rhyme scheme.

'I suppose the Commedia is just about the greatest compliment any man ever paid to a woman.' He had let a few moments pass after she put the book down at the end of a Canto. 'To create Hell, Purgatory and Heaven in your imagination and place your lady in the Seventh Heaven at the top.'

'And yet each of them married someone different and raised a family. It must have been a very strange kind of love.'

'Yes.' He waited till a cart drawn by a clip-clopping horse had rattled past the open window. 'Do you think he ever even told her he loved her?'

Rosalba looked down at the book. Her fingers riffled the corners of the pages. 'You did hear what I said, didn't you? When you were recovering consciousness.'

'You didn't mean me to?'

She raised her eyes. 'That day when you first arrived I came into the room and saw you standing there. I knew then. Poor Jason! I tried so hard but I had changed a lot. You were right when you said that. He must have sensed it. He wanted to make love to me but I wouldn't let him. It was you I wanted and all I could think of was you. Caro Edmundo! Ti voglio tanto bene.'

He made to rise but the wound on his thigh bit him and he winced. She came quickly to his chair, knelt on the floor and laid her head in his lap.

Life in the Lamberti household had returned to normal with astonishing rapidity. The war had almost been forgotten. It was the aftermath of the two murders that loomed largest in the minds of the family. The investigation had been taken on by the civil police. The Questura was once again functioning in Florence under the CTLN and AMGOT. They had plenty of more urgent problems on their hands and the disappearance of old Alessio had provided them with an obvious solution.

The readings from *Paradiso* were continued every day. They had become a kind of ritual which both Rosalba and Edmund were anxious to preserve. As Beatrice led Dante ever higher through the realms of bliss so Edmund's strength gradually returned. Since that day when they had each declared their feelings they had drawn back, as if hesitating on the threshold of a garden which promised too much delight. Edmund kept putting off the moment when he must break the spell and tell her that he was married. She did not understand the reason for his reticence but she sensed it and adapted herself to his mood. Their touching was limited to hands and the supporting arm she offered him when he started walking.

One day he commented that though the *Paradiso* was beautiful stuff it lacked the vividness of the *Inferno*.

'Well, we will read from the *Inferno*,' she agreed at once. She was sitting on the floor at his feet, her legs tucked under her. 'Which bit would you like?'

'You choose.'

She chose Canto V in which Dante encounters the doomed lovers Paolo and Francesca da Rimini. He heard the emotion in her voice as she came to the passage where Francesca explains how she and Paolo yielded to their amorous desire.

'*Ma solo un punto fu quel che ci vinse.*
Quando legemmo il disiato riso
Esser bacciato da cotanto amante,
Questi, che mai da me non fia diviso,
La bocca mi bacciò tutto tremante . . . .'

Her voice broke on the words 'trembling he kissed my mouth'. She looked up at him and he saw that there were tears in her eyes.

'Rosalba. What is it?'

She laid the book on the floor and came up into a kneeling position, her face level with his.

'Why do you never kiss me?'

As in Dante's poem, their first kiss opened the floodgates.

Unclothed her body was as beautiful as her face. Making love to her was like possessing a universe.

As they lay in each other's arms he murmured, 'I always thought her mouth was too voluptuous for a Virgin.'

She raised her head, frowning. 'Whose mouth?'

'My Madonna's.'

'Oh, La Simonetta.' She held him closer. 'That's all right.'

Each day that followed they discovered new pleasures. The small room became an oasis of delight.

'You see,' she said one evening when he wanted her again so soon. 'You have really recovered your strength. Ecco la prova.'

On 31 August Ken returned from the RIP at Siena where Rossi was being grilled. He had called in at 15 Army Group and had more news of Jason. His battalion would be spearheading the advance up the Sieve Valley as Fifth Army moved forward to probe the Gothic Line. Their axis of advance would be Highway 67, which passed through Dicomano on its way to the Appenines.

'There were a couple of letters waiting for you so I brought them along.'

One was from Helen and had been waiting there for a week. Edmund read it first. As usual she played things down but he could guess that the new rockets were giving London a bad time. The Salvation Army van had run a big end but had been repaired. She had been out to dinner with the Warners at the 'Hungaria', had seen the film *In Which We Serve* and was making new curtains for the sitting-room.

I am spending all my spare time trying to get the house as nice as I can for you when you come home. I pray it won't be long now. Life's terribly lonely without you but we press on. Please take great care of yourself.

The second letter was more recent and was dated 20 August. It was from his sister. Luckily he was alone when he opened it.

Dearest Edmund,

We have been trying to contact you through the War Office but no-one seemed to know exactly where you are. I am afraid I have bad news for you. Helen was killed last Friday. A flying bomb landed close to her van somewhere near Stepney –

9

The roaring of the Arno could be heard from as far away as Palazzo Lamberti. The rain had started on 1 September, relentless rain that was to continue for thirty-five days, swelling the river to a bounding flood. There was heavy movement of military traffic on the road westward from Florence to Pontassieve. The little Fiat 1100 was one of the few civilian cars on the move. To spare Edmund's leg, Mario had insisted on driving. He was hunched forward, peering through the windscreen as the Fiat splashed along the Lungàrno Cristoforo Colombo. The windscreen wiper hiccupped to and fro, the tyres sent out showers of spray, rain bounced off the roof. Both men were silent, their thoughts still on the agony of the departure from Palazzo Lamberti.

Edmund had not felt able to tell anyone about the contents of that letter from his sister. His shock and grief had given way to a sense of guilt, as if by falling in love with Rosalba he had in some way precipitated Helen's death. Rosalba of course had immediately seen the change in him. She was hurt and bewildered by his sudden withdrawal, his refusal to tell her what had happened.

The one thing he had known for certain was that he could no longer stay at Palazzo Lamberti. He had to go somewhere, do something, it did not matter what. To apply for compassionate leave back to England was pointless. Helen had been buried the day after he collected the shell splinter in his leg. When he told Rosalba that he was leaving the next day she swayed. He put out a hand to support her but she avoided his touch. As when Aeneas deserted Dido the mere announcement of his departure had been enough to break the magic.

When Mario had heard of Edmund's decision to move up with the advancing army to Dicomano his reaction was the same as on the two previous occasions. 'I'll come too.'

'This is different, Mario. I'm going into the battle zone.'

'I will come,' Mario repeated firmly. The storm of tears and near hysteria staged by Ornella could not persuade him to change his mind.

It was the Countess who had come to see Edmund in the

evening when he was collecting his belongings together. She was poised and courteous as always but there were daggers in her eyes.

'I don't know what has happened to make you decide to leave us, Edmund, I can only assume that you have had some terrible news . . . .'

'Yes.' Edmund agreed tersely.

'I only want you to consider what you are doing to Rosalba. First Jason went away without so much as a word of explanation and now you . . . . I'm not sure that the child can withstand this second shock.'

He straightened up to face her. What he was feeling must have showed because her expression softened. He wondered how much Rosalba had confided to her.

'If I tell her – it may hurt her even more.'

The Countess's experienced eyes looked deep into him. 'There is something you have been keeping from her?'

He paused. 'Yes.'

'For Rosalba,' she said, 'This is what we Italians call un vero grande amore. Is it the same for you, Edmundo?'

'It is.'

'Then you must tell her. When love is true it must have truth.'

Telling Rosalba had been just about the most difficult thing he had done in his life. The physical effort of keeping his mouth firm and his voice under control steadied him. To his astonishment her immediate reaction was not revulsion but compassion, true heartfelt compassion. That was what finally broke his control – the hurt and grief in her eyes as if she was sharing it with him. She reached towards him. He put his head on her shoulder to hide the tears in his eyes.

'All I ask,' she whispered in his ear, 'did you mean – all those things you told me?'

'Every word.'

But her understanding did not affect his decision to go.

The imprint of her stricken face was still before his eyes as the car cleared the suburbs of Florence. Mario had gone through his own particular Calvary. Once or twice he choked on a breath. Why, Edmund wondered, had he insisted on leaving his home if it hurt him so much?

At Pontassieve, where the Arno took a turn southward,

there were still signs of recent German presence. The festoons of signs at the cross-roads pointed to enemy headquarters that had packed up and withdrawn. Tanks and vehicles of 6th (British) Armoured Division were rumbling up from the Val d'Arno and pushing on into the Sieve Valley towards Dicomano. The Military Policeman on point duty made the little Fiat wait nearly five minutes. In the end Edmund got out to have a word with him. The rain was pelting down. His battle-dress trousers were soaked by the splashes from passing vehicles.

'Jerry's pulled back and 6th Armoured is moving up,' the traffic control corporal told him. 'They're bunched like rabbit shit all along the road. I'll let your little bleeder cut in as soon as this lot has gone through.'

'The Germans are pulling back to the Gothic Line,' Edmund told Mario, as he squeezed back into the Fiat. 'Are you game to go on?'

Mario shrugged and engaged first gear. 'Certo.'

'Then turn left. Okay, he's signalling you on.'

The traffic policeman had held up a huge Scammel tank transporter to let the little Fiat dart out and join the column of military vehicles moving up the Sieve Valley. It was the only private car on that whole stretch of road. From here on they were moving into the battle zone.

Edmund was gradually coming to realise that Mario was as little concerned for his own safety as he was himself. 'Mario,' he said after a few miles. 'It's none of my business but – is something wrong between you and Ornella?'

'No.' Mario shook his head. He waited for a moment before adding. 'Nothing.'

Never had a denial sounded more like an admission, but Edmund decided not to press him.

The column ground its way past the deserted slopes of the Chianti Gallo Nero vineyards. Just beyond the town of Rufina a traffic check-point had been set up. The road ahead was under shell-fire.

'I'll get a lift in a military vehicle from here,' Edmund said. 'You turn back, Mario. I know you want to get over to Poppi and see that the deposit with the *Birth of Venus* . . . .'

'Please let me come with you.' There was desperation in Mario's voice. 'I don't want to turn back.'

Edmund looked at him and this time Mario met his eyes.

'There *is* something wrong, isn't there? You haven't been the same since Caterina was . . . .'

Edmund stopped. Mario's lower lip was trembling. He blinked hard and turned his head away.

'Were you in love with her?' Edmund asked quietly.

'Not in love . . . but . . . . We made love. The night the bridges were blown up.' Mario covered his face with his hands.

'So we're in the same boat,' Edmund murmured.

Mario lowered his hands. 'The same boat?'

'Oh, it's just a saying – when someone is in the same situation as yourself.'

'But it's not the same situation at all, Edmundo. With you and Rosalba it was a true great love . . . .'

'You mean you knew?'

'Everyone could see it!' Mario was almost laughing. 'At least, everyone in the family. And Rosalba was so happy again. It was a joy to see. You did not leave Florence for that!'

On impulse Edmund said: 'The night before we left Florence I had a letter telling me that my wife had been killed by a bomb in London.'

The blunt statement shocked Mario and released the tears that were starting from his eyes. They flowed down his cheeks. His friend's sympathy somehow intensified Edmund's own distress. It grew in his breast and threatened to choke him. 'Let's move on,' he said harshly. 'We want to be up with our troops when they reach Dicomano.'

Mario wiped his cheeks with the back of his hand, restarted the engine and waited for a chance to slip out into the traffic. They moved on towards the mountains, now looming dark and threatening ahead.

Between the visits of the King from 24 July to 4 August and that of Churchill from 14 to 28 August, Alexander had moved his headquarters from Lake Bolsena to a feudal estate just south of Siena. A connoisseur of art and himself no mean artist, he liked to spend as much time as he could spare visiting cultural centres. The visits of these two Very Important Persons had done something to console him for the depletion of his forces, and Churchill's support had fortified him in his aim to break the Gothic Line before winter set in. Churchill had already urged Eisenhower, through Ultra channels, to push on as rapidly as possible towards Berlin. Alexander and his armies in Italy offered the best chance of forestalling the Russians in the race to occupy the homelands of the Reich. And there were indications, filtering through intelligence channels, that certain high commanders in the German army might be ready to co-operate in this objective. They preferred the prospect of occupation by the Allies rather than by the Soviets.

After reaching the line of the Arno, Alexander had given his forces a respite of three weeks. He needed that time to fill the gaps left by the seven divisions he had lost to the invasion of Southern France, and to build up fresh reserves of ammunition and supplies. While he paused, Operation Anvil was launched, the American and French forces under General Truscott landing almost unopposed on the French Riviera. Toulon, Marseille and Grenoble were quickly captured as the Germans retreated up the Rhone Valley.

By the end of August he was ready to resume the offensive. His plan was to deceive the enemy by a great show of activity in the Fifth Army area around Florence and then attack with Eighth Army on the Adriatic coast to the east. When Kesselring switched forces to the east, Fifth Army would attack in the centre. If the enemy line could be broken the Germans would have to withdraw all their forces from northwest Italy, where the Italian partisans had already risen in strength. The American divisions in Mark Clark's Army would turn against Mantua and Verona. Eighth Army would take Ferrara, Padua and Treviso, crossing the rivers Po, Adige and Brenta. Alexander would then achieve his objective of breaking into Austria and the Balkans, at one stroke getting in the rear of the German armies in Europe and taking over the entire centre of Germany. This would affect the whole balance of power in post-war Europe.

Between Alexander and his objective nature had placed a formidable barrier. The great mountain mass of the Appenines slanted across the Italian peninsula separating Tuscany from the Lombardy Plain. One hundred and fifty miles long and fifty miles wide with peaks rising to 7,000 feet. It was like a sea of gigantic waves. A mechanised army had to advance on the line of the few roads crossing this range, ignoring the huge areas between. The French North African mountain troops could have fought their way across these empty mountain regions as they had fought through the Aurunci mountains at Cassino; but they were now pursuing the Germans up the Rhone Valley.

Here in the mountains north of Florence was where Hitler and the Oberkommand-Wehrmacht had decided to make their stand; this was the position from which the southern flank of the Reich would be defended. The Todt Organisation had been ordered to build on the southern slopes of the Appenines the most formidable line in Europe. It was named Gothen Stellung, the Gothic Line. While Kesselring fought his supremely skillful delaying campaign from Rome to Florence, the Todt Organisation laboured to complete the fortifications. They used 15,000 Italian workers and a Slovak technical brigade supervised by German engineers. The work was carried out with teutonic thoroughness. The mountains themselves were blasted to make tunnels and galleries. Thousands of tons of concrete were poured to create fortress-like positions. A hundred Todt shelters, each one a small fortress, were placed at key points. There were 2,376 deep concrete machine-gun emplacements, 479 anti-tank guns, mortar and assault-gun positions. Thirty Panther tank guns had been embedded in steel and concrete bases. Mines were laid in areas not covered by machine-gun fire, anti-tank ditches up to three miles in length were dug, 120,000 metres of barbed wire were deployed. Where necessary farm buildings, even whole villages were razed to clear fields of fire for the guns. Behind the Gothic Line rose the tall confusion of mountain behind mountain and beyond that the long straight roads of the Lombardy Plain. Kesselring thus had the facility to switch forces rapidly from one section of the front to the other.

The attack on the Eighth Army front to the east began on 25 August, just in time for Churchill, with his white suit and topee, smoking the inevitable cigar, to see some of the fighting from a Forward Observation Post. Sun-hats would not be required for much longer, for on 1 September began the heavy rain which was to continue for thirty-five days. On that same Sunday, Fifth Army crossed the Arno and began to feel its way towards the Gothic Line. On the right flank of 6th Armoured Division the 2nd Battallion, the Royal Ulster Fusiliers were ordered to advance through the hills on the division's right flank, pushing the enemy back until they bumped into the main defences of the Gothic Line.

As the burning sun and choking dust of summer gave way to rain and slithery mud, the Fusiliers changed from tropical kit to serge battledress. Under their new CO, Lt Col Jason Fitzgerald, they braced themselves once again to face the mountains and the rain, the bullets and the shrapnel, the maiming and the killing, the horror and the glory. They did not know that ahead of them lay the most bloody encounter of the war. The storming of Piano Castle would become one of the regiment's battle honours, but an honour won at terrible cost.

Edmund and Mario entered Dicomano with the Field Security Officer of 6th Armoured Division soon after the tanks had taken it. The enemy had withdrawn, leaving half the town in ruins. A detachment of partisans had assumed control of what was left. They were a Communist group and suspicious of the British. Their leader softened when Mario addressed him in dialect. He was not really interested in the fate of the art treasures of Florence. His real concern was in the ideological struggle for the control of liberated Italy. However, he sent for the ex-SIM agent who had been the partisan's informant on the movement of the Soprintendenza lorry. His name was Pironi. They all took refuge from the rain in a café that had survived the demolitions.

The lorry, the SIM agent said, had been in Dicomano until 1 September. On the day that Fifth Army crossed the Arno, it had been driven away up the road to San Godenzo and the Passo del Muraglione. But the officer in charge apparently did not know that the road at the top of the pass had already been demolished. He had been forced to turn off Route 67 near San Godenzo and take a side road to a hamlet deep in the hills where there was a walled monastery. It was called Castel del Piano. Perhaps he had thoughts of returning to claim his treasure-trove when the tide of war turned in Germany's favour. What he did not realise was that he had entered an area controlled by partisans of the Brigate Fulgore.

The partisans let the Germans unload the paintings and store them in the monastery. Then they killed them.

'And the pictures?'

'They are still in the monastery. We needed the lorry, you see. You want to see them, capitano? I can take you up there. Capitano, you hear me?'

Through the café window Edmund had seen a YMCA tea van come down the battered street and stop opposite a house that had been gutted by fire. The girl driver climbed out and began to open the hinged side. He dragged his eyes away to give his attention to Pironi.

'Can you show me on the map?'

He had already folded the map so that the area round Dicomano was visible through the cellophane cover. Pironi's finger meandered over the place names and came to rest on a point high in the hills east of San Godenzo.

'But that's right in the Gothic Line.'

Pironi shook his head. 'Their defences are in the valleys where the main roads pass. They haven't enough troops to hold the territory between.'

'Why are your troops so slow?' the partisan leader interjected fiercely. 'There is nothing to stop you advancing to the Passo del Muraglione. Nothing! The Germans have withdrawn behind San Godenzo. There are fifteen thousand partisans waiting up there to help you!'

'There's a road up to Castel del Piano which we control.' Pironi ignored his leader's outburst. He was eager to persuade the newcomers to follow his suggestion. 'One of my lads came down that way this morning without seeing any Germans. He and I will escort you up to Castel del Piano. What do you say?'

'Listen, I'll be back in a minute.' Edmund was already moving towards the door that led out into the street. The YMCA van drew him like a magnet. This girl, like Helen, was prepared to risk her life to bring their tea and wodges to the soldiers in the forward area. She was behind her counter lighting the burner under the urn as he walked up. She gave him a smile of recognition.

'I'm afraid the tea's not ready yet.'

'Doesn't matter. I thought you were always with 24th Guards Brigade.'

'I've been switched to 1st Guards. They're with 6th Armoured. Didn't I see you in Florence?'

'Yes.'

'How's your wife? Still driving for the rival firm?'

'She's fine.'

They talked for a few minutes while she lined her mugs up on the counter. Like Edmund she had been impatient to escape from Florence when it became a haunt of administrators and tipsy soldiers on leave. He moved away when he realised that a queue had formed politely behind him.

When he rejoined the group in the Café, Mario told him he had made up his mind. 'I'm going up to Castel del Piano, Edmund.'

'You're taking a needless risk. We're bound to advance soon.'

'I have to get up there before the attack. The pictures must be protected. These partisans are Communists. They do not appreciate their value.'

Edmund stared towards the mountains, grey and hostile under the rain-clouds. The Madonna was up there, not more than eight miles away. Out in the street the YMCA van was doing a brisk trade with the rain-soaked soldiers.

'We'd better make sure we have a full tank of petrol. By the look of those mountains we'll be in first gear most of the way.'

This time Edmund took the wheel with Pironi beside him. Mario sat with the lad in the back seat. The two Italians lowered their windows and poked the barrels of their rifles out. Troops of 6th Armoured Divisions had not pushed on up the road leading north from Dicomano. Soldiers manning the outpost beyond the town stared in amazement as a little black Italian Fiat beetled past them and disappeared up the winding road that led towards the ramparts of the Gothic Line.

'Crazy Eyeties,' a Private of the Rifle Brigade commented. 'Old Jerryl'll make fuckin' spaghetti of them all right.'

A quarter of a mile beyond Dicomano Edmund again began to have that exposed feeling that comes when you push beyond the advance of your own troops. In the back seat the boy was chattering non-stop. It was hard to tell whether he was terrified or simply unaware of the danger. The road had not begun to climb yet but the hills flanking it had closed in and steepened. Here there were not even the signs of recent battle, apart from one burnt-out Sherman tank, evidence of a too-daring thrust by a troop of the Derbyshire Yeomanry. Edmund drove more slowly, expecting at any moment to come round a corner and find himself looking up the 88 mm barrel of a Panther tank's gun. The Gothic Line loomed closer. This was like driving up to the gates of an enemy castle. He felt sure that hostile eyes were watching the car, that they were only holding their fire to be sure of hitting their target.

'How much further to the turning?'

'Half a kilometre. Look! Up there. That is Castel del Piano!'

Just for a second he had caught a glimpse of a squat building with a tower perched on a hilltop surrounded by a wall. It was on a shelf in the hills, poised high above the valley. Like so many of these monasteries it was sited like a fortress.

Even the lad in the back seat had fallen silent by the time they came to the road junction. A sign indicated 'Castel del Piano 9 kms'. Edmund took the turning without slowing. Cross-roads were dangerous places. Gunners usually had the range of them.

It was a relief to be off the main road and under the cover of the pine trees that covered the slopes. The track climbed steeply, tacking to and fro across the slope. A thousand feet up the rain gave way to mist and a few hundred feet higher the sky cleared. Suddenly sunshine was slanting through the trees. The forest floor was patterned with dappled shade. In the glades cohorts of tiny flies, jewels in the sunbeams, had emerged from shelter to continue their jerking, linear quest. Here and there, with unconscious irony, boards nailed to the trees warned DIVIETO DI CACCIA.

'Hunting forbidden! Tell that to the Jerries.'

At about three thousand feet the texture of the forest became different. The pine trees gave place to beeches. The light changed to a translucent green slashed by the lichen-grey tree-trunks. The scents of the forest were strong in the crisp air. The world was a very beautiful place and all at once life seemed precious. In this stillness amongst the high hills Edmund had the illusion that they had left the world of battles far behind.

A jay startled by the unexpected sound of a car screamed 'Rape! Rape!' and fled down a nave of trees.

'Where's the Gothic Line from here?'

'That way, capitano.' Pironi pointed over his left shoulder towards a high peak a few miles to the north.

'I make it another three kilometres.' Edmund was checking the distance on the Fiat's speedometer. 'Why haven't we seen any partisans?'

'There's a bridge very soon. Our outposts will be there.'

They came on the bridge suddenly just round a steep bend. Edmund stood on the brakes. The car stopped a foot short of a jagged rent in the road. Through it raced the foamy leaping waters of a mountain torrent. It was not the stream which had destroyed the bridge but a charge of explosive.

Before the passengers in the Fiat had time to open the doors half a dozen grey figures emerged from the roadside ditches and surrounded the car. On their heads they wore the unmistakeable Starmhelm of the German infantry.

Edmund felt no real surprise. There was an inevitability about it, as if he were watching a repeat of a film he had already seen.

When he could not bear the sounds any longer he jammed his fingers in his ears. Then in the silence he reproached himself for being a coward. It was Mario who was having to endure the beating. Was he so craven that he could not even listen? By participating vicariously in his friend's torment, might he not in a sense share it and thereby perhaps sustain Mario?

The 'interrogation' was taking place overhead, up the flight of stone steps that led from the cellar into the farmhouse kitchen. Edmund himself was in almost total darkness. Chinks of light filtered through the badly fitting door at the top of the steps and a ventilation grill that had been put in at the top of the wall, level with the ground outside. His eyes had become accustomed to the gloom. He could see barrels of wine, sheep fleeces, a stack of logs, discarded tools – all the bric-a-brac of a small farmstead. He had made himself as comfortable as he could on some old sacks and was using the sheep fleeces to keep his hands and legs warm. The cellar was damp and at this height the temperature was not much above freezing.

The memory of what had happened at the bridge was still sickeningly fresh in his mind, though a good three hours must have passed since then. The Germans were certain that they had captured a quartet of the partisans who had been wreaking such havoc behind their lines. The four were dragged roughly from the car, made to stand with their backs to the gash in the road. Edmund saw the Spandau machine gunner taking aim.

'Stop!' he shouted. 'Ich bin ein Britisher Offizier.'

The Feldwebel in charge of the patrol stared hard at Edmund. He peeled off his belted raincoat to show his uniform. That gained a few moments respite, time for him to explain that Mario was not a partisan but an Italian civilian working for the British Army. The Feldwebel barked some order. He was a Bavarian with a strong accent and Edmund could not understand much of what he said. One of his soldiers pulled Edmund and Mario out of the Spandau's line of fire.

There was nothing he could do to save Pironi and the boy. Pironi had already accepted death and was staring wide-eyed at a blue patch of sky amid the rainclouds. The lad had gone down on his knees and was begging for mercy. They had no hope. Their own rifles, which they still clutched instinctively, condemned them.

The march back to the farmhouse where the unit had its headquarters was a real endurance test. The officer at the command post was a young sandy-haired Leutnant with all the bullying arrogance of a Nazi diehard. He listened to the Feldwebel's report with impatience, angry that the patrol had brought in any prisoners at all. How could they deal with prisoners in these remote mountains? The Feldwebel had more sense than his officer. He pointed out that these two captives could provide useful information about the dispositions of the partisans and the intentions of the British.

'Talk to them, Herr Leutnant. We can shoot them later.'

The officer took Edmund first. Nazi though he was, he showed the respect of one soldier for another, especially an Englander. In this sixth year of war, the Germans and the

British were the only nations who had been fighting since the beginning and the front-line infantry had developed a strange sense of comradeship, though it did not prevent them from killing each other with great efficiency. Edmund insisted on his right to give no information beyond his name, rank and number.

'Very well,' the German said pompously. 'You are a British Officer. We Germans recognise the Geneva Convention.' He turned to his Feldwebel. 'Lock him in the cellar and bring the Italian. I've always heard that they are great singers. We'll find out whether this little rat is a tenor or a bass.'

That had been an hour ago. Through the cracked door Edmund was able to follow the progress of the examination. First had come a simple dialogue, one of the unit's Italian-speaking soldiers translating the officer's questions and Mario's answers. These had not satisfied the Leutnant. His voice had risen to a shout as he tried to frighten Mario by moral bullying. When that failed the blows began. Edmund could hear the slither of Mario's feet and the smack and thud of fists as he was knocked to and fro between the encircling soldiers. When Mario still did not provide the answers required, a more systematic method was used. At this point Edmund began to stop his ears. The smack of a metre of hosepipe on human flesh and bones made his gorge rise and Mario's screams tore his mind. It seemed impossible that a man could survive that and still remain conscious. When Mario fell silent Edmund guessed that he had passed out. He rushed up the steps, banged on the doors, shouted: 'Leave him alone, you bastards!' He heard a splash as a bucket of water was thrown over the victim and a gasp. Then the questions and the blows began again.

The light beyond the grill was fading and the yellow glow of a candle was filtering through the cellar door when from the forest outside came the sound of a single shot. It was followed by a short burst of machine-gun fire. Then silence.

From the room above came a series of quick orders and the thud of boots. The cellar door was thrown open. Even the light of a candle was dazzling to Edmund's eyes. He saw the drooping figure of Mario propped between two soldiers with close-cropped heads. He scrambled up as they pushed

143

Mario and was just in time to break his fall as he came down the stairs on buckling legs. The cellar door was slammed shut and the bolt rammed home.

Edmund spread sacks and sheep fleeces to make as comfortable a couch as he could for the groaning Mario. Every part of his body was bruised and bloody. There was no position in which he could find relief.

'I told them . . . all I could . . . . They . . . they would not believe me . . . . The pictures . . . . They thought . . . thought I knew about the partisans . . . .'

It was hardly surprising that Mario's story had not been believed. These tough soldiers could not comprehend that men would take such foolhardy risks just to try and save a lorry-load of pictures.

'Is there any . . . any water?'

'No. I'm afraid not. I could use some myself. There might be some wine.'

Edmund groped his way towards where he had seen the wine barrels. The darkness was total now and he had to rely entirely on feel. He found the circular shape and felt round it trying to locate the bung.

At that moment the whole farmhouse shook from an explosion. Fragments fell from the ceiling. From above came the tinkle of breaking glass. It must have been a mortar bomb, Edmund reckoned, a shell would have done more damage. He knew he was right when three more bombs landed just outside the house. Then came the stutter of sub-machine guns and the roar of a Spandau replying.

'Partisans!' Mario managed to gasp. 'Must be attacking.'

For five minutes the din of a small-scale battle raged round the farmhouse – small-arms fire, the thud of grenades, confused shouting of orders, the screams of wounded men. Then the firing intensified, a couple of grenades exploded in the room above, there was a rush of feet.

Edmund saw the cellar door fly open. The Feldwebel was standing there, a stick grenade in his hand. Before he could throw it, a burst of fire caught him in the back and he pitched down the steps.

In the kitchen a voice was shouting: 'Prigionieri! Dove siete?'

'Qui,' Mario found the strength to shout. 'In cantina.'

A wild figure silhouetted by the flames of the burning farmhouse had replaced the Feldwebel in the rectangle of the door. With his bare head, his unkempt hair, his eyes reflecting the fire-glow, he was a cross between a demon from hell and an avenging angel.

He disappeared for a second and came back with a brand from the fire which he used as a torch to light his way down the steps. He stepped over the dead Feldwebel and saw Mario.

'*Sacra* ....' His eyes flashed at Edmund. 'You are the English officer?'

'Yes.'

'I am Colonel Volpone, Capo of the Brigate Fulgore,' the Italian announced proudly. 'Can he walk?'

'I doubt it.'

Colonel Volpone gave a great bellow. Two more partisans appeared in answer and careered down the steps.

'Take him out quickly. The Germans in the Convento will have heard the firing. They can be here in five minutes.'

Mario yelled with pain as he was hauled roughly to his feet.

'Take it easy,' Edmund warned as he followed the two partisans up the stairs.

In the room above the flames were already taking hold. The first mortar bomb had sent logs and wood from the kitchen fire all over the room. Four dead Germans lay in grotesque attitudes on the floor or against the rough wooden furniture.

Outside, in the dim light of a quarter moon, four more had been lined up against the farmhouse wall. They had their hands in the air and had already been stripped of weapons, money and watches. Two partisans stood guarding them with one of their own Spandaus.

'What shall we do with these, colonello?'

'Shoot them,' Colonel Volpone commanded.

The Spandau roared. The Germans were slammed back against the wall before they crumpled to the ground.

'Jesus!' Edmund exclaimed involuntarily.

Volpone stared at him. 'You do not like it, Englishman? The farmer and his family were shot against that same wall – for sheltering an English prisoner of war.'

The main camp and headquarters of the Brigate Fulgore was high in the hills, well away from any main road. It lay beyond a belt of pine forest on one of those flat shelves which have the name Piano or Pian. It was enclosed by a crescent of steep slopes. A stream raced foaming along one side of it. The approach was by a steep mule-track through thick pines, well guarded by partisan sentries.

In this area the partisans could roam freely. The German forces were concentrated on the Adriatic coast and the valleys to which the mechanised Allied armies were restricted. It was not difficult for the partisans to range deep behind the German lines and return to areas which were only twenty miles from the centre of Florence. Their strength lay in mobility, and their capacity to melt away among the hills if the Germans mounted any concerted operation against them. They had no permanent encampment. They used Italian army tents which could be rapidly struck and moved to a new location. From these remote retreats they were now mounting the operations for which they had been training so long – blowing up arms dumps, sabotaging bridges, ambushing convoys, kidnapping Generals. To these attacks the Germans had a simple answer. As they could not catch the perpetrators they took reprisals against the villagers in the area where these 'outrages' were committed.

The long uphill march was even worse for Edmund than the trek back to the German headquarters. He did not want to claim any help for himself. Mario's need was greater. But after an hour of stumbling over the exposed roots of trees, fording streams and climbing steep gradients he had to confess that he could not keep up the pace.

When he heard that Edmund had previously been injured by a shell splinter, Colonel Volpone detailed a huge partisan named Seppe to support him. With the man's strong arm round his back Edmund was almost carried the rest of the way. From Seppe he learnt that the encounter at the blown bridge had been witnessed by a partisan look-out. Colonel Volpone had only been waiting till dark to mount a rescue attempt and extract vengeance. The bodies of Pironi and the boy had already been recovered. They would be buried with full military honours and one day a stone memorial would mark the spot where they had been murdered.

Edmund's Rolex Oyster had been filched by the German Leutnant. He could only guess that it was around midnight when they at last reached the camp. Here nobody was asleep. There was an atmosphere of bustle and movement, for the partisans usually operated by night and slept by day. Flames danced above a dozen fires. About fifty men were visible, some eating, some cleaning weapons, some devising improvements to their accommodation to make themselves more comfortable. There were women too, mostly young and hardy. The only building of any permanence in the camp was a log hut which served both as a canteen and headquarters.

Volpone led his patrol towards the hut. A partisan guarding the door sprang to attention and executed an elaborate salute. Seppe withdrew his arm from Edmund's shoulder and vanished into the darkness before he had time to thank him.

'You are the first Allied officer to come to our camp, capitano. That calls for a celebration. Fortunately we have wine in plenty and of the best quality.'

'Do not talk of celebration yet, my Colonel.' A tall thin man had come out from the hut to salute Volpone. 'We have bad news from Sant' Anna.'

'Bad news?'

'Yes. The Germans came in lorries. They gathered all the people in front of the church . . . .'

'Wait, Taruffi.' Volpone put up his hand. 'L'Avvocato must hear this. Wait till we are in council.' He held back the flap of the tent for Edmund. 'Favorisca, capitano. S'accommodi.'

The interior of the hut was gloomy. A pile of red-hot embers glowed on a stone plinth in the middle, the small amount of smoke spiralling through a hole in the roof. Edmund noticed a folding desk and chair and near it one of the Number 22 radio-sets the RAF had dropped by parachute. Half a dozen partisans were lying about on bed-rolls, smoking or playing cards. All of them wore predominantly civilian clothes but inevitably with some article of military equipment to give them a martial air. A huge cart-wheel leaning against the wall seemed totally out of place.

Edmund and his host sat down at a long trestle-table surrounded by seats made out of sections of tree trunks. A two-litre flagon of wine encased in basket-work was placed on the table by a bosomy girl in a dirndl skirt. She set a glass tumbler before each man. The council consisted of Volpone and three of his aides with Edmund as a privileged observer. Mario had been taken to the first-aid tent to receive attention from the Brigate Fulgore's medical unit. On the Colonel's right sat a man whom he introduced as 'l'Avvocato.' He wore steel-rimmed spectacles, had flowing grey hair and as befitted a lawyer was the only one wearing a collar and tie. His studious and academic appearance suggested that he was the intellectual of the group. The man named Taruffi was the political theorist. He was tall and thin with sunken cheeks and burning eyes set in deep, shadowed sockets. The third was Volpone's 'chief of staff', and from the start it was evident that he distrusted the British officer. He wore an arrogant and aggressive expression and when Edmund looked towards him his eyes immediately shifted away.

'Now, Taruffi,' Volpone said, when everyone was seated. 'This news from Sant' Anna. It is bad?'

'Yes, colonello. The SS wiped out the whole village. Four hundred old men, women and children were gathered in the piazza in front of the church and then the machine guns were unmasked and opened fire.'

There was a silence. Volpone looked straight at Edmund.

'That is how they fight a war. The Nazis. General Leone's Brigate ambushed a convoy near Sant 'Anna and killed forty soldiers. They murder four hundred innocent civilians in revenge.' He turned back to Taruffi. 'Were there any survivors, eye witnesses? I want this documented.'

'We found one old man, wandering round out of his mind.'

'Where is he?'

'We brought him back, colonello. He's sleeping.'

'I want him here. Bring the bottle round. Our glasses are nearly empty.'

'Where is Sant' Anna?' Edmund asked, as a partisan went out to obey the order.

'Behind the German lines. Tomorrow night, if you like, we'll take you there and you can see with your own eyes.'

'The question is,' Taruffi put in impatiently, 'are we to proceed with the blowing up of the arms dump? It's very close to the village of Puniale.'

Volpone drained his glass. 'What does l'Avvocato think?'

L'Avvocato adjusted the spectacles on his nose and unfolded his expressive hands.

'That depends on our British friends.' He looked challengingly across the table at Edmund. 'It's now six weeks since the Allies captured Florence. We thought then that the attack on the Gothic Line was imminent. Many of our people in Bologna rose against the Fascists and Nazis. Hundreds are dead, broken or deported. But your Army has only advanced to Dicomano and even now seems reluctant to attack. We do not want to fight the Germans alone.'

'We'll attack soon,' Edmund assured him. These people saw only their own little corner of the war. No use trying to explain to them that the Allies' desire to humour Stalin was having its effect on strategy in Italy. 'The offensive on the Adriatic has already begun. The attack on the Gothic Line will start as soon as the Germans switch forces to the Adriatic.'

'If what you say is true we will do all we can to help our liberators. This raid we have planned on the arms dump will hurt the Germans. Why do you shake your head?'

'If you know the Germans are going to take reprisals, would it not be better . . . .'

'Capitano,' l'Avvocato said with earnest patience, 'the war cannot be won without loss of life.'

'Innocent people . . . .'

'My friend, do you know that every day six thousand Jews perish in the extermination camps of Germany and Poland? Six thousand.'

'Did you say *every day*?'

L'Avvocato nodded. 'I said every day and I meant it.'

'But how could you know that?' As Edmund blurted out the question, he saw the Italian's face colour with anger.

'Always it's the same. No-one will believe that this is happening. But I tell you – I tell you solemnly that you have no conception of what the Nazis are doing in Germany today. Reichsführer Himmler is determined on the liquidation of every Jew – man, woman or child – not only in Germany but . . . .'

L'Avvocato's tirade was interrupted when the door of the hut opened and an old man was shepherded in. There was several days' growth on his face. His clothes were tattered, his shoes held together with string. In the brighter light of the big tent he covered his eyes and cringed back, terrified.

'Come in, old man,' Volpone said gently. 'You are among friends here. Get him a glass of wine. Taruffi, find a chair for him.'

Hesitatingly the lone survivor from Sant' Anna came towards the table. Not till he sat down and at last dared to raise his eyes was Edmund able to see his face.

'But – it's Alessio! You are Alessio, aren't you?'

10

Haltingly the story came out. Alessio had fled from Palazzo Lamberti on the night that Caterina had been murdered. He had somehow found his way through the German lines and into the hills north of Florence. All he knew was that he had to find Caterina's husband, who was fighting with the partisans somewhere in the Appenines. It had taken him a week to reach the mountains, sleeping in barns and begging scraps of food from peasant farmers. For another fortnight he had gone from one partisan band to another trying to pick up news of de Angeli. It did not help him that many of the leaders used code-names to prevent reprisals against their families. He had eventually made his way to Sant' Anna, some twenty miles out of Florence. He had found a deserted shepherd's shelter on the hill above the village and was sleeping there, making forays into it to beg for food. By God's mercy he had been hiding in his shelter when the truck-loads of German soldiers arrived.

'Did you see what happened, old man?' Volpone pressed him, more interested in getting an eye-witness account than in hearing Alessio's personal saga.

Alessio seemed to shrink physically as he recalled the scenes he had witnessed. 'They killed everyone,' he muttered, shaking his head. 'Everyone – even the babies. I could hear the shots and the screams but the demons of hell would have turned their eyes from that scene.'

'Even babies, you said,' Volpone persisted. 'Were women raped?'

Alessio lowered his head and screwed his eyes up tight. Tears rolled into the bristles on his cheeks.

'Leave him in peace,' l'Avvocato said. 'We know what happened.' He swung round to Edmund. 'The Germans are an efficient people, capitano. They have developed a technique, a system for these "operations". . . .'

'But Alessio . . . .' Edmund was sure that he was close to finding the answer to what had happened in Palazzo Lamberti on that terrible night of 10 August. 'You say you left the palazzo the night that Signora Caterina and la Nonna were killed. Was that because you saw something?'

The old man's head jerked up. He stared wildly at Edmund. 'I have to find my signore. Capitano, can you help me find my signore?'

More than that he would not say. Whatever dark knowledge he carried in his heart would remain there till he found de Angeli.

During the next few days Mario came out of his shocked state, but he still found it painful to move. No bones had been broken. The main worry was his kidneys which had received several kicks from German jack-boots. Edmund's leg too had mended well enough for him to accompany Colonel Volpone's men on several of their raids. Their methods sickened him, for they took no prisoners and he always had the uncomfortable feeling that when they withdrew to their mountain fastness the helpless inhabitants of the valleys were left to face the reprisals.

Volpone had allocated Edmund a tent to himself and made him his guest of honour. The Rolex Oyster was returned to him without comment. Edmund had his own motives for staying. According to partisan intelligence the Germans had re-occupied Castel del Piano as they withdrew into the Gothic Line. There was a chance he could persuade the partisans to launch an attack and capture it.

'We have our orders from General Leone,' Volpone told

him when he made the suggestion. 'He commands this whole region. He has decided we are to avoid set battles with German troops. Our best policy is to make raids, disrupt communications, ambush convoys, destroy bridges . . . .'

On the third day they netted a big fish. A small hand-picked group successfully ambushed a Corps Commander as he was driving forward in his Kübelwagen to inspect positions in the Gothic Line. Unwisely he chose to wear full insignia of rank and his vehicle carried a General's flag. The partisans killed his ADC, driver and escort, but they brought the General back in triumph to the camp. In his immaculate uniform with shining boots, Iron Cross and medal ribbons, peaked cap and monocle, he was the epitome of a German officer of the old pre-Hitler school. Edmund could not help admiring the dignity and courage with which he faced his captors. Even with his hands tied behind his back he managed to dominate them by his personality.

Edmund declined Volpone's invitation to sit in on his court martial, which took place in the command hut.

An hour later he was talking to Mario in the medical hut. 'I've been trying to persuade Volpone to occupy Castel del Piano as soon as the attack starts, but he won't make any decision without the approval of this General Leone they're all in such awe of . . . .'

Edmund stopped as a ragged volley of rifle fire sounded from the direction of the stream at the edge of the encampment.

'What's that?' Mario winced as he started up from his folding chair. 'Are we being attacked?'

'No. Firing squad.'

The partisans were not the only ones using the high mountains to move from the German-held region to the area nominally re-conquered by Fifth Army. There was a constant trickle of refugees, people who were fleeing from the round-ups still being carried out by the Germans further north. The partisans had their own rough and ready counter-intelligence system and they subjected these itinerants wherever possible to a rudimentary screening. At this stage of the war the Abwehr, the German military intelligence machine, was recruiting attractive girls in the area administered by Mussolini's Salò government. They were given a brief training for their role as tactical spies. Their zone of operations was the forward area. Infiltrated across the lines in the guise of refugees, their orders were to befriend the sex-starved Allied soldiers, if possible seduce them so that they would not be handed over to the American or British security personnel. When they had pin-pointed the location of headquarters and gun positions they were to re-cross the lines with information that would enable the German gunners to straffe them.

It was one of these girl spies that a patrol of the Brigate Fulgore had intercepted on the road to San Godenzo. She was a very attractive eighteen-year-old posing as a member of a Florence family trying to return home. Her Turin accent gave her away. Edmund was in the headquarters hut with Volpone and l'Avvocato when she was brought in by two grinning partisans. She was shivering violently either with cold or terror. Volpone listened to the report of her captors. What he heard enraged him.

'Spia!' He roared the word at her, his face three inches from hers. 'Traitress! What is your mission? What have you been sent to find out?'

'I am not a spy,' the girl flashed back. 'My family is in Florence. I am trying to rejoin them. I am an honest woman.'

'You are no Fiorentina. You are Torinese. Confess it!'

'My parents are Florentine . . . .'

'You are lying!' Volpone shouted. 'We will get the truth out of you!' He turned to one of his aides. 'Tie her to the cartwheel. She may know something about German dispositions and where they intend to establish their line.'

The girl was dragged towards the huge wheel leaning against the wall. Edmund saw now what its purpose was. He quickly stood up and went out of the hut. The light was beginning to fade. The camp fires on which the partisans would cook their supper had been lit. He was walking towards his tent when he heard a hurrying step behind him. He slowed to let l'Avvocato catch up.

'I do not like it any more than you do, capitano.'

'Oh, no? Weren't you one of the tribunal that sentenced General von Gallen to be shot . . . ?'

'He himself requested a firing squad.'

'In preference to a mouthful of sawdust and a bullet in the

back of the head? You partisans claim to be soldiers but you do not observe the Geneva Convention – especially with prisoners of war.'

Edmund had walked past his tent. He knew that if he went in l'Avvocato would follow him and he would then be a captive audience.

'He was the representative of an odious system,' l'Avvocato persisted, falling into step beside Edmund. 'We have evidence that units of the German army – the Wehrmacht – have taken part in atrocities. And I do not mean just the SS and the Einsatzgruppen. A regular officer like General von Gallen does not hesitate to obey the command of his Führer, even when it involves exterminatory reprisals.'

Edmund had chosen a path that led out of the camp along the edge of the stream. He had heard the girl cry out once. He wanted to put distance between himself and the hut where the interrogation was taking place.

'The Germans have learnt after four years that extermination is a difficult task.' L'Avvocato quickened his step to keep up. 'It poses technical problems. How do you kill people and bury them without wasting precious ammunition, time and energy?'

The question was rhetorical. L'Avvocato did not expect an answer. He supplied it himself.

'So you have certain conventions. It is always more convenient if the victims can be induced to gather in one place You know that people will cling to hope even when staring into the jaws of hell? So you tell them that they are being collected to be taken away for forced labour. You may, if you have a sense of humour, even persuade these wretches that they are being assembled for a photograph. A photograph! You do not believe me, capitano? It has worked, many times. But when they are all lined up and smiling it is not cameras that are unmasked, but machine guns.'

Like most British soldiers Edmund tended to regard the enemy as 'old Jerry', a fierce fighter but basically someone you had to respect. Yet l'Avvocato's words carried a chilling conviction. He continued his lecture in the same precise unemotional voice. He had to raise it slightly now because their path lay beside the leaping stream.

'Disposal of the bodies is always a problem, but good

planning will lessen it. You can make them dig their own graves but – you see the difficulty? Who will fill them in?'

Edmund stopped and looked back towards the hut. The sound that had reached his ears was high-pitched enough to cut through l'Avvocato's rasping voice and the rushing of the water.

L'Avvocato had apparently not heard the shriek. 'Of course,' he went on in a reasoning voice, 'it is important that when you are engaged in such work you should enjoy yourself . . . .'

'Oh, come off it, Avvocato.'

'But of course, capitano! It's not difficult to debauch humans. The Nazi specialists understand how to unleash the beast – with pillage, drunkenness, sexual orgies . . . .'

'Is all this based on the testimonies of people like old Alessio?'

'You doubt the truth of what I say, capitano?' Angered, he gripped Edmund's arm and swung him round to face him. 'Shall I tell you what we have seen with our own eyes? We have seen the survivors in a heap of machine-gunned bodies pulled out and told they had two more hours to live, and then shot exactly on time. Why? For the pleasure of watching abject terror. We have seen an old woman burned in her bed because she was too weak to get out of it. We have seen a mother forced to watch while her sixteen-year-old daughter's baby was ripped from her womb. We have seen babies thrown in the air and used for target practice. We have seen girls spread-eagled so that sharpened stakes . . . .'

'All right, Avvocato. That's enough.'

The intensity of the man's ever-quickening speech, his fanatical eyes, the spittle in his breath had got to Edmund's already raw nerves. Without realising it they had walked beyond sight of the camp and were alone in the darkening forest.

Edmund halted in his tracks. From the camp had come the sound of a single shot, the crisp crack of a .45 revolver.

'Would they shoot a girl?'

'I tell you, capitano.' L'Avvocato ignored the shot. He was not going to be denied his peroration. 'We are fighting the blackest, the most demoniac evil the world has ever known. And you are shocked when we execute a General who commands the perverted armies of that monster Hitler and a traitress who would sell the lives of all of us to the enemy.'

One of the German Sappers laying mines on Highway 67 just below San Godenzo was a good Nazi and an atheist. He also had a wry sense of humour. He noticed on a hillock just above the road one of those shrines which the Italians place at intervals along their roads, especially in the mountains. There was always a niche for the statue of the Virgin with room for a small oil lamp and a vase of flowers. This one was enclosed by an iron railing with a small gate. There was a fair chance that some good Catholic in the Allied forces would be moved to go up and say a prayer there. The Sapper decided to provide a surprise answer to that prayer. He buried an anti-tank Teller mine under the gate and wired up a booby-trap so that the first person to open it would be blown to kingdom come.

As darkness fell the following evening, a messenger from General Leone's headquarters arrived with the latest information and fresh orders for the Brigate Fulgore. It was clear that the Germans were withdrawing from all their positions south of the Alpe di San Benedetto, the range of mountains to the east and west of San Godenzo. Astonishingly, they were not manning the fortifications so laboriously prepared by the Todt Organisation.

'But that can't be true,' Edmund protested to Volpone. 'For months we've been hearing about the Gothic Line and how impregnable it is!'

'If General Leone says so it is true,' Volpone declared loyally. 'I have heard that the Italian labourers poured bad concrete and the emplacements are already collapsing. Besides, Kesselring is a wily fox. He has seen what an Italian winter is like. If he stands in the Gothic Line he will have to supply his forces over the Appenines. But if he retreats to the other side he can use the roads of the Lombardy Plain to switch forces and it is you, the Allies, who will have to bring your supplies over forty miles of mountain roads.'

General Leone had ordered Volpone's unit to withdraw to the heights above Castel del Piano to avoid being absorbed by the Allied advance. From there they were to continue their harassment of the enemy. If Castel del Piano was not held in strength they were to occupy and hold it until the Allies advanced.

'You will come with us, of course, capitano. You are a member of our group now.'

'If the Germans are not defending the Gothic Line I must get back to our own lines somehow. That information is absolutely vital.'

Edmund's duty clearly required him to report back with a piece of intelligence that could affect the whole strategy of Fifth Army. British commanders were inclined to be sceptical about intelligence from partisan sources, but if Jason's Roughs were still spearheading the advance there was a chance that he could find his friend somewhere down in the Sieve valley. He had no regrets about leaving the partisans. The shooting of the German General and the girl spy had sickened him. Mario would remain with Volpone's band. If the partisans were successful in occupying Castel del Piano he would be on hand to safeguard the paintings.

'What about Alessio?' Edmund asked Volpone.

'The old man? We'll look after him.' Volpone laughed. 'He may even find his signore up there in the mountains.'

Long before dawn the camp had been struck. Only the log hut and two graves remained when the partisans moved out. The General had been given a proper burial and his grave clearly marked. When the war had passed on he could be taken to lie with his soldiers in a German war cemetery. The girl spy lay beside him beneath a rough wooden cross.

Volpone insisted on allocating Edmund a bodyguard. 'Seppe comes from Montalbano, that's the way you want to go. He'll guide you and he can also bring back messages from your high command.'

Edmund and Seppe set off at first light. They took it slowly as they descended the mule track that led down to the valley. There was not a soul to be seen in the wooded slopes around them. The Germans had slipped back to the high mountains and the British had not yet realised that the Gothic Line had been abandoned. Sound travelled clearly, though the echoes from the hills made it difficult to pin-point the direction. Somewhere on the slopes east of the main road a squadron of tanks squeaked, rattled and roared, disproving the theory that armoured vehicles could not operate in this terrain. From the valley came the inevitable crump of shells but the firing was half-hearted.

The village of Montalbano was deserted. The Germans had evacuated all civilians from the vicinity of the Gothic Line. Seppe was uttering lamentations as they walked down the little street with its broken windows and looted shops. He had just caught sight of his own home when Edmund heard a familiar whistle. Acting on a reflex he dragged Seppe through a door that hung loosely on its hinges. The mortar bomb landed across the street.

'Two inch mortar. There will be more to follow. Some platoon commander softening the place up before he moves in.'

'Mamma mia! Nostra casa sarà destrutta!'

'Keep your head *down*, Seppe!'

The barrage lasted for three minutes, while the two men crouched behind a window. When it stopped Edmund still waited, holding Seppe back. When he heard the crunch of booted feet on broken glass he called out: 'British officer in here. Don't shoot.'

He signalled Seppe to stay put and walked slowly to the doorway, keeping his empty hands well out from his hips. A dozen rifles with fixed bayonets swung in his direction. They were held by soldiers in battle-dress wearing the flat tin hats of the British Tommy. From their height and bearing it was evident that they were Guardsmen.

The Royal Ulster Fusiliers were in the hills on the right flank of 1st Guards Brigade. Battalion Headquarters was temporarily located in a smart modern chalet overlooking the valley. The Regimental Sergeant Major ran his eye disapprovingly over the officer who dismounted from the Jeep driven up by a Grenadier NCO. His uniform was discoloured and covered with mud. He had two days' growth of beard on his face. But the captain's pips on his shoulder were unmistakeable and the RSM rather ponderously addressed him as 'sir'.

'The CO's busy at the moment, sir. He has an order group in half an hour.'

'I've got to see him at once, Mr . . . .'

'Delaney, sir.' The RSM straightened imperceptibly.

'I have some very important information for him. Tell him please that Captain Brudanell is here.'

To the RSM's surprise the CO wanted to see this scruffy visitor immediately. Edmund was escorted to the *salotto* of the chalet. Jason was sitting behind a trestle table with his Adjutant beside him. Edmund pulled out his smartest salute. Behind him he heard the RSM start to breathe again.

There was a certain formality about Jason's manner, as if he was afraid that Edmund might treat him with too much familiarity in front of his staff. He had already grown into his new responsibility and had acquired the confident manner of one who is deferred to by all around him. When Edmund was careful to address him as 'Colonel' he relaxed and brought out a bottle of Haig. Edmund noticed that the glasses they drank from were of the finest Florentine crystal.

'Odd thing about war. It makes the world a small place. I want to hear all about your partisans but my company commanders are coming in at mid-day. And no doubt you want to shave and clean up . . . .'

'I do, but there's something you ought to hear without delay, Colonel.'

Jason listened intently while Edmund told him that the Germans had pulled back from the Gothic Line.

'This information, is it reliable?'

'Well, I can tell you that I walked down from Monte Masaccio this morning and did not see a soul till I met that Grenadier patrol. There's nothing between you and the top of the pass.'

'You'd better be right, Ed, because you're going to stay with us when we advance.'

The Corps intelligence staff believed that the enemy were waiting for them in the much publicised Gothic Line. To prove that the partisan reports were correct an Italian liaison officer attached to 6th Armoured Division walked on foot up the road to the bottom of the Passo del Muraglione. He drew no fire. Those formidable emplacements were empty.

As the country was so inhospitable to tanks, the division had to rely on infantry patrols to regain contact. The Royal Ulster Fusiliers on the right flank pushed forward through mountains that became progressively higher. When they were within two miles of Castel del Piano it became painfully clear that the Germans intended to hold this natural strongpoint. The leading company came under heavy fire from the walled monastery. Traffic on Route 67 was halted by shelling, accurately directed from the observation post in the tower. This feature, which quickly became known as Piano Castle, reared its head spectacularly over the valley and dominated the axis of advance.

The Roughs were ordered to attack and capture it. Jason was given twenty-four hours to prepare for his first major action as Commanding Officer. He included Edmund in the group that comprised Battallion Headquarters; the terrain was familiar to him and he would be a useful liaison officer when contact was made with the partisans known to be waiting on the high ground East of Route 67. So Edmund found himself taking part in a battle that later became a model for military textbooks and elicited a special commendation from General Alexander.

Lt Col Fitzgerald made his personal reconnaissance from a hill farm which afforded a good view of the objective about a mile away. Edmund pointed out Monte Falterona towering to five thousand feet on the right. He passed on what he had learnt about Castel del Piano. The name dated from the tenth century. In those days a medieval castle had crowned the hill, which was shaped like an inverted bowl. The word Piano referred to the flat shelf between the hill and the slopes of Monte Falterona. The fortress had been replaced in the 1300s by one of the innumerable monasteries which were a feature of the Italian landscape. It was a solid building with a tower in the middle. The gardens, about a quarter of a mile in length and breadth, were enclosed by a stone wall from whose base the ground fell away steeply.

Jason surveyed the scene for a long time through binoculars. He scanned the steep slopes below the hill, exploring every possible line of approach, carefully noting the position of the machine gun posts dug in just outside the wall. Then he moved to the monastery itself. His gaze rested for a long time on the tower.

'Those are very solid buildings.' He lowered the glasses and turned to the Gunner Major. Bryce Ayres' battery had been in support of the Roughs since the Sicily landings. He

160

had become almost a part of the regiment. 'Will your guns have much effect on them, Bryce?'

'We can make it very uncomfortable for the people dug in round the walls.' Bryce had been using his own binoculars. 'We won't be able to breach those buildings but our gunfire will make them keep their heads down.'

'The place is like a fortress.' Jason again studied the large-scale plans which had been provided by the air photo interpretation officer at divisional headquarters. One showed the layout of the grounds, the other every detail of the buildings. 'I particularly dislike that tower. It dominates the whole area. A few thousand-pound bombs would soften the place up nicely. I think I'll ask the GOC to lay on an air strike. I'm sure the RAF would oblige.'

'I expect they would, Colonel,' Bryce agreed. 'But gunfire would be more accurate. And we can co-ordinate it more closely with your attack.'

Jason shook his head doubtfully. 'These old castles are built of massive stones. Shells detonate on impact and do little damage.'

Edmund might have remained silent if the Gunner Major had not demurred about an air-strike. As it was he heard himself talking before he realised that he was flouting regimental etiquette. 'At Montecassino the bombing helped the defenders more than the attackers. All it did was bury a couple of hundred refugees under rubble.'

Jason looked at him coldly. 'Are you worried about refugees, Ed, or about your pictures?'

Stung by Jason's sarcasm Edmund spoke more frankly than his rank or position justified. 'Well, a lot of damage could be done for doubtful advantage. If you bomb the place into a heap of rubble, you'll lose the element of surprise. And the Krauts can still defend the ruins – probably better than standing buildings. In fact they'd have better fields of fire if the buildings were flattened.'

Jason had waited in silence for Edmund to finish. Bryce Ayres was listening with polite surprise, but the RSM was clearly outraged by Edmund's audacity. Jason pondered for a few moments, his eyes not leaving Edmund's face.

'Perhaps you're right, Ed,' he said with remarkable calmness. 'Perhaps you're not. Is your Madonna up there?'

'Not my Madonna, Jason. The King's Madonna.'

Jason tapped the two plans with the back of his nails, 'What do you think, Bryce? Can your guns handle it?'

'I think so, Colonel. If my battery is not enough we can always call for an Uncle shoot.'

'That's it, then.' Jason put the plans back in their cellophane holder. 'We'll take Captain Brudanell's advice. No airstrike.'

11

Jason assembled his Order Group at 0915 hours in the water mill which was for the moment serving as battalion headquarters. The rumble of the great wheel provided a rhythmic background as of distant funereal drums. The dozen or so officers who gathered in the grain store were purposeful but quiet. The battallion had already concentrated for the attack and they knew that something big lay ahead. The Adjutant, Richard Skillern, checked his list to make sure that the four Company Commanders were present as well as the commanders of the gunner battery, the tank squadron, the machine gun platoon and the section of sappers.

Jason asked the Intelligence Officer to open the proceedings. Alan Bulmer began by reading a résumé of the BBC news.

'In Normandy the German garrison at Brest are still refusing to surrender, though Allied forces have already reached the river Moselle. In Moscow an armistice has been signed between Rumania on the one hand and the Soviet Union, the United States and Great Britain on the other. On the Eastern Front the Russians are at last dropping supplies to the insurgents fighting German tanks in Warsaw, but the Soviet forces have halted on the Vistula and are making no move to enter the city. In China General Stilwell has inspected Communist positions at Kweilin. In Italy Eighth Army have taken Coriano and opened up the road to Rimini. The BBC is not saying much about the new rockets the Germans are using on London but Goebbels is claiming that the whole area round Trafalgar Square is in ruins. Of course, that's mostly propaganda.'

On a lighter note the IO added that an English Symphony Orchestra under John Barbirolli had played Elgar's *Enigma Variations* to a slightly baffled Rome audience and that demobilisation orders were expected shortly from the War Office. This last item produced an ironic cheer. He concluded by outlining as much as was known of enemy dispositions in and around Castel del Piano. Interrogation of POWs and air photo reconnaisance indicated that the monastery was held in company strength, probably by 104 Panzer Grenadiers.

Edmund gave his own personal description of the monastery and briefed the Order Group on the partisans' organisation and probable reactions.

Then Jason stood up to outline his plan of attack. There was nothing youthful or diffident about him now. Edmund knew that he was watching an experienced and competent soldier in action. The essence of the plan was flexibility so that Company Commanders could act on their own initiative as the situation developed. In the broadest terms it meant that B Company (Captain John O'Dwyer) would first attack and capture the enemy positions outside the west wall; C Company (Captain Donald Lester), following up, would deal with the south wall; whilst A Company (Captain Blake Megginson), moving through the wood to the south-east, took the east wall and went on to clear the northern reverse slopes. D Company (Major Ian Duddington) would be in reserve. The artillery fire would be co-ordinated to harmonise with this programme, whilst the Machine Gun Platoon and the Tank Squadron each had their allotted tasks. It all sounded very neat, very logical.

'No air-support, sir?' Ian Duddington, the senior company commander, inquired.

'No,' Jason said, without looking at Edmund. 'Bryce is confident his gunners can give us all the fire-power we need. Reconnaissance will be carried out down to platoon level. Battalion HQ will move to Monte Picino at 0100 hours. B

Company must be ready to leave the concentration area at 0200 hours so as to be at the Start Line by 0600 hours. Any other questions?'

Edmund fitted in a few hours sleep that afternoon whilst Jason finalised his plans, co-ordinating movements and timings, fine tuning the artillery programme. The barrage would precede the attack and then move forward as it advanced.

An early evening meal was accompanied by some excellent wine which the miller had dug up from its hiding place. Then the personnel who made up tactical headquarters prepared to move off. Major Jimmy Bruce, the Second-in-Command, was left in charge of Rear Headquarters in the mill. There was that atmosphere of unspoken tension and expectancy that makes the mouth go dry and induces irresistible yawning. Having heard the CO's orders, Edmund could visualise the whole battalion stirring out there in the darkness, silent and furtive so as not to alert the enemy. It was raining, as it had done almost ceaselessly since 1 September.

Jason took Edmund with him in his own Jeep, along with his batman, Fusilier Quinn, and the RSM. Quinn had brought a Benghazi Burner to brew up tea, a box of rations and some fresh eggs he had scrounged from a farm. It would be his responsibility to sustain the CO and the RSM during the battle.

It was 0055 hours when they reached the farmhouse on Monte Picino. Bryce Ayres and Alan Bulmer were already there. They knew they had to be on hand five minutes before the stipulated time. The Sanitary Corporal was digging the indispensable latrines. The signallers were setting up the Number 18 and 22 wireless sets which would be used until field telephones could be laid out to the companies. The Doctor and the Padre were down at the Regimental Aid Post just in rear of the start line. From there, the seriously wounded and the dead would be taken back to Rear HQ. The Provost Sergeant was standing by to deal with prisoners.

At 0310 hours the artillery began firing their programme. The flash of the guns illuminated the clouds over the valley to the rear of Tac HQ. The shells could be heard whipping overhead and bursting on Castel del Piano. Edmund hoped that the Germans had stowed the paintings well below ground. The din provided noise cover so that the enemy would not hear the infantry moving up from the concentration area, nor the tanks creaking to their fire positions.

By 0530 Castel del Piano was just becoming visible against the dark mountains beyond. First the tower emerged, then the roofs of the buildings and lastly the perimeter wall. There was little conversation now at Tac HQ and the wireless sets were silent. The battalion was poised. Everyone knew exactly what he was supposed to do. Edmund remembered what it had been like in France in 1940. His thoughts were with the Company and Platoon Commanders and the hundreds of Fusiliers who would soon have to advance against the bullets, mortar bombs and shells.

At 0540, thirty minutes before Z hour, Quinn brought three cups of tea to the bedroom from whose window Jason was surveying the gradually lightening landscape – one each for the CO, the RSM and Edmund. At 0545 the artillery concentrated an intense bombardment on the east end of the wall. This was a feint. At 0600 it switched to the west end and at the same time the tanks opened up from their hull-down positions.

By 0610, Edmund knew, John O'Dwyer's company had left the start line and started to move up the gulley that led to the objective. Bryce Ayres' Forward Observation Officer was with Company Headquarters. Nothing was heard till 0615. Then, as the artillery barrage lifted past them, the Germans under the west wall woke up to the fact that they were being attacked. Their Spandaus began to speak. They were answered by the British heavy machine guns. At the same time enemy mortar and shell-fire began to pour down on the gulley and the neighbouring slopes.

Edmund, keeping discreetly in the background, did not know what messages Jason was receiving. He could tell from his face that things were not going well.

By 0645, he knew, Donald Lester's C Company should have gone through the leading company to deal with the south wall and that Blake Megginson's company should be attacking the east wall. Jason called him over. Both he and Bryce Ayres were looking very tense. 'Ed, do you speak any German?'

'A little. I'm not very fluent.'

'But you can understand it?'

'Reasonably well.'

'B Company have taken some prisoners. I need to know in what strength the Krauts are holding the monastery. Is it a company or a regiment? Would you go down and see what you can find out? Make the bastards talk.'

Down in the valley from which B and C Companies had started their attack, stretcher bearers were bringing the wounded in to the Regimental Aid Post. Ambulances were standing by to take the most serious cases back to the Casualty Clearing Station or the Field Hospital. Some joked and smoked as they jolted along, some lay pale and silent, some screamed with pain. There were men with messy, bloody stumps where arms and legs had been blown off, men with faces that were a mask of blood and tissue, men writhing with bullets in their guts. One man was lying on his stomach with a lump of jagged metal up his arse.

Edmund was glad that his duty took him to the assembly point for prisoners. Every tortured face in the RAP seemed to accuse him personally. How much of this would have been avoided if he had not argued against the bombing of the monastery?

The Provost Sergeant's POW cage was a sheep pen of some farm buildings near the RAP. Half a dozen sullen and arrogant Panzer Grenadiers were being guarded by a couple of trigger-happy Fusiliers.

Edmund interrogated them in an empty cow-shed. The first three were stubborn, refusing to give more than name, rank and number. He ordered one of the Fusiliers to start digging a grave. He made the Germans take their jack-boots off. He told them about the massacre at Sant' Anna. Then, in an outburst of rage that was only partly simulated, he roared an order at them to answer his questions. They talked.

An hour later he sent the Provost Sergeant up to Tac HQ with a message. Castel del Piano had been reinforced the previous day and was now held not in company but in battalion strength. The artillery preparation had not inflicted many casualties because the majority of the troops had been inside the buildings. And Edmund was staying at the RAP to assist the Padre. The wounded were coming in fast and he needed help with the dying. No more prisoners had been taken.

The next three hours were a nightmare. From the casualties being carried back by the exhausted stretcher bearers he learnt that the Fusiliers were being badly mauled. The bodies of John O'Dwyer and two young platoon commanders were brought down and sent back to Rear HQ. Twenty-seven Fusiliers had been killed and two score more wounded. Some of the wounded had a compulsion to talk and from them Edmund gleaned snippets about the battle.

15 Platoon had breached the west wall and were pushing on towards the south when they were counter-attacked and lost half their strength.

The Jerries had put snipers in the trees in the orchard.

The worst of the machine-gun fire was coming from the tower.

Cpl. Lang's jaw had been shot away but he had continued firing his Bren gun.

17 Platoon had got caught in their own artillery barrage.

One of the Germans spoke perfect English. He had been heard shouting, 'I say, you chaps, steady on!'

At about mid-day the flow of wounded ceased. The din on the hill above had slackened. Edmund washed the blood off his hands and forearms and went back up the hill to Tac HQ.

There was no sign of Jason. At the window of the upstairs bedroom Jimmy Bruce was staring at Castel del Piano through binoculars. Bryce Ayres was talking to his own CO who had come up to see how the battle was progressing. Lieutenant Colonel Dudley Freemantle was a seasoned veteran who was unfailingly cheerful and good-humoured. Instead of the customary swagger-stick he carried a mashie-niblick so that he could seize every opportunity to practise his golf shots. While the two gunners conferred, the second-in-command put Edmund in the picture. A, B and C Companies had all managed to breach the wall but at the cost of heavy casualties. Several platoons were still inside, dug in but pinned down by fire from the tower and the monastery. The platoons in the slit trenches outside the wall were coming under fire from artillery in the mountains to the east. When Jason had sent in his reserve company, Ian

Duddington's D Company, he had decided to accompany them himself to co-ordinate the attack. Now D Company also was pinned down astride the south-east corner of the wall.

'Jason should have asked the RAF to bomb it,' Freemantle told the 2 i/c. 'But if you can get your people back outside the wall, I will lay on an Uncle shoot for five minutes. Jerry won't offer much resistance after that.'

An Uncle shoot meant that every gun in the division would concentrate rapid fire on that one target. Jimmy Bruce was not cheered by the suggestion.

'I'm afraid we've lost contact, Colonel. Our field telephone lines have been cut by shell-fire and the companies' wireless sets must have been knocked out. I can't raise any of them.'

'Then,' Freemantle told the 2 i/c, 'you'll have to send a runner.'

'I'll go, sir,' the RSM volunteered immediately.

'I can't spare you, Mr Delaney. If the adjutant hadn't stopped a bullet . . . .'

Edmund realised now that Richard Skillern was nowhere to be seen. 'What happened to him?'

'Went for a jimmy riddle and got hit by a sniper. Only wounded but we had to evacuate him. Mr Delaney, have you seen the Intelligence Officer?'

Before he had time to think Edmund found himself saying: 'I'll take your message for you.'

'This has to be timed very precisely, you understand?' Dudley Freemantle wagged his mashie-niblick to emphasise the point. 'We'd better synchronise watches. I make it 1237 – now.'

Edmund adjusted his own watch to the Gunner Colonel's, made sure it was fully wound.

'The Uncle is timed for 1400 hours,' Jimmy Bruce said. 'That's one hour and twenty-three minutes from now. Say, forty minutes for you to reach D Company headquarters, thirty minutes to get word to platoons and thirteen minutes for them to withdraw behind the wall. The Uncle will be from 1400 to 1405. They must be ready to attack immediately after the shoot.'

'Right.' Edmund was not feeling in a talkative mood.

'Do you mind repeating the message for Sunray back to me. Just to be sure.'

'The gunners will lay on an Uncle shoot from 1400 to 1405 hours. All platoons to withdraw outside the perimeter wall by 1400 hours and be ready to attack as soon as the shoot finishes.'

'That's correct. Now, here's your Verey pistol. When you've delivered your message fire a green over two reds. Then we'll confirm the Uncle.'

Edmund took the Verey pistol and the cartridges.

'A green over two reds.'

'And you'd better take the Adjutant's steel bowler.' Jimmy Bruce gave Edmund the helmet, then held out his hand. 'Good luck. And thank you.'

Edmund happened to glance at the RSM. There was a thoughtful expression in Mr Delaney's eyes, but all he did was nod. Dudley Freemantle was scrutinising Edmund rather as if they were about to drive off the first tee as partners in a foursome needle match.

'Cuppa tea before you go, sir.' Fusilier Quinn had materialised at Edmund's elbow. 'I put a drop of something stronger in it.'

The route Edmund had chosen took him past the Regimental Aid Post and up the gulley via which B Company had opened the attack six and a half hours earlier. Bryce Ayres' guns put down some smoke shells on the slopes to the west. As the smoke drifted over the gulley he knew that he was hidden from the German observation posts. But as he began to choke on the acrid air, shells began to rain down all round him. The enemy had assumed that the smoke was to conceal a reserve company moving up the gulley. Edmund went to ground while the earth shook round him. Shrapnel and rock fragments zinged through the air.

'Why the hell did I open my big mouth?' he shouted at the earth an inch from his nose. He knew the answer. It was Dudley Freemantle's remark about RAF support that had spurred him.

When the stonk lifted he glanced at his watch. God, how time flew! 1245 already and he was due at D Company headquarters by 1317. That was where Jason was presumed to be.

As he climbed, grunting and grimacing with pain, he could see the wall rising above him at the top of the gulley. B Company headquarters was in a captured German sangar outside the south-west corner of the perimeter. The Company Sergeant Major spotted the lone figure clawing its way up the gulley and guided him in by voice. He flopped into the sangar as a volley of mortar shells came moaning down. The half-dozen men in the trench crouched, heads down.

'It's been like that the last two hours,' the CSM shouted. 'We're up shit creek here.'

Edmund saw that the will to fight was burning low. The Company had suffered heavy casualties. The senior Platoon Commander had taken over from the dead John O'Dwyer. Two platoons were inside the wall, unable to advance against withering fire from the monastery buildings and tower. The company's number 22 set had been knocked out by mortar fire.

Edmund took it upon himself to inform the CSM and the very young Mr Roscoe about the Uncle shoot and advised them to watch for the Verey signal. When they saw it they'd know that the shoot was on and had better get their two platoons back behind the wall.

'How can I find D Company headquarters? The CO is there.'

'At the south-east corner, last we heard of them. If you keep close beneath the wall they can't see you from the monastery. But Jerry has an OP on Monte Falterona, so watch out.'

His watch hand was already past 1325. The south-east corner was three hundred yards away. He could see Monte Falterona looming up below the lifting clouds so of course anyone up there could see him. He took a gamble on the regularity of the Germans. Their gunners often took a break at lunchtime. He scrambled out of the sangar, made for the protection of the high dry-stone wall and ran eastward as fast as his aching legs would carry him.

The three hundred yards might just as well have been three miles. A narrow path ran along the base of the wall to his left. It had been breached every now and again by shell-fire. To his right the ground fell away steeply. Across the valley he could see the slopes of Monte Picino and the farm-house from which Jimmy Bruce must be watching him. Sangars and slit trenches had been dug below the wall. Astonished faces under tin hats stared up at him as he blundered past. Frequently he had to step over the corpses of Panzer Grenadiers or Fusiliers. As his vision began to blur he heard voices ahead urging him on. They rose to the volume of a cheer and he had the illusion that he was back at school finishing the long cross-country run with his friends waiting for him at the tape. Those voices solved the problem of locating D Company headquarters.

As he dived into the sangar he was sure that his luck was running out and that a shell with his number on it was already on the way. Blinded with sweat, fatigue and fear he heard a voice exclaim: 'You crazy bloody fool! What the . . . .' Then Edmund's helmet rolled off and Jason realised who it was. 'Jesus God! Ed! To what do we owe the honour . . . .'

'I've got to pee,' Edmund gasped.

'Feel free, old man,' said Jason. 'It happens to the best.'

The Uncle came down at precisely 1400 hours. It was awesome. The fire power of an entire division was concentrated on the Monastery of Castel del Piano and the area within the wall. For Ian Duddington it was an agonising five minutes. One of his platoons, Eamon Corrigan's, had by outstanding valour captured the lodge half way up the avenue. It was impossible to extract them without exposing them to murderous machine-gun fire from the tower. Jason had decided that the Uncle must go ahead, even if the lodge was obliterated.

'I'm sorry, Eamon. Sorry, sorry.' Ian kept muttering as an apocalyptic storm of high explosive rained down. Surely nothing could live, nothing could survive in that inferno of dust, smoke, flame and disintegrating masonry. And it was so near that the ground shook, the revetments of the sangar trembled.

It ended with the same suddenness as it had begun. There was a moment of appalled, shocked silence. Then with a shout of, 'Come on, you Roughs!' Jason was up and over the lip of the sangar. He had a Tommy-gun in his hands. All round the wall the Fusiliers responded to the battle cry, swarming up from their slit trenches and pouring through the breaches in the wall.

'Come on, you Roughs! Come on, you Roughs!' The shout was echoed all round the wall.

Edmund was sandwiched between Ian Duddington and his CSM as they went through the wall. Somehow a Tommy-gun had found its way into his hands. The CSM had given him a couple of grenades to stuff in his haversack. Looking ahead he saw that the outline of the monastery had changed. The tower was gone. All over the orchard and gardens the Fusiliers were racing forward. And still from the buildings ahead there was silence. The trees in the orchard had been stripped of leaves and branches. The ladders the snipers had used to climb into their perches lay flattened, each with a grey-clad corpse beside it.

The group Edmund was with had got half way from the wall to the monastery and still they had not been fired on. Had the defenders all died in that maelstrom of shrieking metal? Then from ground level somewhere to the right, a lone Spandau opened up. Beside Edmund, Ian Duddington staggered, fell.

'Come on, D Company!' Jason shouted. 'Don't falter, we've got them.'

Edmund checked as the Fusiliers, regaining momentum, streamed past him.

The Spandau that had hit Ian was in a low outbuilding on the right flank, about fifty yards away. The machine gunner had swung his weapon round to fire into the backs of the Fusiliers rushing the monastery. Men were still falling. Edmund saw red. He veered towards it and found cover behind a row of low bushes. Crouching and weaving he covered the intervening space in fifteen seconds. He flopped into a hollow ten yards from his objective. He reached into the haversack and found one of the grenades. He pulled the pin and bowled it straight-armed through the window of the outhouse. As it exploded he followed it in. The chatter of the Tommy-gun drowned his own hoarse roar of rage and terror. He rushed into a black, smoking charnel house. . . .

Edmund always maintained afterwards that it was not he who had stormed the machine-gun nest. Some wild demon had entered his body and taken possession of his spirit for those horrific moments.

When he came to his senses a minute or an age later he was limping back to the place where Duddington lay motionless. He gently turned him on to his side, released the helmet strap from his chin, put a supporting hand under his head. With a great effort Duddington opened his eyes. He fought for breath, struggled to rise.

'No good . . . bought it . . . .'

'Stay put, Ian. Don't try to move.'

Edmund looked round for a stretcher-bearer but suddenly the orchard was empty. From the direction of the monastery came a ragged cheer. White cloths had appeared at the windows. The Spandau had fallen silent.

'Have they – ?'

'Yes.' Edmund eased the bare head back. 'Jerry's surrendering.'

'Valerie,' Ian Duddington said with sudden strength and clarity. 'Tell her . . . . They really do come from . . . .'

But he never completed the message.

Edmund stayed till the CSM came back looking for his Company Commander. His tough veteran's face crumpled when he saw the corpse. He brushed the back of his hand across his nose and bit hard on his lip. The two men waited together till a couple of stretcher bearers came running up.

'Has he croaked?'

The CSM nodded, avoiding words. When the bearers, bandsmen in happier times, had carried their burden away the CSM straightened his shoulders. 'Going to see what's happened to our platoon in the lodge.'

'I'll come with you.' Edmund did not want to drift about on his own. He kept thinking about Valerie. Wife probably. 'Wonder what she's doing at this moment.'

'What?'

'Nothing.' He had not realised he'd said it out loud.

There are few things worse for morale than to be shelled by your own guns. Out of twenty-four men in the lodge eleven had been wounded and five killed, including the platoon commander. The survivors were in a state of stunned shock. One man had gone screaming mad. A medical orderly gave him a morphine injection.

173

In the monastery the last isolated shots had died out. The Panzer Grenadiers, stupefied by the bombardment, had no fight left in them. The Roughs were systematically clearing the rooms, assembling their prisoners in the courtyard. From the buildings and the surrounding grounds came the cries and groans of the wounded.

All this was familiar to the Fusiliers. Somehow they were making order out of the chaos, an experienced organisation going about the aftermath of battle. A and C Companies had been sent out to man the perimeter against a possible counter-attack. The Machine Gun Platoon came roaring up the hill in Bren-gun-carriers to support them. The tanks clattered up the road to take hull-down positions on the hill to the east. The Provost Sergeant had marshalled his prisoners in the courtyard, barking orders at them, no nonsense. In the garden the Padre had already started to bury the dead in batches. The RAP had moved up to instal itself in the Chapel.

The battle was over. The smell of cordite and death pervaded the scene. Along with the shock and the grief there was the sense of exhultation at still being alive.

Edmund found Jason in the office under the entrance archway, where he had temporarily set up battalion head-quarters. The RSM had just handed him a sheet of paper with some figures on it. Mr Delaney's attitude towards the new CO had changed. The respect he showed was no longer the formal subservience of an experienced warrant officer to a younger man who carried the King's Commission. Jason had proved in the battle for Castel del Piano that he would not hesitate to share the danger with his men. He was a commander who led from the front. It was his example that had carried the attack through.

Jason looked up bleakly from the sheet of paper the RSM had just handed him. It bore a first estimate of the day's toll. There was accusation and something not far from hatred in his eyes.

Enemy	Own troops
Dead: 27	Dead: 5 Offrs. 56 ORs.
Wounded: 53	Wounded: 8 Offrs. 128 ORs.
Prisoners: 167	Total casualties: 197

'I started the day with 593 men, Ed. Now I've got 396. That's thirty per cent casualties.' For a moment his emotions got the better of him. He slammed the table with his blackthorn. 'You and your bloody Madonna!'

12

There was still a handful of monks in the monastery. They had been prepared to endure deprivation and risk death to ensure the continuity of the community. Thanks to their deep cellars they had survived those terrible five minutes when the artillery of an entire division had been concentrated on Castel del Piano. The roofs had suffered badly and the tower had collapsed but the massive walls had withstood the bombardment. Damage was mostly confined to the upper floors; not one pane of glass had survived.

Even in his shocked state the old Abbot was grateful that his monastery had at least not been bombed. He'd feared it would suffer the same fate as Cassino. 'We thank God and Saint Benedict for our deliverance and pray for the souls of the poor soldiers who were killed.'

Edmund also had been thinking about the Fusiliers whose lives had been sacrificed. It would be a cruel irony if, after all, the Mostra paintings had been removed before the attack or had been destroyed in the bombardment.

'Yes,' the Abbot said in answer to his question. 'Many pictures, beautiful pictures. The Germans put them in the refectory but we moved them down to the bakery for greater safety.' He smiled. 'Since many months we have not flour to make bread.'

Edmund had started to follow the old man towards a stairway that led down to the basement when an orderly came panting along to tell him that he was urgently needed at battalion headquarters. He found Jimmy Bruce in the office

175

Jason had used under the entrance archway. The Second-in-Command explained that the CO had moved on with A and B Companies 'to see the Krauts off Monte Falterona'. Tac HQ was now up on the mountain to the north-east of Castel del Piano. The perimeter round the monastery was being defended against a possible counter-attack by C Company and the remnants of D Company.

'Half a dozen partisans walked in a few minutes ago. Looked as if they could do with an hour on the square under a good drill sergeant. Still, they seem anxious to help. Could you have a word and sort them out, Ed? I gather there are more of them out there in the hills. If we could get them in we could use them to man our perimeter. That would free C Company if Sunray needs them.'

Edmund nodded and made for the door.

'Oh, and Edmund – .'

'Yes?'

The 2 i/c was embarrassed. He was doodling on a message pad. 'Ian's CSM told me. He said you deserved at least a DSO . . . .'

'What on earth for?'

'Dealing with that machine-gun nest. He said you wiped out the Spandau crew single-handed with grenades and a Tommy-gun . . . .'

'All I did was . . . .'

'And taking that message to Jason. Damn good show. I agree you've earned something, perhaps a Mention . . . .'

'Listen, Bruce.' Edmund came back to the front of the desk. 'It was the least I could do. I'd influenced Jason in his decision about air support . . . .'

'Difficulty is,' the 2 i/c was still drawing matchstick men, his eyes lowered, 'if we do get an allocation of gongs they'll be for the regiment. You don't officially belong to us, so it wouldn't be easy . . . .'

'Will Ian get something? I mean posthumously?'

'Oh, yes. He'd be top of the list.'

'That's good enough for me. It would make things, well, a bit easier for his wife.'

'But Ian's not married.'

'There's someone called Valerie. Will you do something for me and forget about Mentions?'

'Certainly, old boy.'

'Try and find out who Valerie is and let her know that Ian spoke her name just before he croaked. It was the last thing he said.'

Edmund found Volpone and two of his officers in the refectory. They were making free of the wine which they had commanded the monks to produce. Alessio was being used as a waiter to bring fresh supplies and fill the empty glasses. Volpone explained that General Leone had ordered them to rendezvous with him at the monastery as soon as it was captured.

'What about Mario? Isn't he with you?'

'Mario? Gone to look for the Padre Abate. His precious pictures. All he can think about.'

'Could your men take over the defence of the perimeter here? Then the Fusiliers could tackle the Germans on Monte Falterona.'

'My partisans are more suited to mobile warfare,' Volpone replied. 'General Leone will decide about our future operations.'

Edmund was heading back towards the stairway leading to the basement when he heard a shout from outside.

'Don't shoot, lads. They're Eyeties! More flippin' partisans!'

A column of men had come marching out of the forest, more or less in step. Those with rifles carried them over their shoulders at the slope. Many wore steel helmets, mostly of British or Italian pattern but some unmistakably German. The man leading them was huge. He wore the almost complete uniform of an Italian cavalry officer with black calf riding boots. Staring straight ahead and ignoring the ribald comments of the Tommies he marched his men through the archway and halted them in the courtyard. At the tail end of the column came a boy leading a mule with empty dangling stirrups.

General Leone left his men under the charge of his Adjutant and strode into the refectory. Volpone leapt to his feet and snapped his heels together.

'Generale! Commandi!'

The General stood at least six-foot-three-inches tall but the massiveness was in his breadth. His body was solid as a barrel, supported on strong, slightly bandy legs. A muscled diaphragm bulged out over his belt. The ends of a wide moustache drooped down at the edges of his mouth. A line of black beard ran round his jowl from ear to ear. Thick eyebrows formed an unbroken bar above his fierce, jet-black eyes. Round his neck a scarlet scarf had been knotted with studied carelessness. Pinned to one lapel was a death's head badge which must have been taken off the body of some SS officer.

He embraced Volpone with a bear hug. 'You have done well, colonello. I will see that you receive recognition for this. Castel del Piano will make an excellent headquarters for our next operations.'

Leone's voice was so resonant that his statements echoed like recitative delivered in a large auditorium. He was too large for this life. He would have looked out of place anywhere except on the stage of an opera house.

'We only obeyed your command, my General.' Volpone did not disillusion Leone in his assumption that the partisans had captured the monastery. 'Alessio!' he shouted. 'More wine for the General.'

Volpone was introducing Edmund when the old man came trotting in to obey the order. His arrival was heralded by a crash as both bottle and glass fell from his hands.

'Signore!' he exclaimed, his eyes lighting up with joy. 'At last! At last I find you!'

Leone was puzzled for a second and then he roared: 'Alessio! But how ever do you come to be here?'

Tears were already on the old man's cheeks as he stumbled towards de Angeli in his best attempt at a run. He took the big man's right hand in both of his and kissed it.

'Oh, signore, è successo una cosa terribile.'

'Cos'è successo? Dimmi subito!'

'La signorina Caterina. E morta assassinata!'

The news that his wife had been murdered could not have been broken with more brutal suddenness. De Angeli's face muscles twitched as if he had been struck by an invisible whip.

'Morta? Assassinata?' The great voice was not much more than a whisper. 'Ma come?' Quando? Alessio, dimmi, dimmi.'

For five weeks Alessio had been bottling up his terrible secret. The command to speak at last offered him relief. The story came spilling out in a rasping Florentine accent.

'Mi raccomando, signore. There was this Jewish girl. The Fascists were after her. She was only fifteen. She begged me to save her, to hide her. I put her in the attic you reach through the trapdoor on the top landing. I took her food, sometimes talked to her . . . . No harm in it, signore, mi raccomando, I did no wrong . . . .'

'Great God, Alessio! Come to the point. What about my wife?'

'Well, from up in the attic, signore, it's possible to look down into the bedrooms . . . .'

Alessio stopped, terrified. De Angeli's formidable brows had lowered.

'What did you see, Alessio?'

The old man stared mutely. Edmund knew for certain that he had watched Ken disporting himself with Caterina and was fighting to prevent himself blurting it out.

'Speak!' de Angeli roared. 'What did you see?'

'I was up there that night. No harm, signore, I swear to you! Only at night could I take food to la piccina . . . .'

'Alessio!' de Angeli raised his fist. 'It is a matter of total indifference to me whether you fondled the little Jewish girl, even fornicated with her if you were up to it.'

'La signorina Caterina was asleep in her room. The English officer had gone – '

He stopped himself just in time.

'What English officer?' de Angeli demanded.

'There was an English officer billetted in the house, but he was away that night so only la Nonna and la signorina were there. I heard la signorina Caterina call out. I went to the crack where you can look down into the nursery. Il signorino Guido and his partisan friend Federico were there. They – '

'Come on, man.' De Angeli's fists were still clenched.

'Federico. He was beating her –'

'Beating her?'

'Sisignore. Aveva una frusta.'

De Angeli strode to the wall and struck it with his clenched fist. Alessio stared at him fearfully. When he turned round his knuckles were bleeding.

'Why did you not stop them, old fool?'

'How could I, signore? They had guns.'

'Did Guido beat her?'

'No signore. Only Federico.'

De Angeli's eyes had widened so that the whites were visible all round the pupils. His mouth had begun to work involuntarily.

'And then – ?'

'Then, signore . . . .' Alessio twisted away from his master's stare, hiding his face. 'I cannot say it.'

'TELL ME!'

'Federico had got very excited. The beating had aroused him. He – he – '

'TELL ME!'

'Ha violato la signorina – '

'Aaach!' de Angeli gave vent to a roar that was more animal than human. He strode rapidly about the room as if searching for an escape from a truth that was unbearable. Alessio watched him, expecting a blow. De Angeli stopped, towering above him.

'Did Guido . . . ?'

'No signore. Guido ran out of the room.'

'Was it Federico who killed her?'

Alessio nodded.

De Angeli swung his eyes towards Edmund but he was not really seeing him.

'How long ago?'

'Il 10 Agosto, signore.'

'More than a month. My wife has been dead more than a month and I did not know it.'

Then at last the big man crumpled. He slumped down on the long refectory bench and pillowed his head on his arms. His body shook to racking sobs that seemed to tear his throat.

Mario was guided down the dark stairway to the basement by one of the younger monks. He moved cautiously, holding onto the stone bannister. Even a week after the beating his body was tender and he was fearful of falling. The monk put out an arm to support him. The feel of the rough habit reminded him that this man was a priest as well as a monk. What would his verdict be if he heard Mario's story?

When they were safely at basement level the monk strode ahead to open the heavy shutters covering the windows. The fading daylight filtered through the shattered panes. Beyond them he could see the stone wall of an area below ground level. The bakery was a low but spacious room with a vaulted ceiling. A long pine table stood in the middle. Huge black ovens filled one wall at the far end.

Even in the gloom Mario knew at once that he had entered a treasure house. The pictures in their ornate gilded frames had been placed against the centre table and the walls – fifty or more masterpieces by the greatest Renaissance artists. He walked along the line of gilded frames with the young Benedictine following silently behind, passed a *Christus Patiens* by Cimabue, an *Adoration of the Magi* by Fra Angelico, a *Virgin adoring the Christ Child* by Leonardo, an *Annunciation* by Filippo Lippi.

When he came to a dramatic *Resurrection* by Michaelangelo, in which Christ was shown leaping from the tomb, he paused, so deeply absorbed that he did not notice when the young monk slipped quietly away and went back up the stairs. Only the realisation that the light was fading spurred him to begin a more sober assessment of what was there. He had counted thirty-seven of the Mostra paintings, virtually undamaged, when he became aware that someone else had come into the bakery and was standing behind him. He turned round, showed no surprise when he saw who it was.

'A miracle, Edmund!' He had at last learnt to drop the final O. 'Nearly everything is here!' In his excitement Mario forgot that the two men had been separated for three days by the surge of battle. 'And look! Your Madonna. She is safe.'

Tugging Edmund's sleeve he towed him round the table till they were under the windows. He had propped the *tondo* up so that the light fell on it. The tender colours of Botticelli, so much more subtle than in any reproduction, seemed to glow with a radiance of their own. Mario watched Edmund's expression as his gaze wandered over the serene faces of the adoring angels, the glimpse of mediaeval Florence in the background, the chubby Child innocently clutching three crude nails. When at last he looked at the Madonna herself he became so still that even his breathing seemed to have stopped.

The sharp crack of a field gun rattled the windows, brought them both back to reality.

'One of our own guns,' Edmund reassured Mario. 'Still, we'd better close the shutters.'

Mario sensed Edmund's urgency as he was led up the stairs again. At ground level the light was fading rapidly. From the chapel came the rhythmic sound of male voices raised in Gregorian chant. To a background of gunfire the Benedictines were singing Evensong. On Monte Falterona the enemy shelling had intensified. Castel del Piano itself was enjoying a period of comparative peace.

Volpone was sitting on an old mounting-block in the courtyard. His men were standing or squatting against the walls and fountain, not sure what they were supposed to do next. They were out of place amidst the purposeful chaos of the British Army. The Tommies tended to regard their bizarre dress, their dramatic postures and gestures, their archaic weapons with sceptical amusement.

'What's happened to de Angeli?' Mario asked.

'Disappeared. Took the mule and went off by himself.' Volpone had been helping himself over-generously to the Benedictine's Chianti Classico. 'No one was allowed to accompany him.'

Edmund asked in which direction he'd gone. Volpone stood up to point southward but thought better of it and sat down again rapidly. 'He's no longer the General Leone we know, Mario. I was to take command, he said. But without precise orders what am I to do?'

Edmund said, 'I can tell you what to do.'

Mystified, Mario watched as he walked out through the archway. A couple of RASC lorries were parked under the lee of the walls. They had chugged up the winding road bringing ammunition for the guns now deployed on the flat stretch of ground that had given the place its name. Edmund talked to the Sergeant in charge of the small convoy, showed him the special pass signed by the Commander-in-Chief. When he came back, accompanied by the Sergeant, he was smiling.

'These lorries are returning empty to Pontassieve. I've persuaded them to make a detour through Florence. It's our chance to get the pictures out of here.'

'Aren't they safer in the basement?'

'What I'm afraid of is that the enemy may have lured Fifth Army into the foothills so that they can attack from higher ground. That might be the reason why they withdrew from the Gothic Line.'

Mario could not follow this tactical reasoning. He suspected that Edmund was absolutely set on getting his Madonna back to Florence.

'This is Sergeant Henderson.' Edmund was introducing the RASC man. 'He says he's keen to practice his Italian on someone.'

'Ciao,' the Sergeant shook Mario's hand. 'Molto piacere. Haven't had a chance to visit Firenze yet, but I'm due for leave soon. You don't happen to know any nice signorinas, do you, mate?'

Volpone pulled himself together when Mario told him that his partisans could make themselves useful by loading the paintings onto the lorries. The 3-tonners were reversed into the courtyard. Under Mario's supervision the framed pictures were brought up from the basement and carefully packed with blankets lent by the Abbot. The Italians could see that most of the subjects were religious. They did not need Mario's warnings to handle them with reverence. Edmund, watching for the Madonna, insisted on the *tondo* being especially well padded and placed just inside the tailboard of the leading lorry.

By the time the job was completed the guns nearby had started to fire. It was dark enough for the flashes to illuminate the sky. Mario was hardened to gunfire now but some of the partisans, shocked by the deafening noise, clapped their hands over their ears.

'Let's move.' Edmund had to shout to make himself heard. 'These 25-pounders may attract counter-battery fire. I'll ride in the front lorry. You take the second one. We'll go straight to the Uffizi.'

Mario nodded obediently. He was moving toward his lorry when he saw a pathetic figure come stumbling out of the monastery.

'Capitano!' Alessio went up to Edmund with his palms pressed together in his customary beseeching gesture. 'You are going to Florence? Please, please take me with you. Don't leave me behind. My signore – he has lost his reason. I must get back to the *palazzo* before he does.'

'All right, Alessio. Get into the front lorry, up there beside the Sergeant.'

Edmund was about to climb up after him when he paused. During a lull in the artillery fire the blare of battle could be heard up on Monte Falterona. Mario saw him walk quickly to the little Rear HQ office in the archway. The drivers had started their engines before he came back. His face, pale against the dark walls behind, was illuminated fitfully by the flashes of the guns. It reminded Mario of the flickering images of the early horror films.

'Edmund! What's the matter?'

'Same bloody story. The Roughs are being counter-attacked'. Then less brusquely he added. 'Let's get started, Mario. We'll meet at the Uffizi. I've given the drivers instructions.'

'Edmund . . . .' Mario's voice was drowned by a salvo from the guns. Edmund was already walking towards the leading truck and the chance was lost. Mario climbed in beside the Lance Corporal.

The RASC man grinned at him. 'Paura?' he said, nodding towards the 25-pounders.

Mario shook his head. 'Niente paura.' Never again would he be frightened by mere noise. The most terrifying thing on earth was the personal violence of man against man.

Ahead, the leading lorry was moving away. He could see Edmund sitting near the rear tailboard where the Madonna was stowed. There was no need to ask his friend for assurance that he would never betray those confidences about Caterina. He knew he could trust him. But there was something else he had wanted to say. The days they had spent together up here in the mountains had been, in spite of all his sufferings, *una esperienza preziosisima*. Edmund knew of his transgression but he also knew about his Calvary. It made a unique bond between them. But the English were not like the Italians. You could not easily confide the deeper emotions to them.

As the lorry began to descend the hill the monastery faded into the gloom. He would have liked to make some act of contrition back there, but he felt the monks had not been in the mood to hear confession. The vehicle lurched, one wheel half in the ditch, and he was thrown against the door. The narrow road up to the monastery was crowded with vehicles as the service units moved up in support. Half-way down a petrol lorry had been hit by a stray shell and was on fire. Bursting jerricans were hurtling through the air like monster squibs. When the truck reached the main highway leading from Dicomano to the Passo del Muraglione it met a steady stream of lorries and armoured vehicles climbing the winding road. Word had got back that the Gothic Line had been abandoned and the key point of Castel del Piano captured. The driver had to stop frequently to give precedence to the huge tank transporters. Edmund's vehicle was already several places ahead of them.

Three miles below San Godenzo where the road crossed a narrow bridge a Military Policeman was controlling the traffic. He had held up the south-bound stream to give precedence to a battery of heavy guns moving towards the pass. The RASC driver pulled to the side and stopped his engine. He fished for a packet of cigarettes and lit up. The other lorry was stopping a hundred yards ahead.

'Looks like we'll all be here for a bit. What's it you Italians say? Pazienza.'

Through his window Mario could see a shrine on the side of the hill above the road, only twenty yards away. It was the usual stone construction with a little niche for the statue of the Virgin. This one was surrounded by a railing with a wrought-iron gate.

'Have I time for . . . ?'

On the driver's nod he opened the door and climbed down onto the stony verge of the road. To hide his real reason for dismounting he unbuttoned his flies and directed a jet against the front wheel. Then he turned and walked slowly towards the shrine. Perhaps here he could find an answer to the question he had not been able to ask the Benedictine.

There was no light burning in front of the statue. The oil in the lamp had run out long ago. The flowers in the vase had withered. But the face of the Virgin was faintly lit by the gleam of passing vehicles. As he stood outside the little gate it seemed to Mario that she was smiling.

By the middle of September Florence had settled down into

185

its role as a city behind the lines. The battles *in montagna* were still close enough for the people to feel involved. The pleasure-loving aristocrats of high society had opened their houses and their arms to the officers of the Cavalry and Guards regiments who were now coming in on leave. Many units had established rear echelons in the city or its outskirts so that they could send parties back for a period of rest. The officers' club in the Hotel Principe e Savoia emitted the sound of revelry by night. The madama of the bordello in Via dei Volpi was trying to recruit more girls to meet the demand. The food shortages were forgotten. The ordeal of those grim days sandwiched between two armies was now just an exciting memory. With their genius for improvisation the citizens had made good much of the damage. Twenty years of Fascism had ended. The war had passed on. Only the devastated area around the Ponte Vecchio remained silent and sad.

The bag-pipes and drums of a Scottish regiment had played in Piazza Signoria, to the baffled astonishment of the populace. The big cafés had opened up in Piazza della Republica. Their tables spilled out over the pavements and on warm evenings the square was filled with the music of their orchestras and singers. Many British and American soldiers were living a life of violent contrasts. One day they could be shivering in the driving rain and mud of the Appenines and the next lounging in the drawing-room of some gracious Florentine hostess.

On the night of Monday 8 September, a family party was taking place in Palazzo Lamberti. It was the twenty-fifth wedding anniversary of the Count and Countess. They were all still officially in mourning for la Nonna, and for Caterina too. But five weeks had passed and this was after all a joyful family occasion. The Countess was as charming as ever and looked ten years younger. She had acquired a new admirer in the shape of an AMGOT Colonel from South Carolina. She was wearing a long dress, low cut to display her splendid décolletage. She had refrained from wearing her jewelled necklace – the famous Lamberti rivière. The Count was dressed in a dark suit rather than the white tie and tails he would have sported in happier times. He was now well in with the officers of Allied Military Government, especially the Americans. He had recovered almost all his former bounce and confidence.

The family had eaten well. Provender from the black market had been reinforced by some American army rations. Susanna had brought up some of the best wine from the cellar, half a dozen bottles of the Léoville-Barton 1928. Now they were all assembled in the *salone*, their glasses charged with newly acquired Bourbon whisky. Prodded by Rosalba and Ornella, Guido walked to the front of the fireplace. He now had a job as liaison officer between the Allied and Italian forces and was very full of his new importance. The tassels and épaulettes of his dress uniform glittered in the light of the crystal candelabra.

'Please – quiet everybody.' The babble of conversation died down. 'I want to propose a toast. Today, as you know, is Papa's and Mamma's silver wedding.' A flurry of clapping, led by Ornella. 'I have been doing some research and I think I am correct in saying that it is almost exactly five hundred years that de'Lambertis have been living in the Palazzo. Now, I know that we have recently suffered great tragedy, but all things considered . . . .' Guido faltered. The sound of the knocker on the front door below had echoed up the staircase.

'Mezzanotte,' the Count muttered. 'Chi puo essere? Susanna, go and see who it is.'

As the old servant hurried out, the insistent knocking was repeated. The days of the Black Militia and the Gestapo were recent enough for the sound to send a shiver down every spine. Guido had lost the thread of his discouse. That did not matter as no one was listening to him. They were all trying to make sense of the voices on the stairs. Two spots of colour appeared on Rosalba's cheeks.

Then, with a dramatic flourish, Susanna flung open the double doors. On the landing outside, Edmund and Alessio were standing on either side of a circular gilded frame, holding it by the rings screwed into the back. Edmund was almost as dishevelled as Alessio, his uniform muddied and torn. As they came in the light fell on the *tondo*. No one in the room spoke or moved. The picture had a tremendous presence which imposed an awed respect. In dead silence the two men set it down on the carpet. Edmund signalled Susanna to bring a chair to support it. Then his eyes sought Rosalba. 'Rosalba, would you come over?'

The silence still held as, watching his face, she came and stood shyly beside the painting.

'Yes.' Edmund stepped back, looking from the painted face to the live face. 'It has been worth it. I brought it here because I wanted to see you both together.'

'Pardon me.' The AMGOT Colonel had come to stand opposite the *tondo*. 'Is that a genuine painting or . . . ?' He cocked his head at Rosalba. 'It looks uncommonly like this young lady.'

'You think so?' Edmund smiled at Rosalba.

'It is not so surprising, Harvey.' The Countess was smiling with pride. 'Both Rosalba and I are direct descendants of Simonetta.'

The tension had been broken. Everyone began to talk again. Ornella came and seized Edmund by the arm. 'Is Mario with you?'

'No.' Edmund hedged, avoiding her eye. 'Mario is – he's . . . .'

'Where is he? Tell me, Edmundo. Is he all right?'

'He's – he went straight to the Uffizi with the other paintings. Excuse me, Ornella. There's something I have to tell Guido.'

She let her arm drop. The resentment she'd felt ever since he had taken Mario away showed plainly in the glare she gave him.

Edmund drew Guido away from the Count's side. He saw that the Countess was watching, her wise eyes missing nothing. He turned his face away from her. It would not have surprised him if she had been capable of lip reading.

'Guido,' he said quietly. 'Get out of here.'

Guido stared arrogantly. 'Are you telling me what to do? I'm an officer in the Army now, not just a partisan.'

'De Angeli is coming.'

'Wha – what?'

'He has a score to settle with you.'

Guido's head jerked round. He saw Alessio staring at him and knew what Edmund meant.

'I came here to warn you. Not for your sake, believe me, but for Rosalba's.'

Guido turned and began to push his way towards the door.

The Countess had seen the change in his manner. 'Guido, what is it? Where are you going?'

'Nowhere, Mamma,' Guido stuttered, head down. 'Please excuse me.'

'Guido!' The Count's call was peremptory. 'You cannot leave like that. Where are your manners?'

'I have to, Papa. I'm not feeling . . . .'

'You were all right a minute ago. Now, pull yourself together!'

As the Count strode forward to bar his way to the staircase, Guido twisted round and made a dart for the door that led to the servant's quarters. Before he got there it burst open with a crash.

De Angeli stood in the opening, an apocalyptic figure. His bulk filled the narrow doorway. Rage seemed to have added another three inches to his stature. He still wore the uniform and accoutrements of the campaign. His shirt gaped over a chest matted with hair. The knee-length boots were slimy with muck. Blood oozing from a slash across his cheek had congealed in a black smear. He wore no headgear and his streaming wet hair sagged over his ears and brow. His huge fist gripped a heavy Luger .45 automatic. His eyes were maniacal.

Guido stopped, then recoiled as if he had bounced off an unseen wall.

'Meno male.' De Angeli had spoken quietly but his deep voice rumbled through the room. 'I prayed you would be here.' His eyes swept the gathering. 'But where is Federico?'

'Federico?' Guido echoed the name stupidly. 'I don't know.'

De Angeli took two steps forward. His left hand seized Guido by the lapels of his uniform. His strength was enough to lift him clean off his feet.

'Where is Federico?' This time the voice was a roar.

'Teo!' the Count rapped out in his *commendatore's* voice. 'What does this mean?'

De Angeli shook Guido like a rat. 'Now, tell me! Where is your brave and heroic friend?'

'Teo, you can't behave like this.' The Count raised his voice but he was keeping his distance. Rosalba and Ornella had clasped each other in terror. 'We have order in Florence now. You will force me to call the police.'

'Call them!' De Angeli thundered. He lowered Guido till his feet rested on the floor. 'Will you or I tell them that your son is – un rapinatore e un assassino!' The last word was spat out with such emphasis that Guido's face was sprayed with saliva.

Then with a calmness that was more frightening than his rage, De Angeli relinquished his grip of Guido. He released him gradually as if he feared that the boy would crumple at his feet.

'Tell them, Alessio.'

'Signore mio.' Alessio, still standing beside the Madonna, shook his head. 'Non posso.'

'Tell what?' The Countess had begun to divine a dreadful truth.

'Alessio was keeping a little Jewish girl in the attic above Nonna's house . . . .'

'Alessio?' The Countess turned to Alessio with surprise. 'Is this true?'

'Signora contessa.' Alessio's head was bowed and his hands were again clasped in supplication. 'Mi raccomando. It was to save her, she was being hunted by the SS.'

'Giulia!' De Angeli raised his voice to command attention. 'Alessio was in the attic when Caterina was killed. He saw what happened.'

'And . . . .' The Countess hesitated. She knew that when the question was answered her pride in Guido would be shattered forever. 'What did Alessio see?'

The eyes of everyone turned towards the old man. He shrank and cast a spaniel's imploring look at De Angeli.

'Speak, Alessio!'

'Federico and il signorino came into the room of la signorina Caterina.' Alessio was talking rapidly, anxious to get this over as soon as possible. 'They covered her mouth. Il signorino held her down while Federico beat her . . . '

'No! No!' Guido whimpered.

'Yes, you did, Guido.' De Angeli gritted his teeth. 'The beating excited them and Federico raped her. Then Federico killed her – with sadistic viciousness.'

'Is this true, Alessio?' The Countess was standing erect but she had put one hand on a chair for support.

'Sisignora.'

'And la vecchia contessa?'

'Ma!' Alessio wagged his head disapprovingly. 'La vecchia contessa could walk better than she would like you to think. She must have heard something and come out of her room . . . . When I ran down from the attic she was lying in the stairway. It did not seem right so I lifted her and carried her to her chair. I could not stay in the house . . . .' He began to sob with dry, wheezing gasps.

'He ran away then,' De Angeli explained. 'Came to try and find me. Only today I learned of this – this bestiality.'

Guido suddenly found strength. He twisted out of De Angeli's grasp and skeetered across the room. Instinctively seeking sanctuary he took refuge behind the *tondo*, as if the Madonna could offer him protection.

'I did not kill Nonna. And Ì did not rape Caterina. When Federico killed Caterina I was trying to help Nonna, but she was already dead. It was not my fault! I did not want that to happen.'

'But you let him beat her,' De Angeli growled. 'You held her while he beat her.'

'She dishonoured you!' Guido flung back at him. 'She was a slut. She dishonoured Ornella. She seduced Mario.'

'*No!*'

Even Ornella's anguished cry did not stop Guido. 'Yes, she did!' he screamed at her. 'You saw that too, Alessio. Tell them.'

'I did not see that, signorino, but the girl Maddalena, she saw them.'

'I do not believe this,' de Angeli bellowed.

'It's true. She'd been sleeping with SS officers also. That's why we went to punish her. For the honour of the family. She was a whore!'

De Angeli drew in a breath. His mouth opened. His lips were drawn back from his teeth. No sound came out. Ornella was in a chair rocking to and fro with her head in her hands. Rosalba was sobbing with shock and bewilderment.

De Angeli was like a ship that had been first bombed and then torpedoed. The powder magazine was about to explode.

Brandishing the Luger he thrust Edmund aside and lurched towards the *tondo*. Guido ducked away out of sight behind the frame. It was a pathetic and childish instinct. The canvas offered him no protection. As the Countess rushed forward to throw herself on his arm, De Angeli fired. The bullet smashed through the picture, puncturing the patch of sky behind the Madonna's head. The Count's roar and the screams of four women mingled with the deafening report. Edmund strode between De Angeli and his target.

'STOP IT, ALL OF YOU!' he shouted with the full power of his lungs. 'Mario – ' in a sudden frozen hush eight startled faces turned towards him, ' – Mario is dead.'

During the seven weeks since Edmund had last driven back to Alexander's headquarters the tortuous road from Florence to Siena had deteriorated. The rain that had fallen almost continuously since the beginning of September had added to the damage done by heavy military vehicles. Frequently the 15-cwt truck had to follow a rutted deviation to avoid a demolished bridge. Near San Donato a bare-headed priest driving an ox-cart had been crowded into the ditch by a six-wheel-drive lorry. In one river valley a squad of kneeling women were slapping their washing on the flat stones. There were knots of refugees on the roads, struggling back to their homes with their entire wordly possessions on their backs. In the ruined villages life was returning to normal. For these Tuscan peasants the war was past history. The Committee of Liberation had posted up placards headed RICOMIN-CIAMO, with pictures of hammers, nails, saws and screw-drivers. Already the Italians were working for their economic miracle.

He was still chiding himself for announcing Mario's death with such brutal suddenness. Ornella's tormented cry would echo forever in his memory. At the time it had seemed the only way to stop the mayhem. He had been more concerned for the Madonna than for Guido's skin. The boy had been lucky to escape with nothing more than a bullet wound in his arm. It was the honour of the Lamberti family that had been destroyed during those bitter ten minutes. Even the Countess had crumbled and for two days would speak to no-one. With Ornella heavily sedated by the doctor, Rosalba had been landed with looking after the children. Rather than call at the locked and shuttered *palazzo*, Edmund had chosen to write to the family. He had been sincere when he asked them to believe that Mario had sacrificed his life no less valiantly than a soldier – for the sake of the art treasures he loved.

Sitting at the back of the RASC lorry on the road down from Castel del Piano Edmund had seen the flash and felt the shock-wave of the explosion the instant before he had heard it. He had run back to find the driver of the second vehicle bleeding from a score of splinter wounds. A hail of shrapnel had ripped through the canvas cover of the 3-tonner. Opening the little gate in the railings Mario must have activated the booby-trap and detonated the Teller mine. His body, when Edmund had found what was left of it fifty yards from the pulverised shrine, was a bloody pulp.

The sun was low now as he came within sight of Siena. He directed his driver round the town. Alex's Advanced HQ was at Le Ropley on a hill a few miles outside the city. If he had gone through proper channels Edmund would have reported to Colonel Parkinson, who was comfortably installed at Main Headquarters in the Excelsior Hotel. Parkinson would create merry hell about his not reporting back as ordered and swanning off on his own initiative to Dicomano. The man was capable of putting him on a charge for 'conduct prejudicial to good order and military discipline'. Edmund regarded the Madonna as something private between himself and Alex and he intended to hand her over in person.

Alex had been away on one of his sorties to the Adriatic front. He was expected back shortly. The delay gave Edmund and his driver time to unload the *tondo* from the Bedford.

The C in C arrived in his open staff car with his flag flying on the radiator. The shorts and shirtsleeves of July had been discarded in favour of field boots and breeches, a battle-dress blouse and a fur-lined flying jacket. He was slightly taken aback by the COPAT officer turning up complete with the King's Madonna.

'Did I say that?' he asked, when Edmund reminded him of the conversation with the King.

'Yes, sir.' A little stiffly Edmund added, 'I took it as a personal directive.'

With his characteristic ease of manner Alexander recovered quickly from his surprise. He put his scarlet-banded cap on his desk, hung his flying jacket on the back of the door, then listened intently while Edmund recounted all the Madonna's adventures. The two men spent a further five minutes admiring the picture, discussing Botticelli's technique and style. The hole made by de Angeli's bullet had been expertly repaired in the Uffizi's Gabinetto di Restauro.

'You've done well, Brudanell. The King will be pleased. But I'm sorry to hear about your Italian friend. We must do something for his widow.'

Edmund could only nod.

'And now,' Alex's voice was brisk. 'I think we'll get this back to His Majesty without delay. I would like to show my appreciation of his visit. If you can arrange to have it crated, I will authorise a flight so that you can take it back to England and return it to the King.'

'Is that – ' Edmund began, startled, ' – is that a direct order, sir?'

Alex's avuncular smile gave way to a frown. 'I don't understand you. Most people would be delighted at the chance of a posting home.'

Edmund stared out of the window at the silhouette of Siena against the deepening crimson of the clouds. The sun was catching the roseate brick of the towers and the black and white marble of the cathedral.

The bearer of evil tidings is seldom forgiven. He had followed the coffin to the cemetery with the rest of the mourners. Only he knew how little of Mario was inside the splendidly ornate box. All the family were there except Guido, who had been disowned by the Count and expelled forever from the *Palazzo*. When the service had ended Edmund was aware that the Lambertis had drawn closer together, excluding him. Rosalba's face was hidden by a heavy black veil. He did not try to speak to her. The time for that would come, when memories were less fresh, less painful. . . .

'Well?' Alexander's impatient voice cut across his thoughts.

'With respect, sir.' Edmund's eyes had switched to the Madonna. 'I'd rather finish the job in Florence than return home. Half the pictures we recovered from Castel del Piano are going to need repairing and . . . .'

'Very well,' Alexander cut in, anxious to get this matter settled. 'As a matter of fact I think you're wise to stay out here.' Edmund glanced up and met his eyes. The frown had been replaced by a faraway look. 'If I can break into the Lombardy Plain before winter sets in – you could be in Berlin for Christmas.'

Author's postscript

This novel is a blend of fact and fiction. An invented plot with imaginary characters has been set against a background of historical fact.

The principal characters in the story, including the Lamberti family, are fictitious. There was no such regiment as the Royal Ulster Fusiliers and the battle of Piano Castle was based on an action fought elsewhere by a real regiment. The Buckingham Palace Madonna was inspired by a Botticelli painting in the Uffizi Gallery.

The background, however, is based on histories, diaries, letters and personal recollections. The demolition of the bridges and buildings in Florence, the ordeal of the city, the dispersal of the art treasures, the military background are all as authentic as research could make them.

I am particularly indebted to three people who recalled personal experiences for me. Professor Ugo Procacci, formerly Director of the Soprintendenza, gave me a first-hand account of the dispersal of the Florentine art treasures. Signora Elia Masti, who still lives at Montegufoni, told me how her father, Guido Masti (later Cavaliere), saved the *Primavera* and several hundred other works. General Sir Geoffrey Musson made available his records of the battle for the monastery at Incontro, fought by the Duke of Cornwall's Light Infantcy in July 1944, and this provided a basis for the fictitious battle of Castel del Piano.

The Imperial War Museum was as usual a rich source of material – histories and personal documents from the library, B.B.C. reports on the entry into Florence from the sound archives, pictures of the visits of George VI and Churchill from the photographic and film departments. The Sikorski

Museum made available their detailed information on the Gothic Line.

In June 1984 an exhibition opened in Florence showing a selection of the works of art recovered between 1945 and 1976. Of the 3,600 paintings removed from Italy in 1943 and 1944, 600 are still missing. Many are of major historical and artistic importance.

James McConnell
MONXTON
20 August 1984